Hauntings and Havoc

Witch Haven Cozy Mystery - book 8

K.E. O'Connor

K.E. O'Connor Books

HAUNTINGS AND HAVOC

ISBN: 978-1-915378-35-4

Written by: K.E. O'Connor

Preface

The Witch Haven series has been created so you spend time with four amazing witches:

Books 1-3 tell Indigo's story: Spells and Spooks, Hexes and Haunts, Curses and Corpses

Books 4-6 tell Luna's story: Muffins and Moonlight, Cupcakes and Cauldrons, Pancakes and Potions

Book 7-9 tell Odessa's story: Hauntings and High Jinx, Hauntings and Havoc, Hauntings and Hoaxes

Book 10-12 tell Storm's story: The Case of the Screaming Skull, The Case of the Poisoned Pumpkin, The Case of the Cursed Candy

And there are two bonus origin stories to enjoy:

Fire Fang and **Silvaria**

Chapter 1

This was one of the worst days of my life. And although I'd had a few stinkers, lying in a locked cell under Magic Council scrutiny had to be tying for first place. My business had been shut down, my scarecrows taken, and I was waiting to be charged with who knows what, alongside Sol, my hardworking employee and friend. Well, friend with complications attached.

And to top it all, I had unpleasant magic attached to me, making me want to scratch myself raw. It got slapped on me before I went into the cell so my power was dampened. Maybe I shouldn't have attacked Selma Black when I discovered what she was doing at my farm, but that was my safe place, and it shouldn't have been invaded.

Why was the Magic Council picking on me? There were genuine criminals out there who needed bringing to justice. Instead, they went for an easy target. And now everything lay in tatters, and I couldn't see a way out.

My cell door opened, and Selma Black's sharp face looked in at me. "Are you ready to confess?"

I swung my feet over the edge of the hard cot I'd been resting on. "Nope. I have nothing to confess. And I shall ask for a written apology from you when this is over. It should include glitter and hearts. Maybe even a lipstick kiss."

Selma's cold gaze hardened. "Follow me."

"Where's Sol? Are you still holding him?" I hurried out of the cell, looking for a friendly face, but there was none as we walked along the chilly white painted corridor. I'd been brought to the main holding cells at the Magic Council headquarters, where everything was done by the book and filed in triplicate.

"He's safe."

"But where is he?"

"Somewhere you can't influence him."

We walked through several doors that needed unlocking with magic before we got to an interview room. Selma led me in and gestured to a chair set against a table. She spent a minute getting her paperwork laid out in a neat row in front of her before sitting opposite me.

"Your name is Odessa Matilda Grimsbane?"

"You know it is."

"And you're the owner of the Grimsbane farm on Pokey Lane?"

"Of course. But I won't answer any more questions until you tell me about Sol."

Selma's lips pursed a fraction. "Your partner in crime is being questioned. His answers are illuminating."

I gripped the edge of my seat. "Unless you have an interest in scarecrows, you won't find anything exciting at the farm."

"It's not so much the scarecrows, but it's what you do to make them so powerful. And Sol has provided me with plenty of information we can use against you."

I shook my head. Sol wouldn't say anything against me. I'd always treated him well and considered him a friend. My breath stuttered. Maybe he'd had enough of me. After all, I'd rejected him when he said he loved me. Or he could be angry about Brodie and my plan to bring him back to life. Would Sol turn against me?

He'd be hurting because I couldn't love him. Not that he wasn't easy to love. Sol Vossen was a great guy; he just wasn't my guy.

"What's on your mind?" Selma said. "Feeling guilty about something?"

"The last time I checked, I had nothing to feel guilty about."

She ran a finger down a piece of paper in front of her. "Tell me about the magic you use to animate your scarecrows."

"I use nothing illegal. I form a kind of magical umbilical cord with my scarecrows and channel reanimation magic into them. It makes it easier to keep track of them and get to them quickly if they ever struggle."

"What do you mean by struggle?"

"Not struggle. I'm not describing how it works all that well." I shuffled on the hard seat and released my grip on the chair's edge. "My magic has life-giving properties. It connects us."

"I want to know about their struggles."

"Forget I said that word."

"I can't. Explain."

I huffed a breath through my nose. Selma wasn't letting my tiny slip of the tongue go. "Just like all magic beings, my scarecrows have their ups and downs. I expect you have bad days, don't you?"

"No. You make yourself sound like a god with your magic. That's dangerous."

I raised my hands as I shook my head. "It's not that. I know I'm no goddess. My magic restores. It nurtures."

Selma clicked her tongue against the roof of her mouth. "It does a lot more than that. Are you able to raise the dead, just like your scarecrows?"

"No!"

"Are you certain? We've had incidents of the undead lurking about in the nearby village of Silver Steeple."

"That has nothing to do with me."

"But you could do it?"

I twitched my nose. "I mean, I've never tried, but raising the dead isn't my specialty. My magic isn't dark."

"You must get a thrill from having so much power," Selma said. "You have an army of dangerous creatures at your command."

I hid my hands under the table as I clenched my fists and took a few seconds to deep breathe away my annoyance. "It's always rewarding to see a scarecrow come to life. And they're great protectors. That's their job. They're here to look after the vulnerable, not cause problems."

"Yet they are. These reports show your scarecrows aren't under control. Maybe they never have been. Or maybe you're using a new kind of magic. Something dark and unstable." Selma cocked her head like a bird, her neck sinews bulging.

"I'll give you a list of the spells and potions I use. It's nothing dark, just a powerful combination mixed in with my magic."

"I'll take that information." Selma arched an eyebrow. "And I want to know about the locked barn."

The cold plastic of the chair dug into the back of my legs. "Which one? I make sure all my barns are locked."

"The only one we couldn't get in. I found a gap in the wood. There are scarecrows in there. They look strange, and several were dismembered."

I snorted out a laugh. "You make me sound like a scarecrow serial killer. I create life. I don't destroy it."

"You can destroy your scarecrows, though. If they become unstable, you take the magic back. Isn't that a kind of murder, if you consider them alive?"

"I... no! And I only do that as a last resort." Although I'd been doing it more frequently. I'd been distracted by my continued plight to bring back Brodie, my dead love.

"Someone as powerful as you needs monitoring. Much more monitoring than you currently have."

"I fill in my quarterly appraisals as requested by the Magic Council. You can't expect me to do more."

"You will if you want your business open again. Which is looking unlikely." Selma flicked through a file. "Once I've completed the tests on the scarecrows we collected, I'll know exactly what I'm dealing with."

"You can't do that."

"Because you claim they have feelings?" Selma tapped her fingers on the table. "Is that all scarecrows, or just the ones you're hiding in that locked barn?"

"Um... I consider them family." I'd meant to conceal that barn but had run out of time thanks to a ghost in distress. And although I was eternally grateful they hadn't been able to look inside, I couldn't figure out why the doors wouldn't open. It was a simple spell and a padlock keeping people out.

"What are you doing with those hidden scarecrows?" Selma leaned closer, her nostrils flaring.

Sweat prickled on the back of my neck. "I'm... testing a theory."

"What would that be?"

"I haven't patented it yet, so I can't risk the idea being stolen by talking about it." Selma wouldn't understand I was creating a vessel for Brodie's ghost. What I was attempting broke magical law and would give Selma her reason to lock me up.

"You're running a dangerous operation you have no control over. Your scarecrows are too powerful.

If that power is coming through you via a... what did you call it?"

"A magical umbilical cord."

"Exactly. Since you're the source of that power, there's the possibility you'll lose control, just like your scarecrows. Is your power becoming unstable?"

"Do I look out of control to you?"

"You look like a witch who's panicking. This investigation would have gone more smoothly if you'd told the truth. The Magic Council appreciates honesty. When it comes to your sentencing, it's looked on favorably."

I didn't believe that. All Selma wanted to do was shut down my business and send me to jail. She had me in her sights and wasn't planning on losing focus.

She pushed a piece of paper and a pen over to me. "Write down the list of spells and potions you use on your scarecrows. I'll check it tallies during my tests."

"Don't experiment on my scarecrows. It'll destabilize their magic. It could kill them."

"You make it sound like they're alive."

I gripped the pen. "They are to me. And they're valued by people who take them into their homes."

"We're auditing all sales you've made in the last two years. We want to see how valuable people consider these scarecrows and the troubles they've had with them."

"Then you'll be disappointed. My customers are happy. You only have to check my website to see the glowing reviews."

"Maybe there are some customers who didn't survive after taking in one of your scarecrows. If a rampaging giant straw-filled monster had murdered them, they couldn't leave a review."

Selma was goading me, but I wouldn't let her make me angry. I knew my scarecrows. And sure, they were capable of killing. It was how I made them. They were powerful, bold, fearless, and protective of their masters. They had to be. Being in the magic community wasn't without its dangers, and people needed protecting. That's what my scarecrows did. But they were made to protect, not destroy.

I spent a few minutes writing down my spells and potions, making sure I missed nothing so Selma wouldn't trip me up. I passed it back to her, and she tucked it into a file and stood.

"That's it?" I said.

"For now."

"Can I leave?"

"Not yet. I'm going back to see Sol. From the way he's talking, I won't need anything else from you, other than your signed confession."

"Sol won't betray me." Despite the confidence I pushed into my tone, I was wavering. I'd known Sol less than six months, and after rejecting him, he might be done with me. And I wouldn't blame him.

"We'll see. After this mess, he won't want to stick around."

I scowled at Selma's back as she led me to the cell and locked me in. She was right about Sol. He had no reason to stay. I'd pushed him away repeatedly, and my business was locked up tight thanks to the

Magic Council and their ridiculous bureaucracy. If I could get out of this, I may not even have any work to offer Sol. The guy had said he'd work with me for nothing, but I didn't want to test that theory.

A small black spider scuttled out from under the single cot and waggled a front leg at me. It looked like it was beckoning me closer.

I ducked down until we were almost eye level. "Hilda! How did you get in here?"

She scuttled over, and I held out my palm so she could climb onto it. "Indigo sent me. She's worried about you."

I smiled. Trust one of my closest friends to be looking out for me. "She's not the only one. Selma Black has just grilled me. She's got it in for me. She's also questioning Sol. The Magic Council is trying to find something wrong with my business."

Hilda's black legs quivered. "Indigo and Olympus are working on getting you out."

"They're here?"

"They are, but Selma's got them tangled in paperwork. It could be another few hours before you get free."

"But they can get me free? The Magic Council will realize their mistake and let me go?"

Hilda waggled her two front legs. "Hopefully. They're doing their best, but you know what the Magic Council is like. There are so many rules to comply with."

I sighed and headed to the cot. I sat on it and leaned back against the wall.

Hilda jumped onto my knee. "Indigo wanted to know if there's anything that needs fixing."

I tilted my head. "Fixing?"

"At the farm. Olympus only found out at the last minute about Selma's plans to shut the place down. He was too late to stop her from sending in her team."

"I doubt he could have done anything, but I appreciate the thought. Selma is on a mission to destroy me."

"So, is there anything? Indigo's sure she can creep in and deal with things if you need stuff kept under wraps. Anything, you know, that might not be strictly legal."

Indigo was an amazing friend, but there'd be questions to answer if I revealed what I was up to. "No, it's best she stays out of this."

"There's nothing to hide? You're sure?"

"There are... things that'll need explaining. But I'm working on a plan." Which currently involved refusing to talk to Selma, turning invisible, or faking memory loss.

There was a muffled thump against the side of the cell wall. It was followed by a fizzing noise.

I gathered Hilda up and slid off the cot. "You hear that?"

"I do. It sounds like—"

A flash of white light dazzled me, and I raised my hand, shielding Hilda as chunks of rock blasted around us. A few seconds later, the fluffy black head of Tuffin, a cat familiar I'd adopted from a ghost recently, appeared through a hole in the wall.

"Huh! That dumb scarecrow got it right. He said he could sense you behind this wall," Tuffin said.

I stared at her, my mouth open.

"What have they done, silenced you with magic?" She stepped nimbly over chunks of rock. "We need to move. In case you hadn't figured it out, this is a jail break."

"I... What?"

Shamrock, my ever faithful scarecrow companion, poked his head through the hole. He waved at me, then slammed his fist against the wall twice, making the hole bigger.

"Let's go," Tuffin said. "The guards will be all over this place in a couple of minutes. We disabled two of them, but there'll be more."

"Err... Is this a good idea?" I said to Hilda.

"Don't ask the creepy spider. I spent ages coming up with this plan. Well, a few minutes." Tuffin turned and flicked her fluffy black tail. "Although if you want to stay here and rot..."

"It won't look good if I break out of jail. I can still turn this around."

"Doubtful. This could be your only chance to get free," Tuffin said. "Of course, if you want to plead your case in front of a bunch of poker-faced Magic Council members, who I'm sure will have no problems with the freaky scarecrows you've been creating, then stay. Explain away."

"You're right. Let's move," I said. "But we need to get Sol."

"I knew you'd say that. That's being dealt with. He's next door. Marmaduke is blasting a hole through the wall as we speak."

I looked at Hilda, who was staring at Tuffin, looking undecided if she was friend or foe. "Tell Indigo and Olympus I'm okay, but I need to find a place to hide out for a while until I figure things out. I can't go back to the farm."

"Sure, and we'll figure out a story to explain this hole. We could say trolls attacked the Magic Council headquarters, and your cell just got in the way. I've heard a rumor that trolls sometimes abduct witches for fun."

"Thanks, Hilda. Anything you can do to cause a diversion would be amazing." I set her on the floor, and she dashed through the hole.

Shamrock grabbed my arms and heaved me through the hole before wrapping me in a punishing embrace, the scent of warm straw and pumpkins covering me as he huffed hot breath into my hair.

"It's good to see you too, buddy. I don't want you getting in trouble over this, though. You should have stayed away."

"We were already in trouble," Tuffin said. "The Magic Council is hunting us. I barely got away when we found them poking about at the farm."

"Thanks for coming back for me."

Her nose crinkled. "As if I had anywhere else to go. And Eldridge left me in your care. Besides, we're testing this whole witch familiar thing. Isn't this what I'm supposed to do? Get my witch out of trouble?"

"It is. Nice work." I tried to wriggle out of Shamrock's grip, but he wasn't done squeezing me.

"There's an alert out for any scarecrows you've created," Tuffin said. "I'm included in that alert since we've been spotted hanging out together. I'm a wanted cat."

"Sorry to hear that. Shamrock, you can let me go," I wheezed out. My scarecrows were enormous and sometimes forgot their own strength.

Shamrock lowered me to the ground but kept a tight grip on my arm as we hurried along the wall. There was a second smoking hole through which Sol's head was poking. Another of my scarecrows, Marmaduke, stood beside the hole. I also got a bone cracking hug from him.

"Odessa! Did you arrange for this to happen?" Sol said.

"Nope. But I'm glad it did. We need to get out of here."

He shook his head. "Selma has more questions for me. She'll be back soon."

"Let's leave Mr. Goody Two Shoes behind," Tuffin said. "He'll only slow us down."

"No. We go together. Sol, we have to get out of here before we get charged."

"With what? When I was interviewed, Selma said there was nothing to worry about."

"Don't believe anything Selma Black has to tell you. She wants my farm shut down and the scarecrows destroyed." There was no time for being subtle. "Marmaduke, grab Sol."

"What? Wait!" Sol yelped as all seven feet of hulking scarecrow loomed over him and dragged him through the hole.

Marmaduke slung Sol over his shoulder and took off running.

I wasn't sure this was a great idea, but people were shouting and footsteps were drawing near, so we were out of time. I grabbed Tuffin, jumped on

Shamrock's back, and clung on. "Let's get out of here. Make it fast."

Shamrock took off like a rocket, and my head flipped back so hard I worried I'd get whiplash. Within minutes, we were out of sight of the imposing Magic Council building. The Magic Council headquarters moved around whenever the workers inside felt under threat, which happened on a weekly basis since no one liked them, so it took me a minute to get my bearings, but I soon recognized the surroundings. We weren't far from my home village of Witch Haven.

"Head for the forest. We can hide out there and figure out our next move," I said.

Marmaduke and Shamrock changed direction and sped along.

Tuffin scrambled up, settling her butt against my collarbone and hanging her front paws over Shamrock's shoulder as the wind flicked her whiskers back. "We should get out of here while we can. You can start again somewhere else. I've always wanted to visit a tropical island."

"I'm not abandoning my home or the scarecrows," I said. "I'll take on the whole Magic Council if I have to, but I'm clearing my name."

"It's just a building. And you can make scarecrows anywhere. They'll follow you."

"Nope. My friends are here."

"Odessa, I can't get Marmaduke to put me down." Sol was clinging to Marmaduke, his arms wrapped around the scarecrow's middle. "He's not listening to me."

"It's quicker this way. Just hold on and you'll be fine."

The look Sol shot me suggested he was unhappy with this plan, but we had to get away.

"Go to the distillery," I said to Shamrock. "It's been closed for renovations for at least a week. No one will be there."

"Good thinking," Tuffin said. "We use it as a base. You gather your assets, assuming Selma hasn't frozen everything, and then we leave for our island sun paradise."

"No leaving. But I do need time to think. Once Selma understands how my business runs, she'll back off." Although I was wondering if I'd see Hell freeze over before that happened.

"There's no chance of that. Selma Black wants your head on a pole."

My nose wrinkled. "That's a disturbing image. Although she does hate me. Maybe I wronged her in a former life."

"Most likely. You can be annoyingly cheerful. I reckon Selma plans on tearing apart the farm and the scarecrows until she finds enough evidence to ruin you."

"Selma needs a fun hobby," I said, "one that doesn't involve persecuting innocent witches."

"Or a boyfriend. After all, you get distracted when there's a good-looking guy around." Her gaze landed on Sol.

"That's not true." I'd always been loyal to Brodie. He was my one and only, even though we'd been parted by his death over three years ago. I hadn't given up hope we'd get our happily ever after.

My gaze cut to Sol, and my cheeks flushed. I had experienced a moment or two of weakness with him. I'd even considered becoming more than his employer, but it was wrong to betray Brodie. And once Brodie was back, I'd be focused. No one else would tempt me. Not even a good man like Sol.

Marmaduke made short work of smashing the lock on the closed distillery entrance door. The place was quiet and dark as we entered, and I decided to keep it that way, so I pointed to the lights and shook my head.

This wasn't an alcohol distillery, but a magic distillery run by the Frost family. It wasn't a popular business, but it had made the family rich, and they had sites around the world. The Frost family offered payment for magic. People's powers were distilled out of them and sold to the highest bidder. It was an enterprise you only used when you were desperate and had no other option.

"Marmaduke, you can put me down," Sol said. "There's no threat here."

Marmaduke grunted and looked at me for his orders.

"Let me down, Shamrock. Marmaduke, let Sol go, too. Both of you go look around." I patted Shamrock's arm. "Make sure we're alone. Then come back."

Shamrock set me on my feet, while I kept hold of Tuffin so she didn't fall, and he dashed away with Marmaduke.

Sol raked a hand through his hair. Despite looking disheveled, he was still a handsome man. Big, broad, kind of hairy in a manly way, with several days' dark stubble on his chin. "Listen, Odessa. We should go back to the Magic Council. I was making things right with Selma and explaining what you do."

"What were you telling her?" I jammed my hands on my hips. "When she interviewed me, she said you were singing like a canary. You could have gotten me in trouble."

His expression hardened. "I wouldn't do that. You know how I feel about you."

I huffed out a breath. "I also know I rejected you. You told me you..." I couldn't bring myself to say the L word.

"Yeah. I love you. And that hasn't changed, no matter the crazy mess we've found ourselves in."

"It should. If you weren't involved with me, you wouldn't have been arrested."

Sol's walk was confident as he approached. "I'm prepared for everything they throw at me. But I'm not happy you suggested I'd tell the Magic Council something bad about you to save my neck."

I bit my bottom lip. "I'm panicking. And I never said that exactly."

"But you meant it. You don't trust me?"

Guilt gnawed at my insides. I had doubted Sol. "I trust you. But it feels like everyone has turned against me."

"Not everyone." He cupped my face in one of his big, tanned hands. "Sure, this is a mess. But we could have stayed and straightened things out with the Magic Council. Running looks bad."

"And given them time to find something to charge me with? Maybe you, too. And then my business would never reopen. What will I do without my farm, scarecrows, or my amazing pumpkins? It's all I've ever known. I'm not letting that go."

"But was running the best thing? Doesn't that suggest we're guilty?"

"We'll cover that up," Tuffin said. "That spider said something about trolls. Or we could blame the scarecrows."

"Spider?"

"Indigo's familiar came to see me," I said. "Olympus and Indigo were trying to get us out, but it didn't sound like it was going well."

"You can thank Wonder Cat for your rescue," Tuffin said. "Is there any fish in this place?" She leaped out of my arms.

"I doubt it," I said.

Tuffin's nose crinkled again. "I'll go look for fish. You two focus on figuring out a good cover story to clear your names."

"We don't need a cover story," Sol said.

I rested my cheek against his warm hand, reassured by his presence.

Sol smiled down at me. "We'll figure a way out of this together."

Tuffin hissed, and her fur puffed up. "Something is in here."

I looked around the dense blackness of the distillery. "I don't sense anything."

She hissed again, then yowled as she was dragged back by her tail and slung out the door. A few seconds later, Shamrock and Marmaduke suffered the same fate, growling and snarling as they were taken outside, and the door slammed behind them.

Sol grabbed me as I sparked up a spell. "You see anything?"

"Not a thing," I whispered. "But something doesn't like us being here."

He yelped as an inky black shadow grabbed him and pulled him away from me into the gloom, leaving me alone.

Chapter 2

After shock had frozen me in place for a few seconds, I took off running. "Where are you?" I held up a huge orange ball of light, frantically searching for any sign of Sol.

There was no reply to my repeated calls of his name.

"Who else is in here? Show yourself." My skin was prickling all over as if someone, or something, was watching me. And whatever that was, it was unfriendly.

I hurried along, peeking behind storage boxes and distillery vats. Sol hadn't just vanished. He'd be here.

"We don't want trouble. Give me back Sol, and we'll leave." I kept running, searching every dark corner and storage area. Where was he? What had taken him?

"It's too late for that." A low, female voice echoed around me. "This is private property."

I spun around, trying to find where the voice had come from. "We didn't mean to trespass. If this is your home, then I'm sorry."

"You will be."

That was rude. "Where's Sol?"

There were several seconds of silence, only filled by my panting breath as I continued to search. I froze as a light flicked on. Sol was suspended against a wall. His eyes were closed and his head slumped down.

I raced toward him, but the light went out, and Sol was gone by the time I got to the wall.

"You won't find him unless I want you to," the disembodied voice said. "What are you doing here, Odessa Grimsbane?"

"Making a mistake. How do you know me?" I traced my hands along the wall but found no sign of Sol.

"I make it my business to know every powerful magic user. It helps to have them on my side. I even bought scarecrows from you. They were excellent."

"We've done business?" I said.

"We have."

"Did you buy directly from me?"

"I don't get my hands dirty with small purchases. But I supervised. I approve of your scarecrows."

"Thanks. I'm always happy to meet a satisfied customer. Show yourself."

The woman laughed. "Let me give you a hint about who I am. You're standing in a building I own."

"This place belongs to the Frost family."

"Correct."

"You work here?"

"Pay attention. I own the place."

"It's a struggle to focus when you're threatening my friend and you tossed my familiar and scarecrows out the door." The Frost family had bought several scarecrows from me over the years, but I still didn't recognize this voice.

"I should have invested in a scarecrow for my private security. Perhaps I wouldn't be in this situation if I had."

"Situation? Are you in danger?" I crept along the wall, still seeking Sol.

"Give the witch a medal. She's almost figured it out. Although I'm not in danger, anymore. The dead are rarely in danger."

I pulled up. "Hold on, are you Arietta Frost?"

"Congratulations. I'll have to polish that medal." There was a sharp inhalation of breath close to my ear. "Do you know what happened to me?"

"I don't know the details, but I saw your obituary." Arietta had been fifty when she'd died. She was filthy rich, a ruthless business woman, and disliked by everyone.

"Let me give you another clue. I was murdered."

"Um... I'm sorry to hear that. But that doesn't mean you can hurt my friends. We didn't realize you were haunting this place. We'll get out of your hair."

"No one knows I'm here. I've been keeping a low profile. Figuring out how to get revenge for what happened to me."

"If you think someone killed you, I understand why you'd do that." Maybe if I got her talking, she might warm up to me and let Sol go.

"I know I was killed. I just don't remember who did it."

Even though this ghost was being a pain in my behind, I felt a trickle of sympathy for her. When someone died, they didn't remember the last few minutes of their life. It was easier that way, especially if the end was dramatic and unpleasant.

"Well, good luck with your search for justice. We'll go. If you just show me where you've hidden Sol—"

"You came here for a reason."

"Well, we did. But this isn't the right place for us."

"Wrong. You came here to help me. You're a ghost whisperer."

"Not exactly. I'm more of a pumpkin whisperer. Scarecrows, too."

"I know about your farm and your strange little pumpkins. That doesn't interest me. But I'm fascinated by your affinity with the dead."

"It's life I focus on. I bring life to my scarecrows."

"That's not the only thing you can do. As I said, I ensure I know who the most powerful magic users are, in case I ever need them. And I need your help now."

"To do what?"

"Help me get revenge for my murder."

I snorted a soft laugh. "I don't think I will. I've got my hands full." I lifted the orange orb higher.

"I won't let your boyfriend leave until I get what I want."

My gaze narrowed. "You can't hold him here. That's against the law."

"What will the Magic Council do, arrest me? I'm dead." A rumbling growl echoed around me. "Someone I trusted killed me. I will get payback."

"Can't the Magic Council help you figure this out?"

"They're useless. They've asked a few questions, but they mainly sit behind their desks, scratching their heads and taking too many coffee breaks."

"Have you got any idea who killed you?"

"Someone I let get close. A family member, most likely."

"You're sure about that?" If the way Arietta was treating me was her typical mode of operation, she must have made plenty of enemies along the way. And she exploited vulnerable magic users through the distillery business. That would have made her a target for a lot of people.

"I'm certain. Now, you will help me, or you'll never see your lover again."

"I... um... Sol is a friend."

"Friend, enemy, lover, I couldn't care less. You have a connection with him, and I plan to exploit that."

"Threatening a person won't get you what you want."

"It will. It always worked in my business." She cackled out a laugh. "You care for this warlock, and you care for the creatures I evicted from my distillery, so you will help. And I know people like you. You're that annoying kind of witch who has to do right by others. You always put yourself at the bottom of the list. You might not even be on the list. It's a mistake to care for everyone else before yourself. What does it leave you with? Or does that sense of self-righteous do-goodness make everything perfect?"

"You're... a mean person."

"That's almost a compliment. And I've been called a lot worse over the years. But this behavior has always gotten me what I wanted."

"Murdered by someone you trusted?"

An icy fist slammed into my stomach, and I wheezed out a breath and doubled over, black dots shunting across my vision. For a new ghost, Arietta had power.

"My judgment slipped, and I learned my lesson the hardest way possible. But I will have my revenge. And if you ever want to see that warlock again, you'll help me."

I rubbed my stomach as I eased myself upright. Arietta's ghost stood in front of me, and I stepped back to avoid the chill radiating off her and any more of those punches. She'd been an imposing figure when alive, but in ghost form, she was magnificently scary. Tall, willowy, with silky vibrant red hair and a long face with fierce green eyes.

"Your death was about six weeks ago, wasn't it? I remember reading about it in the paper."

"That's right. They should have had my murder as a front-page feature after all I've contributed to this village."

I wrinkled my nose. "I know what kind of business this is. It's not popular."

"It is to the people who use it. And I always had repeat customers. I pay for quality magic." Her gaze flickered over me. "You have power. I could make you wealthy if you give it to me."

"I'm happy with my powers right where they are. And I need them." To blast this ghost in the butt the second I got the chance.

"For your ridiculous scarecrows?"

"Among other things. Now, if you could just let us go—"

"No. You're staying. You're helping me." Her form shimmered out of focus. "The Magic Council is inefficient. Despite everything I've given this village, they don't seem fit to use all their resources to solve my murder."

"And you're sure you were murdered? Death can be confusing. You could have made a mistake about what happened to you."

She growled again. "I don't make mistakes. And the idiots on my case can't even see me. They're using poorly trained, lazy agents to investigate."

It wasn't the first time I'd heard about incompetence at the Magic Council, and since I was currently on the receiving end of it, Arietta had my sympathy. "What actually killed you?"

Her frown slid into a creepy smile. "You're helping me?"

"I'm considering helping." And buying time to find a way out of this place.

She gave a nod. "I don't remember. But I felt an intense pain in my chest." Arietta pressed a hand against her heart. "It felt like fire, and then nothing."

"Could you have had a heart attack? Running this business must have been stressful. You dealt with a lot of miserable people."

"My heart was fine. You must find out who did this to me. My death wasn't from natural causes."

No, I wasn't working for this ghost, but I tried for a soft approach to see if she had an agreeable side. Although from what I'd seen so far, I wasn't too hopeful. "If you were killed, that's awful, but I have my own problems. I have to focus on them."

"They're not as important as solving my murder."

"They're problematic enough. It's why we came here."

A gleam of wickedness entered Arietta's green eyes, and she flicked her hair over one shoulder. "Go on. I love a scandal."

I didn't want to share my secrets with this ghost. "It's a private matter."

The darkness faded to a gloomy gray, and I spotted Sol pinned against the opposite wall. I raced over, but slammed into a hard barrier of magic before I could touch him. "Sol, wake up! We have to get out of here."

"Sol is in my thrall, and he'll stay there until I decide otherwise. The only way you're getting your boyfriend back is if you help me." Arietta's words drifted over my shoulder in a plume of chilled air.

My fingers flexed. I considered myself a friendly witch, but this ghost was pushing her luck. "Let Sol go."

"I'll consider it if you tell me why you hid in my distillery. You must need to keep a low profile. The site has been closed for weeks, so you'd have known it was empty, and no one would have seen you sneaking in."

"Maybe we did need a temporary refuge. You don't need to know any more than that."

Arietta whizzed to Sol's side and yanked his head back, using his hair. She licked down his face and grinned at me. "I can make him do anything. I could get him to dance naked or eat grapes off my stomach. I could also get him to hurt himself, or you. And if I did, it would be your fault. All I want to know is why you're in my distillery. Surely, that isn't too much of a request."

"Fine. Just let go of Sol." It made me sick to watch the way she was pawing at him.

Arietta kept a tight grip on Sol's hair and simply arched an eyebrow.

"Fine. I got in trouble with the Magic Council. It's a misunderstanding, but they closed my farm and are investigating my work."

"What do you do at that boring little farm that's of interest to the Magic Council?"

I shrugged. "My scarecrows are powerful."

"And..."

A sigh slid out. This ghost wasn't letting us go until she knew everything. "Selma Black searched the farm and took away my scarecrows. She thinks my magic is unstable and I can't control them."

"Hmmm. Your creations are powerful, I'm not denying that. But we never had trouble with ours. Give them a clear order, and they know where they stand."

I deeply regretted ever trading with Arietta. She wouldn't have been kind to my boys. "I don't disagree, but there has been a couple of complaints from residents. Selma took them seriously and is looking for trouble."

"And will Selma Black find any trouble? Have you got secrets on your farm?"

"She found something that made her arrest me and Sol. And my business has been shut."

"Which doesn't answer my question. But I have another. If you're under arrest, why are you here?"

"Maybe we got out on bail."

"Or you escaped. Is that what happened? You're on the run from the Magic Council?" She hooted a laugh.

"It's not that simple. There was an... accident at the Magic Council. I used it to get out so we could clear our names."

"You are on the run. And you're hiding here." Arietta jigged up and down, taking Sol with her in a creepy dance as one of her hands settled on his butt. "You were sent to me. I don't know what demon or angel is on my side, but you picked this building for a reason."

"Yes, I did. It was close, and I knew it was empty."

"No, it was because you're meant to work for me. I've always had good luck on my side."

"Was that good luck around when someone murdered you?"

Arietta draped an arm over Sol's shoulders and pinned him back to the wall. "Someone stepped out of line, and you're going to help me make them pay."

"I won't hurt anyone."

"You will if I tell you to. And if you refuse to help, I'll let the Magic Council know where you are."

"Then I'll go."

"And leave behind this cute chunk of pie? I see you're fond of him. You can't keep your eyes off him for more than a couple of seconds. And why should you? He's delicious." She licked him again.

"That's unhygienic. And assault. Keep your tongue in your mouth."

"I'll lick every inch of him if I choose to do so." Arietta raked a hand through Sol's hair and then shoved him away. "How about this for an incentive? If you don't help, I'll tell the Magic Council you killed me."

My jaw dropped. "You're unbelievable. Are you really that hateful?"

"If you don't give me what I want, I'll do it. You mean nothing to me."

"I don't believe you will. And since it's unlikely you had real friends while you were alive, you won't get anyone to help you frame me now you're dead." I jammed my hands on my hips. "And how will you plant evidence when you don't even know how you were murdered?"

She bared her teeth. "I'll figure it out."

"If you could do that, you wouldn't be demanding my help. You can't do this alone."

Arietta shimmered and growled, twisting in the air, clearly hating me for pointing out the flaw in her plan. "Very well, then I shall kill your boyfriend."

My heart felt like it lodged in my throat as I looked at Sol. He was unconscious and helpless against Arietta, and I couldn't get to him through the magic barrier.

"What will it be, witch? You have the solution in your hands. You solve my murder and your life can go back to normal."

I couldn't stand the thought of Sol being hurt, but I wasn't giving up. I placed my hands behind my back as I sparked a disintegration spell. A direct hit on Arietta's head should do the trick. It wouldn't force her to cross over, but it would be enough to fragment her form. While she was getting back together, I'd break through the magic, grab Sol, get out of this building, find my scarecrows and Tuffin, and get the heck out of here.

"You can't care about him much if you're having to think so hard about this," Arietta said. "I could turn him into a ghost, and we could spend quality time together. I'd be an upgrade from you."

"He's not into older women." It was a bitchy thing to say, but this ghost was pressing all my buttons.

She hissed at me. Her fingers elongated until the tips were pointed, and she wrapped her hands around Sol's throat and squeezed.

"Wait! Don't do that. Sol shouldn't even be involved in my mess. He only works for me. We're not even together."

Arietta kept her hands wrapped around his throat, but was no longer choking him. "I can see you're interested in him. Why fight the inevitable?"

"I'm fighting nothing. I'm just trying to help a friend."

"Sure you are. You keep telling yourself that. One day, it may even come true. You friend zone a guy enough times, and he'll get the hint." Arietta kissed Sol's cheek. "So, do I have your loyalty?"

"No. But I won't let you hurt Sol. And I won't let him down." I thrust the disintegration spell straight at Arietta's head.

She moved at the last second, and the spell skimmed her left shoulder, knocking her back so she dropped Sol.

I raced forward, hurling more disintegration magic at Arietta as she bounced around the room.

My attention switched to Sol as he hit the floor and groaned. "Sol! We need to move. Get up."

An inhuman shriek filled the air, making my ears ring. But I kept slamming magic at Arietta. This ghost had to back off, or I'd destroy her. I wasn't rolling over and being her lapdog.

"You'll pay for that, witch." Arietta vanished, and the room plunged into darkness.

I lost my bearings, tripped over something, and face planted onto the cold floor. I groaned and pushed to my feet. "Sol, where are you?"

A quiet moan led me closer to him.

"Are you hurt? Can you get up?"

There was no reply as I inched forward on my hands and knees, my cheek throbbing from where I'd slammed into the floor, and my knees burning.

A heavy weight smashed into my back, crushing me. I tasted dirt as I struggled to get up, but I couldn't move. I sparked another spell, but a cold, sluggish sensation exploded from the base of my neck and traveled down my spine, taking away my desire to fight.

"I will kill you," Arietta hissed in my ear. "Keep fighting me, and I'll drain you of everything. You'll be a pointless husk and thrown into the world of mortals, who know nothing about magic, if you don't agree to help me."

I couldn't speak because my face was smooshed on the floor. I tried to buck Arietta off, but her hand was wrapped around the back of my neck as she sucked out my magic. Every second that passed, I grew weaker and more certain she'd carry out her threat to extinguish my magic for good.

"Bow to my will. Your magic will be saved, and your wannabe boyfriend will be protected. Work for me and all the pain will be taken away."

I couldn't lose my magic. I needed it to bring back Brodie. Without my ability, everything I'd worked so hard to achieve would be gone. And I couldn't allow Arietta to hurt Sol.

"Last chance, witch. Save yourself and your boyfriend, or this is over."

I raised my right hand in defeat.

"Yes?"

"It's a yes. I'll help you," I muttered into the cold concrete floor. The weight vanished from my back, and I rolled over.

Arietta stood over me, an annoyingly smug look on her face. "Excellent choice."

"Promise me you won't hurt Sol anymore." I scrambled to my feet, feeling so weak my knees wobbled.

"I'll look after him as if he's my offspring," Arietta said.

"And he comes with me when I look into what happened to you."

"No, he's my collateral. Once you leave, I need a reason for you to return. Despite you repeatedly saying you're not involved with him, you want to be. I could feel it when I took your magic. Which, by the way, is excellent." She sucked on each finger as if she'd just devoured a bargain bucket of greasy fried chicken.

I looked at Sol, who was slumped on the floor. "Feed him and let him sleep. And stop groping him."

"Isn't it adorable how much you care. Don't worry, I know how to take care of someone. Although I have staff who usually do that kind of thing."

"Just do your best. But I have a problem to deal with before I can solve your murder."

"Another one? How tedious."

"I'm a person of interest at the Magic Council. I escaped from my cell—"

Arietta clapped her hands together. "You admit to a jailbreak. This is even better. Now I have a corrupt witch on my side."

I really hated this ghost. "Not corrupt, just misunderstood. My problem is, how can I investigate your death when I'm a wanted witch?"

"My family don't live in Witch Haven. They're all in Crown Copse."

"The gated development where houses cost about ten million each?"

"Try fifteen. And, yes."

I whistled. "How does that help me get about without being spotted?"

"Use a concealment spell to get out of Witch Haven. Once you're in Crown Copse, no one will bother you. We keep to ourselves, and the neighbors are never any trouble. I kick them out if they are."

"I'll be bothered if the Magic Council question residents. They might think I've left the village and am hiding out somewhere close by."

"No. Crown Copse is a private village, and I have trolls who guard the entrance. If you don't have permission to go in, you don't get in. You can work for the Magic Council or the Devil herself and you still won't get through."

"That could be useful." My gaze went back to Sol. "Can't I take him with me?"

"He'll be safe here. And he's not waking up anytime soon."

"You need to make him comfortable. He's on the cold floor."

"You're demanding for someone who has no power." Arietta's grin was sharp. "I admire that. When your back is against the wall, you keep on fighting. I should have hired you while I was alive. Perhaps I wouldn't have been killed if you were watching my back."

"I may have killed you if I worked for you," I muttered.

"There's no need to be petty. We're both getting something out of this. I get revenge, and you get your boy toy back."

I was about to protest, but shook my head. Arietta could assume all she liked. "What about Tuffin and my scarecrows?"

"What's a tuffin?"

"The cat familiar you ejected."

"Oh, very well. I won't destroy them. They're outside."

"Then we have a deal. I'll solve your murder, and you let everyone go."

"We do indeed have a deal. Welcome to my world, Odessa Grimsbane. But be careful. Once you've walked on the dark side, you may never want to leave."

"I'm hightailing it out of here the second I can." It seemed I was now a ghost whisperer for a monster, and I didn't like it one bit.

Chapter 3

After an uncomfortable night of barely sleeping in the distillery, I was awake at dawn, ready to leave. Arietta had been her sarcastically unpleasant self all night, although she'd kept her word and made Sol more comfortable. She'd found a blanket to cover him and a cushion for his head. He hadn't stirred all night. I tried talking to him on and off for hours, but whatever she'd done, he wasn't waking up from it.

I rolled over and almost shrieked as I found Arietta by my side, staring at me. I scrambled away. "What are you doing so close? Trying to examine my tonsils?"

"You look tired. You have to be on top form today. My death is your priority."

"I'm aware of that, but I can hardly help the way I look. This isn't a spa. And sleeping on the cold floor all night didn't do my back any good."

"Suck it up, buttercup. The rewards will be worth it. And you were the one who insisted on staying near Sol so you could stare at him like a lovestruck teenager. I told you where the staff room was. There's a couch in there."

"You refused to lower the barrier so I could get near Sol, and I wasn't letting him out of my sight. I don't trust you not to lick him again."

"That's probably sensible." Arietta's gaze flicked between us. "If you behave yourself today, I'll wake him for you. You can have cozy chats and talk about your future together."

"Sol won't want a future with me after this. He should have left when he had the chance."

Arietta's lips pursed. "This hunk of sturdy farmhand candy didn't want to be with you?"

I stood slowly and stretched out my back and arms. "First off, he's not farmhand candy. He's a person who deserves respect. Don't label him because of the way he looks."

"He'd preen like a peacock if he heard me describe him that way. All men have egos that need stroking. And you have absolutely noticed this big, rough farmhand and thought about what you'd like to do with him. I expect that was a key criteria when you hired him. Must be buff was a tick box that had to be filled." She arched an eyebrow.

"You're being crude and disrespectful to both of us."

"Get used to it. So, are you planning a future with this guy?"

"There's no future for us." I turned and looked at Sol. "He was helping me one last time before he left. Sol wasn't happy working on the farm. He'd even applied for another job, although I'd convinced him to stay. I'm sure he's changed his mind since the whole getting arrested mess up."

Arietta yawned. "My heart is breaking. You have such a tragic life."

"No more tragic than a person getting killed by someone who should have looked out for her."

She cackled a laugh, not seeming to mind my jab. "I don't know why you're holding back. Grab him while you can. I sampled a little of his magic, and although there's not much there, it's full of annoying goodness. There's not a bad thing about this guy. I'd find that boring, but you, you're a good little witch, too. You'd be perfect together."

"It's not like that. I'm... with someone."

"But you're not married?"

"Yes. No. Well, technically. In my head, I am married."

"What a way to complicate things. Other people's love lives are so tedious. Take a leaf out of my book when it comes to romance. Get the men while they're hot, use them for everything they're worth, and move on to the next gorgeous guy. Or girl. Whatever takes your fancy."

I dug my fingernails into my palms. If I hadn't been so exhausted and drained of magic, I'd make Arietta sorry. But I was running on empty. My head hurt, my stomach growled, and my eyes felt gritty from lack of sleep. I had to deal with this ghost and move on with my life, which would mainly involve avoiding the Magic Council until I figured out a solution to my little snafu.

Arietta clicked her fingers in my face. "Stop staring at lover boy. You'll get him back soon enough. And if we shake my family up enough, one of them might confess today. Then you can forget this ever happened."

"I can't wait. Let's get out of here and see what they have to say about your death. I reckon I've got just enough energy left for a concealment spell."

"Then use it. I expect you want to say a sickly sweet goodbye to this burning hunk of yumminess, so I'll meet you outside. Don't be long." Arietta blinked out of sight.

I pressed my hand against the magic barrier surrounding Sol. "I'll be as quick as I can. If you can hear me, see if you can figure out a way to escape. Then we can take Arietta down between us."

He didn't stir, not even a flicker of an eyelid.

With a sigh, I turned and headed outside. I almost stumbled over my feet at the sight in front of me. My scarecrows were frozen, and Tuffin was unconscious on the ground. "Arietta! What have you done to them?"

She swirled around in front of me. "Removed a threat."

"I didn't realize you'd trapped them. That's unfair on Tuffin. She's just getting over being frozen and imprisoned."

"Is that so? Do we have a bad kitty on our hands? I hope so."

I stalked toward her. "You must stop hurting people. I don't work that way."

Arietta pouted and flipped her hair. "I was hurt. Why was that allowed to happen? Maybe I'm not the nicest person in the world, but I deserve justice. I shouldn't have been killed."

Her change of attitude surprised me so much I didn't know what to say.

"Do you think I wanted to run a place like this? To take magic from those who had nowhere else to turn. Do you know how many sleepless nights I had because of this business?"

"I... No. I assumed this was what you enjoyed doing."

A wicked smile crossed Arietta's face. "Are you that gullible? Of course, I loved doing this. I provided a service to people stupid enough to get themselves in a bind. It's not my fault they messed up and had to give away something so integral to their identity. I often wondered if they even deserved to keep existing, frittering away their gifts for money."

"Yes! Of course they do. And everyone gets in trouble at some point in their lives. What's wrong with you?"

"Nothing. I have the world figured out. It's a mean place, and people will stab you in the back." Arietta jabbed a finger at me. "And you need to become savvier. If you don't, my family will run rings around you. They'll throw you a dubious alibi, and you'll believe it. You can't. People lie to you, they deceive you, and they cheat you. Even your closest friends. And I can guarantee that anyone you've ever loved has done the same."

"You're wrong. There's only one man I loved, and he never lied or deceived me."

"They all do. You just don't know about it because he got away with it."

"Restore my scarecrows and Tuffin and let them go," I said.

"No. They make interesting ornaments."

"If they stay out here, they'll attract attention. And if I get discovered, I won't be able to help you. You can threaten me all you like, but you'll be on your own. Then you'll never get your revenge."

Arietta's gaze flickered over Tuffin and the scarecrows. "If I do, you must send them away. Give them an order to leave. I know you can command your scarecrows to do anything. They'll listen to you."

As much as I wanted to set Shamrock and Marmaduke on Arietta and destroy her, it was too much of a risk with Sol unconscious and trapped inside the distillery. "Agreed."

She flicked a hand, and Shamrock and Marmaduke came to life.

I rushed over and caught hold of their hands. "Listen to me, both of you. Leave immediately and keep a low profile from the Magic Council."

Both scarecrows were glaring at Arietta, but I knew they were paying attention.

"Go back to the farm. If it's safe, and there are no members of the Magic Council around, find a place to hide and remain there. If you don't, they'll catch you and pull you apart."

A buzzing filled my head as Shamrock formed a link with me. "You need help?"

"I'm good. I'm dealing with things. You have to look after the farm. Watch what the Magic Council is doing."

"You not safe."

"I will be. But I can't worry about you two. I'm concerned about the business. And check on the far end barn."

"Not allowed. Always tell me no entry," Shamrock said.

"I'm overriding that order. See if the Magic Council has gotten inside yet. Selma has been having problems getting in, and I can't figure out why."

"And you?"

"I'm helping Sol. And this ghost. She thinks she was murdered."

Shamrock growled. "She bad. Deserve to die."

"We're wasting time," Arietta said. "The longer we delay, the more likely your boyfriend is to find himself in trouble."

"Go," I said to Shamrock and Marmaduke. "Don't come back."

They hesitated, but my order overrode their protective instincts, and they raced away. I looked at Tuffin. "And my cat familiar."

"That mangy moggy attacked me. She stays where she is."

Poor Tuffin. Everyone she tangled with ended up freezing her. "At least let me make her comfortable."

"Why? She can't feel a thing."

I walked over to Tuffin. Her fuzzy face was frozen in a snarl, and one paw was raised off the ground, the claws extended. "She's not happy."

"You're too soft-hearted. That'll get you in trouble." Arietta flicked out a hand, and Tuffin wriggled.

I eased her onto her side and settled her on a comfortable-looking pile of moss. "Try to get away if you can," I whispered.

"No more speaking with the enemy. Let's get out of here." Arietta's icy hand wrapped around the back of my neck, and she hauled me to my feet. "Move it."

After another quick look around, I cast my concealment spell and hurried away from the distillery. "You'd better fill me in on everything leading up to your death. Leave nothing out."

"It was a murder, not a simple death."

"An alleged murder."

"Definite murder. And you should know everything about me already. I'm the most famous magic user around here for a hundred miles."

"Humor me. Was anything special happening in your life or with your family? Something that unsettled one of them?"

"I'd recently sold the business. I told my family over dinner the night I died."

"You were getting rid of the magic distillery? Everything?"

"I was selling it to someone. The deal would have made me ridiculously rich. It took months to organize, and I kept quiet about it until the night of my murder."

"Your family knew nothing about the plan to sell?" I skirted through the trees, glad it was still early because there were so few people around. And the Magic Council kept regular nine-to-five hours, so most of them would still be in bed at this time of the morning.

"It had nothing to do with them. It was my business."

"Did you set it up?"

"No, my mother handed it to me. It's been in our family for generations."

"What about family members who worked for you? They might have realized something was going on."

"My niece, Regan, works for the company. She's my brother's daughter. She handles the marketing and PR."

"Anyone else?"

"No. She's the only one directly involved in the business."

"Your brother didn't take an interest or sense something was going on?"

"I don't let him get involved. Derwin is incompetent, and he has no backbone. The women in my family are the strong ones. Besides, it's best to keep people in the dark until they have to know things. It gives you an edge over the competition."

"You see your family as competition?"

"You don't?"

"Nope."

Arietta chuckled. "You should have seen the looks on their faces when they found out about the sale. I wish I'd taken a picture."

"It must have been a shock. Did no one know?"

"My husband did. Chay. He was more excited than me about the money. Not that I was planning on giving him much. I'd have gotten him some gifts and treated us to a vacation, so he wouldn't have been left wanting." Arietta flitted ahead of me.

I kept my voice down as we left the trees and hurried along deserted streets toward the edge of Witch Haven. "You made the announcement about the sale at dinner, and then what?"

"We celebrated. At least, I celebrated. The others joined in, eventually. My adorable but stupid son, Fontayne, was there. Chay, my husband, my niece, Regan, and my brother, Derwin."

"What did you do after the announcement was made?"

"I had a few drinks and then did what I always do in the evenings. I sat in the pagoda in the backyard with a drink and worked on a voodoo plushie."

"I'm sorry, what? A voodoo plushie?"

"I know, it's a little unusual. When you think of plushies, you imagine some little old lady making felt dolls, but these are different. I was given a kit when I was a child and took to it. And there's a community of voodoo plushie makers all around the world. We have quarterly meetings and show off our designs."

"You use these toys in voodoo magic?"

"They're like puppets, but more elaborate. And more powerful. At least, mine are. I have a room in the house dedicated to them."

"You have a room of magically enchanted toys? That's not at all creepy."

"Everyone needs a useful hobby. And if someone ever wrongs me, I pull out a voodoo plushie and make sure they know never to do it again."

"You'd better not have a plushie of me."

"I barely know you. But if you get on my wrong side, you'll join my voodoo plushie collection."

"You can't make them now you're a ghost."

She scowled. "Don't underestimate me, witch. I'll figure out a way just to spite you."

I had no doubt she would. And having seen Arietta's power, I wasn't underestimating her. I'd never met such a strong ghost before.

"You should ask the housekeeper to look at my plushies while you're there. It's a unique collection."

"I'll pass on that, thanks. Although that could be a reason someone wanted you dead. If you'd created a voodoo plushie of them and used it, you wouldn't be on their friend list."

"It's your loss. But if I was killed because I made a plushie in someone's image, you'll have a thousand suspects to investigate."

"You made a thousand plushies? I don't even know that many people."

"I did. Let's hope you won't need to check all their alibis, or I'll be keeping Sol for a very long time."

I groaned as we got to the edge of Witch Haven. Why could murder never be straightforward?

I slowed and looked around. "I have a question. Why will your family talk to me about your murder?"

"Because you're in my employ. Therefore, you're acting as my voice, and they do everything I tell them to do."

"Can they see ghosts?"

Arietta was quiet for a few seconds. "No."

"So why will they believe a tired looking witch when she shows up talking about your murder?"

"I still have power. When I became a ghost, I didn't lose all my abilities. I'll shake them up so they know I'm still in charge." Her laugh had a mean edge to it. "Whoever killed me thought they'd gotten rid of me, but they'll soon see that, even though I'm dead, I'm still the alpha around here."

"I'm sure they'll be happy to know that." This ghost was an awful individual. I had to get out of this situation as quickly as possible.

I kept walking until we got to the edge of Crown Copse. I could tell there was a different class of magic user living here. Every house was immaculate and looked the same. The front yards were pristine, and all the cars looked like they'd just been valeted.

"There's a guard post ahead," Arietta said. "Give me a minute, and I'll make sure your name is on the approved list of visitors, or you'll never get in."

I hung back under my concealment spell, briefly considering making a run for it. But that would mean abandoning Tuffin and Sol, and I wasn't doing that.

Arietta returned a moment later. "It's all clear. You can drop your magic. You'll have no trouble getting through. And the magical tracking is lowered, so you can get in without being recorded."

As promised, when I announced my name to the guard, he waved me through with a grunt.

"Which house is yours?" I said.

"It's in the center of the village, with white columns outside the front door and a unicorn statue in the yard. You can't miss it. It's twice as big as the other properties."

Why wasn't I surprised to hear that?

A barrier of dense, glossy foliage surrounded Crown Copse. It felt more like a model village than a place people actually lived. And although I didn't see anyone, several curtains twitched as I walked past houses.

"Ignore the neighbors. They won't trouble you," Arietta said. "If anyone questions you, say you're doing business for me. They'll soon scamper away."

I nodded. "How do you want to play this? I doubt your family will be receptive if I blunder in and talk about your murder."

"They will. I'll deal with them. You simply get the answers. And they appreciate a direct approach, so no small talk. Make sure they know you can't be messed with since you're working for me."

"Technically, I'm not working for you. You're blackmailing me into doing this by threatening to frame me for murder, and you're holding someone I care about against his will. Two people, if you include Tuffin, which I do." Tuffin may be a furry sassy frass, but I'd taken her under my wing, and that meant she got looked after.

"How perceptive you are. I've gotten you over a barrel," Arietta said. "It's just where I like my employees to be."

This dispute felt like it could go round in circles in an ever decreasing spiral of annoyance. "Come on, let's go have some conversations about murder."

"Perfect. And don't let me down, Odessa. Sol and Tuffin's lives depend on you."

Chapter 4

The bell I rang on the front door of the Frost mansion echoed a tuneful note that resonated through the house as I waited outside with Arietta.

"You'll meet the housekeeper first," she said.

"And does the housekeeper have a name?"

"Eva. She's been with us since she left high school. She's not a talented magic user but knows the basics and keeps the place running smoothly."

"How long has Eva been with you?"

"Twenty years, maybe. She knows how to behave herself."

I'm sure she did whenever she got near Arietta. I couldn't imagine anyone wanting to get on the wrong side of her.

Arietta blasted me with chilled air. "Ring the bell again. What's taking so long?"

"Cool your icy pantaloons. You live in an enormous house. Maybe Eva's upstairs."

"She knows I hate it when I'm left waiting."

"But she doesn't know it's the ghost of her former employer demanding attention. She'd be racing to the door like a unicorn stallion after his mate if she knew it was you."

Arietta smirked. "Naturally."

A few seconds later, the front door opened. A tall, plump woman in her mid-forties, dressed in a traditional black-and-white uniform, her hair pulled back in a tight bun, looked at me. "Good morning. May I help you?"

"I hope so. I'm here on an urgent matter. It's about Arietta Frost. Is the family in? I need to speak to them all."

Eva's eyes flashed with fear. "Did you work for Arietta?"

"No, we never worked together."

"If this is a business matter, contact her legal team. They're dealing with those kinds of things. The family can't be disturbed at this difficult time."

"Well, this is interesting. The housekeeper has gotten courageous since I've gone," Arietta said. "She normally wouldn't say boo to a ghost."

I stepped away from Arietta. "It's not a business matter. It's concerning Arietta's death."

"My murder. Call it as it is. I was killed!" Arietta yelled in my ear.

I shot her a glare and then turned back to the open door. "It's Eva, isn't it?"

"That's right. And... I know you. Odessa, from the scarecrow farm?"

"Yes, that's me. Odessa Grimsbane. I didn't know Arietta, but she has asked me to help her."

Eva stepped back. "I'm sorry, but you must know she's dead."

"I do. It's the reason I'm here. I must speak to her family. Hopefully, this won't take long, but it is important I meet with them all."

"Oh! Well, of course. Give me a minute, and I'll check with Mr. Frost. Not everyone else is awake yet, though."

"Don't waste time talking to that idiot," Arietta said. "My brother has no say over what goes on here."

"Thanks, Eva. I'll stay right here until you get Mr. Frost's permission." I waited until the door had closed before turning to Arietta. "This will go badly if you keep barking orders at me. We must keep things calm. If a family member killed you, we don't want to put them on the alert straightaway."

"We should. Then if anyone makes a run for it, I'll know they're guilty. I can chase them down and make them regret what they did to me."

"Which is what, exactly? You can't remember the cause of death. This could all be a misunderstanding. No attacking anyone until I have all the information."

"Misunderstanding my Aunt Tilda's goblet. This was cold-blooded murder. And I will take my pound of flesh."

"No. We'll make sure justice is done."

"I have my own form of justice figured out."

The door opened again before the argument could continue, and Eva ushered me inside. "Right this way. Mr. Frost is in the study."

Arietta shot ahead and disappeared into a room, which I assumed was the study. A few seconds later, there was a yelp and something hit the floor.

I hurried after Arietta, alongside Eva. As I entered the room, I discovered a pile of books tossed on the floor and a chair knocked over, the former occupant standing and staring at it as if it had just bitten him.

"Let me introduce you to my pointless older brother, Derwin," Arietta said. She was swirling around Derwin, a malevolent look on her face as if she was working up to something big.

"Is everything okay, Mr. Frost?" Eva hurried over and picked up the books.

"I'm... I'm not sure." Derwin was short and stocky with the same vibrant, shiny red hair as Arietta and a wobbly jowl. He wore a bright green and pink flowered shirt.

"He says that a lot. Derwin's favorite phrases are: *I'm not sure, in my humble opinion, and let's consider it some more.* The man never takes any action." Arietta swiped another book off the desk, and it landed on Derwin's slippered foot.

"I can't explain what's happening." Derwin rubbed his toe. "One minute, I was sitting here reading, and the next..." He gestured to the fallen books.

Eva set the books back on the desk and stepped away. "This is Odessa Grimsbane."

"Oh, of course. I recognize you. We sometimes come into Witch Haven to shop. And I visited your farm not so long ago. We had a couple of your excellent scarecrows for a time." Derwin nodded at me.

"I hope they serve you well," I said.

"They did. They were excellent."

"Did? Aren't they still around? My scarecrows come with a lifetime guarantee. If anything went wrong with them, you let me know and I'll fix them. No extra charge."

"Ah, that might be a problem." Derwin rubbed the back of his neck. "You see, my sister had an issue with them."

I glowered at Arietta. She'd conveniently forgotten to mention that. "What kind of issue?"

"Arietta wanted them to attack people. People who didn't deserve it." Derwin chuckled. "I mean, not that anyone warrants being attacked. She soon discovered they weren't mindless killing creatures that did everything they were told. When they didn't obey her orders, she set fire to them."

My heart stopped for several painful seconds as the words hit me. "She did what?"

"I suggested we keep them, but she put them on a bonfire, anyway." Derwin nodded, a glimmer of sympathy in his eyes. "Sorry."

"What was I supposed to do? I expect loyalty from those I hire," Arietta said.

"Oh! Are you feeling well?" Derwin stepped closer, his hand hovering in the space between us. "You've gone pale, and there are bright red blotches on your chest. You're not getting sick, are you?"

"No, I'll be fine. It's just a shock when I hear about people mistreating my scarecrows." The scarecrows were my babies. Arietta would pay for that. "If you look after them, you're guaranteed loyal scarecrows for life."

"They weren't loyal enough for my liking," Arietta said. "Stop stressing about your scarecrows. They're long gone. Order the housekeeper to get everyone else and focus on me."

"Give me a minute," I muttered, still processing my anger.

Derwin glanced at Eva. "Perhaps you'd like some refreshments? I haven't had any breakfast yet, so you're welcome to join me. We can sit and let the color come back in your cheeks."

"Thanks. I am feeling lightheaded." And sick to the stomach over Arietta's cruel behavior.

"Eva, help Odessa to the dining room," Derwin said.

I waved away her hand. "I'll be fine. But a strong coffee would be great."

"That's something I can happily help with." Derwin looked at Eva again and smiled. "Is breakfast ready?"

"As always."

"Then we shall eat." Derwin clasped his hands together. "And Eva mentioned you wanted to discuss some matters concerning my departed sister."

"That's right. The situation is complicated, though. It would be easier if everyone was present to learn what I have to say."

"Um... It's been a traumatic six weeks since Arietta died. I don't want to worry people. She had a son, you know? He's not that old. He doesn't say much about her death, but he must miss her."

"I understand. And I'm sorry, but this can't wait."

Arietta kept poking my ribs with a finger until I waved her away.

Derwin looked at me oddly. "I see. Well, it has been distressing but, in my humble opinion, also peaceful. My sister could be a difficult woman to be around."

"How dare he!" Arietta shot forward and punched straight through her brother.

He staggered back with a groan and hit the wall. "What was that?"

"That is the reason I'm here." I hurried over and helped Derwin to his feet. "Arietta has asked me to help her. She approached me in her ghost form."

Derwin gulped and forced himself to stand. "She's here? As a gggghost?"

Arietta swirled around us in an icy cloud of indignation. "I gave this family everything. They wouldn't have this house or all the money if it weren't for me."

"Settle down," I muttered to her. "Derwin, I'll explain everything. But you all need to hear this."

Eva hurried over, her face pale and her hands trembling. "Perhaps you should rest, Mr. Frost. You hit your head on the wall when you were pushed by... the ghost."

"Stop mothering him," Arietta yelled in Eva's face.

Although Eva couldn't see Arietta, she jerked back and shuddered.

Derwin ran a hand down his face, his gaze tracking around the room. "Arietta's really not gone?"

I nodded. "She's here."

He leaned back against the wall and sighed. "Of course, she was never going to make her passing simple. Eva, fetch the rest of the family, please. We all need to know what's going on." Derwin's words came out shaky.

Eva dashed out of the room, leaving me with a quivering, pale looking Derwin.

"He always was a spineless toady," Arietta said. "If you raise your voice right now, he'll wet his pants."

"Hush. There's no need to be mean." Now the secret was out, I no longer needed to hide the ghost in the room.

"You really are talking to Arietta?" Derwin said. "You're a ghost whisperer?"

"Sometimes. Arietta made contact yesterday in unusual circumstances. She's unhappy and needs a problem solving. She thinks I can help her do that."

"Well, with my dead sister back, we need something to fortify ourselves. Let's go for breakfast. At least we can have a nice view and a decent coffee while I hear everything. I have a feeling it won't be good news."

"That sounds like a great plan." I wanted to make this as easy on the family as possible. It was clear Arietta had terrorized them while she was alive, and I wanted to make sure she didn't keep doing it now she was dead.

I entered a bright, warm room with pretty pastel pink wallpaper. At the back of the room, a long table had been laid out with breakfast trays. There were terrines of bacon, eggs, sausages, hash browns, and everything you could imagine for a delicious breakfast. There were also croissants, fresh pastries, and a huge bowl of fruit salad.

"Help yourself to anything," Derwin said. "Would you like a coffee?"

"Yes, please. And I am hungry. I haven't eaten much since yesterday." I flashed a glare at Arietta.

"Don't hold back. There's always too much food. I keep telling Eva we can cut back now Arietta's not here. She always liked things extravagant, didn't you?" His unfocused gaze went around the room.

"There's no harm in enjoying my wealth," Arietta said.

I helped myself to a smoked cheese filled croissant and a large bowl of fruit salad and sat at the table, eating my food and sipping my coffee as I waited for the rest of the family.

Derwin kept looking at me, then paced to the window, his coffee in his hand. "Did you know my sister when she was alive?"

"Only by reputation. Of course, I knew about the magic distillery."

"Yes, a profitable but unpopular venture." He sipped his coffee. "Arietta could be difficult. She had big ambitions and worked hard, but it was to the detriment of everything else. And she didn't have the best people skills."

"That moron realizes I can hear him, doesn't he?" Arietta said. "Can he really be so stupid as to talk about my perceived failings in front of me?"

"It would appear so," I said. "Arietta isn't happy with your description of her."

Derwin turned from the window. "She never liked to listen to anything other than glowing reviews. She surrounded herself with yes people, so she never had to hear anything bad. As a result, her behavior toward others only grew worse."

Arietta whizzed over and knocked a tray of toast to the floor.

"And, as you can see, she could be petty." Derwin sighed as he scooped up the toast and set it to one side. "But she was still my sister, and I loved her, even though she didn't deserve it."

I turned my head as voices approached the room.

Arietta returned to my side. "Let me introduce you to the rest of the idiots." She pointed to an incredibly handsome man of around thirty, with dark hair, broad shoulders, and a charming smile that lit up the second he saw me. "That's Chay. My latest husband. He always smells good. Like a tropical beach at sundown."

I nodded. "And final husband."

"Beside him is Regan. That's my niece. My brother's daughter. She's naïve but works hard."

I nodded and smiled at the attractive young woman dressed in a soft gray catsuit, her face free of make-up. She couldn't have been more than about twenty-one.

"The cretin who just tripped over his feet is unfortunately my son, Fontayne," Arietta said. "I overindulged him when he was young, and now he's an entitled fool with barely a useful brain cell in that dopey head."

"Don't be mean," I whispered.

The young man she was disparaging had a mess of floppy red curls that he kept pushing out of his purple eyes. He looked like he'd slept in the jeans and sweater he had on and kept yawning and rubbing at his face.

"What's this all about?" Chay said to Derwin. "Eva says there's a family emergency, and it's to do with Arietta." His gaze flicked to me, and he winked.

"There is. We have a situation," Derwin said. "Everyone, grab some breakfast and take a seat. I'll let Odessa explain."

I gave everyone a nervous wave as they stared at me, curiosity written across their faces. I swiftly polished off the rest of my fruit salad as everyone assembled their breakfasts and sat around the table.

"Get on with it," Arietta said. "Ask which one of them killed me."

I eased back my seat and stood, standing behind the chair and resting my hands on the back of it. "I think I'm familiar with all of you. But for those of you who don't know me, I'm Odessa Grimsbane."

"The scarecrow lady," Fontayne said. "Those things are awesome."

"Thank you. That's right, I manufacture enchanted scarecrows. I also run the large pumpkin farm on the edge of Witch Haven."

"They don't care about you," Arietta snapped. "I'm the focus. This is all about me."

"It's nice to meet you, Odessa. But what does your visit have to do with Arietta?" Chay said. "This is about her, isn't it?"

"It is." I flashed my eyebrows up at Arietta. "I have an ability to see ghosts. And I was approached by Arietta's ghost recently."

"No! She's passed over," Fontayne said. "Mom is dead. She's not a ghost."

"Her ghost is right here," I said. "Arietta didn't cross over because she has unfinished business."

"What's that?" Derwin said. "Why has Arietta not moved on?"

I looked at each of them. "Because she believes one of you murdered her."

Chapter 5

No one spoke, and everyone stopped eating as they stared at me.

"Arietta was killed, but not by anyone here," Derwin finally said, his words stuttering out. "It happened outside in the pagoda. But that's being investigated by the Magic Council."

"Have you all been included in that investigation?" I said.

"We've all been spoken to," Derwin said.

Everyone else nodded.

"There's no easy way to say this, but Arietta is convinced one of you was involved in her death. It's the reason she's still here."

She prodded me with an icy finger. "Ask which one of them did it. Get the sneaky killer to confess."

I shooed her away. "Arietta has sort of hired me to solve her murder. So, would anyone like to make this easy and confess right now?"

Again, I was met with a stunned silence. No surprise there, but I had to try the easiest option first.

"This is wrong," Chay said. "It would have been impossible for any of us to do it. We were all inside.

The investigator from the Magic Council believes an intruder killed Arietta. They're talking to local criminals to see if they know anything about it."

Arietta zoomed around the table and swiped at Chay's plate, shattering it and scattering the contents everywhere.

He jumped out of his seat and tugged at the collar of his shirt. "Arietta, sweetheart, be reasonable. You know none of us would hurt you."

"Order him to behave," Arietta said. "Chay doesn't get to tell me what to do."

"Everyone stay calm." I mainly directed that comment at Arietta. I helped Chay pick up the plate and got a strong whiff of coconut and suntan lotion. Arietta was right. He did smell like a tropical beach. "As you can all see, Arietta is unhappy about what happened to her."

"It took a lot to make her happy," Derwin mumbled.

Arietta slammed into him, almost knocking him to the floor.

"Arietta! Please, let me deal with this." I helped Derwin back into his seat. "Are you okay?"

"Don't worry about him. I'm the dead person around here," Arietta snapped. "Stop treating them so well. We have a killer in this room."

"Thank you. Yes, I'll be fine. I'm used to Arietta being demanding." Derwin straightened his plate and smoothed down his hair.

I held a hand up to Arietta to try to get her to stop flying about and making the room so cold. She ignored me. "It would be helpful if I could find out your alibis for that night. Even if it's to discount you all as suspects."

"The Magic Council has already done that," Regan said. "They questioned us right after Aunty Arietta died."

"Would you mind telling me?" I said. "This could be what Arietta needs to hear so she can be reassured no one in this room hurt her."

"I want to hear a confession, not a lie," Arietta said.

"We have nothing to hide. And our alibis are simple," Derwin said. "We were all together. Well, most of us."

"Where was Arietta when she died?" I said.

"In the backyard. She did the same thing every evening. She'd eat dinner with us and then take a plushie outside with a stiff drink and sit in the pagoda. She'd spend time on her own, winding down after a busy day of work. In my humble opinion, it helped her relax."

"Aunty Arietta did little relaxing," Regan said. "She worked every day. Most evenings, too."

"Arietta was out there alone the whole time?" I said.

Derwin nodded. "And we were all in the house."

"Together?"

"I'd gone to bed early," Derwin said. "I have a sensitive stomach, and something I'd eaten wasn't agreeing with me. I got an early night in the hope I'd be better in the morning."

"He claims he has an irritable bowel," Arietta said. "It's his nerves. Ridiculous man."

I shook my head at her and tutted.

"Did Arietta say something about me?" Derwin said.

"She did, but it wasn't important. When Arietta mentions anything useful, I'll let you know." I wasn't passing on the irritable bowel comment in case it embarrassed Derwin. "Were you in bed alone?"

"Yes. I said goodnight to Regan, excused myself from the celebrations, and went upstairs."

"And we were downstairs," Chay said. "Arietta revealed the news about the business being sold, so we celebrated."

"Some of us were celebrating," Regan said. "I wish I'd known about what was going on, since I work for the company."

"If Regan was important enough to know about it, she would have been told," Arietta said.

"You weren't celebrating with Chay and Fontayne?" I asked Regan.

"I had a drink with them but then grabbed a book and settled on the couch at the back of the games room, while they got wasted on shots and cocktails. Chay kept pressing drinks on me, but I didn't want to get drunk. I'm not a huge drinker."

I looked at Eva, who had remained by the breakfast table since her return from gathering the family. "And what about you?"

"I served the evening meal and then left. I usually finish my duties around nine at night. I have a small chalet behind the house. I've lived there for years."

"You live there with your family?"

She shook her head. "I live alone. I never married."

"This isn't getting us anywhere. The housekeeper didn't do it," Arietta said.

I gestured at her to be quiet, and she jabbed me again with an icy finger. "When did you all know something had happened to Arietta?"

"When we heard the gunfire," Chay said. "We ran out and discovered Arietta dead in the pagoda."

"A gun!" Arietta stopped moving, shock registering on her face. Anger swiftly replaced it. "Those sneaky turncoats. They used my gun on me."

"Arietta was shot? It wasn't magic that killed her?" I said.

They all shook their heads.

"But you can all use magic?"

"We can," Chay said. "We're all warlocks and witches. Although none of us are that powerful."

"Why was Arietta killed with a gun? A weapon like that leaves evidence," I said, more to myself than anyone else in the room. "Was the bullet that killed her found?"

"One of the investigators found it," Fontayne said. "They poked around and dug it out of a piece of wood in the pagoda."

"I was shot with my own gun." Arietta shook her head. "I never expected it to end that way."

"Arietta just told me she owned a gun," I said. "Was that the murder weapon?"

"Yes. And it was her gun," Chay said. "It was supposed to be something special. It was used to assassinate someone high up in the Magic Council years ago. I wasn't sure I believed the story, but she had a certificate of authentication."

"Where is the gun now? Was it found?"

"It was in the wishing well. It's around the back of the house, close to the pagoda. It got submerged in water, so there was no useful evidence on it," Chay said.

I looked at Arietta. "Why own a gun? Magic is more powerful than a weapon like that."

"Why not? And it can be effective," Arietta said. "It had such a wonderfully dark history that I couldn't resist. It's amazing what a small piece of metal can do at high speed."

"Arietta had a thing about guns ever since we were children," Derwin said. "There's a shooting range out back, and she was always going out to practice her aim. She liked to have a backup in case anything went wrong with her magic."

"Did her powers often malfunction?" I said.

"No, but Arietta liked to be prepared for the worst and wipe out any weakness."

"And that worked for me for a long time," Arietta said.

"Until you were shot by your back-up plan," I muttered.

She glared at me and spun away, leaving behind an icy backdraft.

"As the business Arietta ran proved, magic can be drained. If you lose enough magic, you become powerless. She never wanted to put herself in that position," Derwin said.

"Aunty Arietta was happy to do it to other people, though," Regan said, the note of disapproval clear in her tone.

"And my actions made her a wealthy young woman," Arietta said. "Regan should be more grateful."

"Was anything else found with Arietta when her body was discovered?" I said. "Any clues to suggest who wanted her dead?"

"There was nothing important," Derwin said.

"Only her voodoo plushie," Chay said. "She was obsessed with those things. She has a room for them upstairs."

"She told me about her toys," I said. "It's an unusual hobby."

"It suited her character," Fontayne muttered.

"What do you mean by that?" I said.

He shrugged and pulled a piece off his croissant. "She always liked to have the upper hand. She had to make sure she had complete control."

"Don't listen to my boy. He's panicking because his free ride could be over. My baby boy may have to face the real world if he gets cut off from my wealth." Arietta swirled around the table. "One of these traitors did it. They're hiding things. Get them to answer you."

"I noticed you have magic barriers in certain parts of the estate and guard patrols," I said. "Did they see anything that night? Maybe someone coming in who wasn't supposed to be in the village."

"The guards were questioned," Derwin said. "Nothing came of it. The trolls always record people who come and go. You may not be aware, but Arietta owned this village, and she decided who got to live here. She could also decide to kick people out."

"And she often did that," Regan said. "I've had to cover up some unpleasant threats because Aunty Arietta decided she didn't like the look of one of her neighbors."

"I always believe in judging a book by its cover," Arietta said. "But sometimes, people turn into nightmares. Of course, I'll evict them if they can't keep up the high standards of my neighborhood."

"Arietta made a lot of enemies?" I said.

"She did. And I must admit, in my humble opinion, I'm not surprised this hasn't happened before now," Derwin said. "My sister wasn't popular."

"I wasn't popular because I spoke my mind. If people didn't like what I had to say, then that was their problem." Arietta scowled at everyone, but there was a flicker of sadness in her eyes. She must have noticed that no one had shed a tear yet.

"So, to be clear, you were all together when you heard the gunshot?" I said.

"We were," Chay said. "We were in the games room, which has the best sound system. We were playing music, dancing, and drinking. When I heard the bang, I went outside with Regan and Fontayne. Eva and Derwin were a second or two behind us."

"Did you see anyone running away from the scene of the crime?"

"There was no one," Derwin said.

"No one ran, because the killer is right here," Arietta said. "Someone is lying to you."

"Arietta's still not convinced," I said. "Could I check the trackers you have around the house? Maybe something was picked up on them."

"They're broken," Derwin said. "They've been down for about eight weeks, and I've been meaning to deal with it. I spoke to the company who installed them, but they've been busy and had to cancel on me twice. I thought we'd be safe enough without them."

"Idiot! He should have told me about that," Arietta said. "Look what happened. I was killed because of his stupidity."

"Excuse me, Mr. Frost, but the tracking system has been repaired," Eva said. "The village is being monitored again, including this house. The trackers recorded anyone coming and going."

"I didn't know that." Derwin sat up straight in his seat. "When were they fixed?"

"A couple of days after you reported the fault," Eva said. "I got someone to deal with it when you mentioned how unhelpful the repair company was being. I'm sorry. I should have mentioned it to you."

"The trackers were working when Arietta was killed?" I said.

"They were," Eva said.

"Has anyone from the Magic Council checked the recordings?"

"No. I didn't give it to them. When they asked about it, I told them it was broken," Derwin said. "They never looked at it."

"Could I look at it?" I said.

"Don't ask permission. Demand to see it if they won't let you," Arietta said. "My killer could be recorded on those trackers. Who's sweating the most?" She buzzed around the table, staring at everyone's face for several seconds.

"Eva, please fetch the recordings connected to the house," Derwin said.

"Of course." Eva hurried away.

"This is what we need. I knew the Magic Council had behaved incompetently," Arietta said. "You're not a smart witch, but you've only been here ten minutes and already discovered a key piece of information. I'll keep you around for a little longer."

I huffed out a laugh. This ghost was unbelievable.

"This situation must be driving Arietta mad," Derwin said. "She hated not being able to solve a problem. She always loved to prove she was the smartest one in the room."

"That was hardly a challenge when you're surrounded by morons. Let's get out of here," Arietta said. "I'm sick of listening to these losers. Go look at my voodoo plushie collection."

"No thanks," I said under my breath.

"I insist. I miss them. They're one of the few things that brought me pleasure. It'll take Eva twenty minutes to gather the tracking recorders. You might as well make yourself useful." Arietta kept prodding me until I swatted her away.

"Would someone mind showing me Arietta's collection of plushies?" I said. "She's keen on seeing them."

"I'll take you," Regan said.

"Thanks. I'll be back soon for the recordings." I headed out with Regan and up a large, sweeping marble staircase.

Regan glanced at me. "Is Aunty Arietta here, too?"

"She is. She tagged along."

"I am sorry about what happened," Regan said. "I hope this gets figured out and you can move on and be happy. Maybe find some peace."

"It's pointless groveling to me," Arietta said. "And if Regan killed me, she'll get what's coming to her."

I ignored her. "Arietta is glad to see you. She misses you."

Regan pursed her lips. "She'd never say that, but I appreciate the comment." She led me to a room along a long, wide corridor painted in a deep vintage green and opened the door.

I didn't step inside as a gleaming sea of angry eyes confronted me. In fact, I wanted to run away and never look over my shoulder. The plushies were all a similar size, apart from a few giant teddies, but they all emitted the same furious vibe of hatred.

"It's something else, isn't it?" Regan gave a mirthless chuckle. "Aunty Arietta had a real thing about creating these monsters. There's even one of me. She made one for each member of the family."

"And you had no problem with that?" I flinched as a weird crocodile type plushie growled.

"I may have done, but I had no choice in the matter. And she used magic in them. Aunty Arietta took personal items from us, usually our hair, and infused it into a plushie."

"As a method of control, nothing more," Arietta said. "Aren't they beautiful? I dedicated so many hours to my creations. You must feel the same way about your scarecrows, Odessa. You infuse them with your power and become more powerful yourself."

"No, that's the opposite of what I do to my scarecrows. I bring them to life and set them free. I don't hold them over people's heads and threaten them."

"Then you're missing a trick." Arietta floated into the enormous room, which was lined floor-to-ceiling with shelves stuffed with creepy plushies.

"I'm not sure what we'll do with these," Regan said. "We can't give them away. Imagine what someone could do with a thousand voodoo plushies. In the wrong hands, they'd be able to take control of the village and have an army of terrified magic users to control."

"You should decommission the magic in each of them. Turn them into harmless toys and donate them to a children's charity," I said. "Make sure something good comes from them."

"Aunty Arietta would hate that. She couldn't stand children. She even sent Fontayne to a boarding school until he was eighteen because he was too noisy. He's only been back here a couple of years."

"My niece knows me well," Arietta said. "And these plushies aren't for children. Don't donate them. They stay here."

"You can take a closer look if you like," Regan said.

"No, I'm creeped out enough just standing in the doorway," I said. "There are too many things growling in there for me to get any closer."

"There's nothing to be afraid of," Arietta said, an evil grin on her face.

There was a heck of a lot to be afraid of. I could feel the magic radiating off each plushie. Arietta had clearly dedicated time and powerful magic into each one. And she hadn't done it for a positive reason.

"Let's go back downstairs," I said. "I'll get the tracking information and then leave you all to it."

Regan nodded and closed the door. She walked along beside me. "Do you really think someone in this house killed Aunty Arietta?"

"It's possible. But it's also likely she made a lot of enemies. Maybe the Magic Council is right and someone did sneak in and do this to her."

"If that's true, I'll be sneaking up on them to enact my vengeance," Arietta said.

I waved away her threats. I was getting used to them since she spat them out every few minutes.

As we headed back to the dining room, raised voices came from inside.

I entered the room to see Fontayne standing over Derwin, jabbing his finger in Derwin's face. "It was you. I heard you say it."

"What's going on?" I said.

Fontayne turned toward me, his cheeks pink and anger in his eyes. "It was Uncle Derwin. He threatened to kill Mom, and a few hours later, she was dead."

Chapter 6

The roar of laughter from Arietta hurt my ears. "That's impossible. Derwin wouldn't dare kill me. He's too pathetic to stand up against me."

I took note of Derwin's pale face and clenched hands. "Did you threaten Arietta the night she died?"

"He did," Fontayne said. "And he said it in front of everyone. We were eating dinner when Mom told us about the sale of the business. Uncle Derwin protested and said he should have been told about it."

"Which Arietta didn't do." I directed my comment to her.

"Derwin has no backbone for hard work. If a problem needed sorting, I had to have someone I could rely upon. Derwin isn't reliable."

"I knew nothing about the sale," Derwin said. "I'd noticed Arietta was having more meetings away from the house than usual and receiving lots of paperwork through the post, but it wasn't uncommon for her to get caught up in a new proposal. And when I asked her about it, she said it was nothing important."

"He'd have tried to stop me by whining and begging," Arietta said. "My brother hates change."

"Why did you threaten Arietta?" I said.

"I was angry. This business has been in the family for generations. Arietta never cared about that. Her only interest was money and how obscenely wealthy she could make herself. And I expect she had no plans to share that wealth with us."

"She'd have shared with me," Fontayne said. "I'm her son."

"And me," Chay said. "She'd promised me a vacation and a new wardrobe of clothes."

"They'd have gotten a little, but Fontayne would have needed to prove himself first," Arietta said. "Just because he's my son doesn't mean he gets to have an easy ride."

"I spoke those words in the heat of the moment," Derwin said. "If I'd been planning to kill Arietta, I'd have kept quiet about it. It's a coincidence we argued, and then she died." His gaze flashed around the room. "The actual killer used that fight to their advantage. They wanted me to look guilty."

"Are you accusing one of us of murder?" Chay said.

"Not Regan. But you or Fontayne could have done it."

Chay rose from his seat, but Arietta shoved him back down. "Derwin didn't do it. Rule him out."

"Are you sure? He doesn't have much of an alibi," I said to her.

"What's Arietta saying?" Derwin said. "She must know I'm innocent."

"She does think you're innocent," I said.

He pressed his lips together. "Did she say I was a coward? Is that why she thinks I wouldn't kill her?"

I winced as I nodded. "Something like that."

"Arietta! Calm down." Chay squirmed in his seat as she kept shoving him. "Don't be angry at me. I'm defending you."

Arietta moved away and rolled her shoulders. "Keep questioning them. We're getting somewhere."

I glanced at Arietta. "Derwin, you have no solid alibi for when your sister was shot. You've got to admit it looks suspicious. You fought with Arietta, and then she was killed."

His jaw wobbled, but he nodded. "I can see that, but I don't benefit from Arietta's death. She has everything tied up in a complicated will. We're still waiting for the final details, but I'm certain her money won't come to me. For all I know, I may get nothing."

"That's true," Arietta said. "I wouldn't trust Derwin to invest the money from the sale of the business wisely. He'd probably donate it to a local animal sanctuary."

"I still think it was you." Fontayne glared at Derwin. "You only live here because you have no choice. It's not because you liked my mom."

"I live here because I like being close to my family, and Regan works for the distillery."

"Were you happy that Derwin and Regan lived here with you?" I asked Arietta.

"Not happy, but it made it easier to keep tabs on them. And Regan isn't hopeless."

"What did Arietta say?" Derwin said.

"She had no problem with you being here," I said.

"Arietta complained about me being here most days," Derwin said. "She said I needed to pull my weight, but every time I made a suggestion about the house or the business, she hated it. Eventually, I gave up. A person can only get knocked back so many times before he learns it's better to keep his head down and his mouth shut."

"At last! He's said something useful," Arietta said.

"Dad wouldn't hurt Aunty Arietta," Regan said. "She could be mean to him, but we were still family. We stick together. And I know she loved us. She just had a hard time talking about it."

"Your aunt had a heart of stone," Derwin muttered, "but we do stick together. There were many times when I didn't like my sister, but I'd never kill her."

"Only because, if you tried and failed, you'd have been terrified about her getting revenge," Chay said. "Let's be honest here. Arietta was tired of you. She wanted a fresh start without her brother tagging along."

"A fresh start! So why didn't Arietta move away and take you with her? She could have left us here. We'd have been happy."

"That was never going to happen."

"Why not? Or did she sell this village, too?" Derwin said.

Chay smirked. "You are out of the loop. We have two magic distilleries in Crown Copse. They're included in the deal."

Derwin stood from his seat. "Arietta sold everything? What about the houses?"

"Those, too. It's why she got such a good price."

"Does that mean everyone who lives here will be forced to leave?" I said.

"It's possible," Chay said. "They all work for Arietta anyway, so some will keep their jobs, but that'll be up to the new owner. They'll have to wait and see what plans they have for changing the business."

"Do the villagers know about this?" I said.

"They don't. Arietta didn't want protests and petitions slowing things down," Chay said. "She planned for a quick sale, and then we were going on vacation for two months."

"To let the dust settle and leave us to deal with the angry neighbors who were about to become homeless," Derwin said.

"Something like that. And Arietta figured it would give you something to do." Chay's smile was smug as he lounged in his seat.

"Even though I didn't kill Arietta, I'm glad she's gone," Derwin said. "She was planning to ruin so many lives by being so callous. She had no plans to look after anyone who worked for her. She threw them away for money."

"It's a serious amount of money," Arietta said. "Anyone else would have done the same."

"Unlikely," I muttered to her. This information wasn't what I'd hoped to hear. If any of the villagers in Crown Copse had discovered Arietta's plan to sell their house from under them, they could have come for revenge. That made the case much more complicated.

"Are you going to arrest Derwin?" Chay said. "He looks guilty to me."

"He's a spineless toad. He didn't do this," Arietta said. "But someone in here did. Chay is pointing the finger a lot."

"No one's getting arrested," I said. "Arietta simply wanted me to find out more about what happened to her. The Magic Council will make an arrest when the time is right."

"Tell them to be careful. I'll be watching. They'd better sleep with one eye open, or they'll regret letting their guards down, just like I did." Arietta hovered by each family member in turn.

"Arietta thanks you for your time," I said. "She appreciates this is a difficult situation you're going through and hopes it's resolved soon."

Chay sniggered. "She'd never say that. I bet she's threatening us and telling us to be careful."

Arietta cackled a laugh. "My husband knows me so well."

"Thanks for trying to soften the blow, Odessa," Regan said. "But we've lived with Aunty Arietta for a long time. We all know she'll be out for revenge. I also know how determined she is when she wants something. She'll keep haunting us until this is resolved, won't she?"

"I suspect she will," I said. "I'll leave you to it for now, but if I could take the recordings from the magic trackers, I'd appreciate it."

Eva stepped forward and handed me a pouch with a number of small, smooth items inside. "The magic trackers were attached to stones placed around the perimeter. Several cover the house, and the rest cover the grounds. You need to swipe your hand over them to activate the recordings. I gave you the ones for the night of the murder."

"Thanks. If anything useful shows up, I'll take it to the Magic Council."

"Don't waste your time on them," Arietta said. "If there's anything on these trackers, I'll come back and deal with the killer."

I didn't pass on that gloomy threat. "I'm basing myself in the distillery in Witch Haven. You can reach me there if you think of anything else useful in this investigation." After saying goodbye to everyone, Eva led me to the door, and I headed outside.

"Odessa, you will see this through to the end, won't you?" Arietta said.

"I shouldn't. You're so mean to your family." I glanced at her. "Are you doubting me?"

"It's clear you're on my family's side. You're as happy as they are that I'm dead."

"That's not true. But from everything I'm learning about you, you weren't kind to them."

"Kindness makes a person weak. You need to toughen up. This world isn't unicorns and fairy dust. There are bad people out there who exploit kindness."

"You're one of those bad people," I said.

"I'm a smart business woman." Arietta turned and looked at the house. "We're making progress. Don't back out now, or I'll haunt you for eternity."

"I'm not backing out. Not while you have Sol and Tuffin. But if something shows up on a tracker,

I'll have to hand over the evidence to the Magic Council. I can't make a formal arrest."

"You won't have to. You leave the arresting part to me."

"That's not happening. Your family has been through enough. You can't keep terrorizing them."

"It has to be this way. I don't want the Magic Council poking around in my business affairs too closely. They love to snoop into things that don't concern them."

"What don't you want them to find?" I said. "I thought the distillery business was reputable. Although you are preying on vulnerable people who have nowhere else to turn. Did you cut corners?"

Arietta went to shove me, but I dodged out of the way. She swirled around me several times, prodding me with cold fingers.

"Stop!" I batted away her hands. "You're only angry because you don't like hearing the truth. It sounds like not many people were brave enough to tell you what they really thought about you when you were alive."

"Brave, or sensible." She got in one more jab. "Perhaps one or two of my business dealings bent the rules, but no one was harmed. The Magic Council won't understand what I was working on."

"Which was?"

"A secret."

"I have no interest in going into the magic distillery business. I promise, I won't steal any ideas."

"Make sure you don't, because I know where you live. And I won't cross over out of spite while I make you pay."

"Enough with the threats! And my scarecrows make me plenty of money. I have no plans to diversify."

"Hmmm... I suppose you are a successful businesswoman in your own right. Very well. It would be good to talk through the idea with someone who has a brain."

"Wow! A compliment."

"I didn't say it was an effective brain." Arietta sort of smiled at me. "I was working on a design for a mobile unit that would take a magic user's power. The way the business is set up, anyone who wants to trade their power for cash has to come to a distillery. We have them all over the world, so it's not usually a problem, but it costs a fortune to run the distilleries and have the staff maintaining things. If I had mobile units that traveled to where people lived, it would free up money in the business."

"So you could reach even more vulnerable people. There's a kind of horrible logic to that."

"I'm providing a much-needed service. Get over yourself. And I expect you don't do everything perfectly with your scarecrows. I know from experience that the magic you pump into them is freakily strong. Is that legal?"

"About my scarecrows. You burned them!"

She tittered. "I knew you were holding onto that nugget of information."

"Why do that? You should have sent them back. I'd have returned your money and had them recommissioned."

"So they could disobey their next owner? Not likely. I did the world a favor by getting rid of them."

My heart throbbed unhappily. My boys would have been scared when they got burned. Arietta was a monster.

"Oh, don't start crying over some straw and pumpkins. If it's any consolation, I made sure they were out cold. They didn't feel a thing." She drifted in front of me. "Do your scarecrows even feel?"

"Not pain, but that's not the point. They were works of art. And you destroyed them."

"They'd served their purpose. I simply took out the trash." She drifted beside me. "And you didn't answer my question. Is the magic you use legal?"

I decided not to comment. There were vague gray areas I chose not to think about, especially when it came to bringing back Brodie. "Why do you have such a problem with the Magic Council?"

She smirked. "Still avoiding the question. Very well. It only makes me more interested in you."

"I'm delighted." I gestured her to keep talking. "The Magic Council?"

"I have a tedious code of conduct they make me stick to. Everyone who uses my service goes through several assessments before their magic is taken. Alongside my mobile units, I was petitioning to speed up that process. Everything would be moved online."

"That doesn't happen now?"

"No. The Magic Council insists on customers having a face-to-face meeting with a qualified professional to make sure they're of sound mind and judgment. Blah, blah, blah."

"That sounds fair to me."

"It's expensive, and it's slow. An online assessment would make everything much smoother."

"And you much richer."

"You talk about wealth as if it's a bad thing. You do well with your scarecrows. You're not poor."

"I won't do well now my business has been shut down."

"Then you know what it's like to get on the wrong side of the Magic Council. They ruin you with their rules and admin."

"They haven't ruined me. It's just a setback." One I had no clue how to fix.

"You won't get any sympathy from me. It's your own fault. You should have been sneakier about hiding things you weren't supposed to do."

We were on such different pages that there was no point in looking for any middle ground with Arietta. I created a conceal spell as we neared the border of Witch Haven, and we walked the rest of the way in silence.

I mulled over everything I'd heard from her family. There was no love lost when it came to Arietta, and none of them were unhappy she was dead. And although Derwin's threat was odd, he'd made a valid point. If he'd been planning to kill Arietta, he wouldn't have said a word.

While we walked, I messaged Indigo. *Hey. Need a favor.*

The reply was instant. *Where are you? We're all worried.*

Waiting for the dust to settle. How bad is it?

Not great. Selma's mad as hell. Let me help.

You can. Odd request. I need evidence on an open murder investigation.

???

I know. Long story. Can Olympus help me?

What are you up to?

I glanced at Arietta. *Helping someone who doesn't deserve it. I need any pictures of the evidence found by Arietta Frost. Do you remember her being killed?*

Sure! But why?

Ghost business.

There was a long pause.

He'll send it. But he's asking questions. Come to mine. I'll hide you. Bring the ghost if you have to.

No. I'm safe for now. And thanks for getting Selma off my back.

We're trying, but she's still after you. Are you sure we can't help? Storm and Luna are also worried about you.

No, but thanks. Just the photos would be great. Once I've dealt with this ghost, I can focus on other things.

Stay safe xxx

We got back to the distillery, and I checked on Tuffin. She was still snoozing on the bed of moss. I picked her up to take her inside, but Arietta blocked the way.

"What are you doing?" Her glare lasered on Tuffin.

"Tuffin can't stay out here. She'll be vulnerable to predators. The woods are full of nighttime creepies."

Arietta scowled. "It's no more than she deserves."

"Tuffin comes inside. You can see she won't be any trouble."

"If I hear one squeak out of her, I'm tossing her outside to the werewolves and night imps."

"You can try." I hurried into the distillery with Tuffin in my arms and dashed over to Sol. My heart sank when I saw he hadn't moved. I'd hoped to find him on the other side of the magic barrier so we could do battle with Arietta, but it looked like I was on my own with this pesky ghost.

"There's a laptop and TV screen in the staff room," Arietta said. "You can project the information from the magic trackers onto that."

I followed her to the staffroom and settled Tuffin on the couch. I pulled out the first magic tracker. After Arietta showed me how to activate the TV, I skimmed my hand over the tracker, and a beam of light shone onto the screen. After a few seconds, images appeared, and we were looking at the back of the house.

"This is it." Her voice was hushed. "This was where it all happened."

I settled on the couch next to Tuffin. The time signature on the tracker showed it was ten-thirty on the evening of the murder. "What time were you killed?"

"Just after midnight," Arietta said. "You can scroll on."

I sped through the footage, not seeing anyone appear. While I was waiting, I checked my email and found two pictures from Olympus. The first showed an empty glass and the second a green plushie.

"What are you looking at?" Arietta said.

"Evidence from your murder." I showed her the picture of the plushie.

She looked at it and shook her head. "I didn't make that."

"It must be yours."

"No, I don't have that design."

"It was found by your body."

"The Magic Council probably messed up the evidence. See how incompetent they are. That's why I need you around."

I found a printer, linked my phone to it, and printed out the two images. I showed the plushie to Arietta again. "Take a closer look."

She stared at it. "It's cheap. And the stitching is bad. I didn't make that. Stop wasting time and look at the tracker."

I set down the image and slowed the recording at just before midnight.

"Come on. Show yourself," Arietta muttered.

My eyes widened as a figure came into view. I paused the recording and stared at it, not believing what I was witnessing. "It's Derwin!"

It was as clear as day. Although he had a hat on, his distinctive red hair stood out, as did the vibrant flowered shirt he wore.

"I can't believe I'm seeing this." Arietta zoomed to the screen.

"Does Derwin always wear shirts like that?" I jumped up and joined her to get a closer look.

"Unfortunately, yes. The man has no taste."

"Arietta, it was him! There's your gun, the distinctive shirt, and his red hair. It was Derwin! We've solved your murder."

Chapter 7

We'd watched the footage a dozen times and were both convinced Derwin was the murderer. Although he hadn't looked at the tracker, so we didn't have a clear view of his face, it couldn't have been anyone else.

"I'm going to kill him." Arietta zoomed to the door.

I threw out a restraining spell to stop her. "Wait!"

She spun toward me. "Why? This is what I needed."

"Take a few minutes. I'm still amazed it was him," I said. "Could this have been faked?"

"No. I have state-of-the-art security. No one can mess with it."

I turned back to the screen, still stunned by the discovery. "Derwin must have figured he could get away with your murder because he thought the trackers were broken. He was surprised when he learned from Eva they'd been fixed. If he'd known they were working, he wouldn't have breezed past for everyone to see him."

"Exactly. So why delay things? Derwin must die."

"No." I pushed everything I had into keeping Arietta in the room. "You're not thinking straight."

"My thoughts are straight. I got you to find my killer, so your services are no longer required. I'll take it from here."

"Stop! You can't kill him."

Arietta snarled at me, her eyes glowing with a ghostly rage. "Are you going to stand in my way?"

I really didn't want to. I was tired, hungry, and running on magic fumes, but I wouldn't let this ghost go while she had murder on her mind. "Yes. I'm not letting you leave."

"I want him dead."

"And I understand why you're angry. But the Magic Council needs to make this arrest. I'll take the evidence to them. Derwin will go to jail for the rest of his life. That's enough of a punishment."

"It's not enough. He needs to suffer."

I eased back my magic, and Arietta didn't make a break for it. "He will. He's about to lose everything. I can't imagine the rest of the family will stick by him after they learned what he did to you."

"I'm no fool, Odessa. I noticed none of them were sad I was gone. And I've been snooping around the house since I died. They're living their lives as if I never existed. They're just waiting for the money to come through. I expect they're secretly congratulating Derwin for having the bottle to do something about me." She shook her head. "How did he find the courage? He's so weak."

I wanted to find a way to soften this blow, but Arietta had been truly horrible to her family; from Eva, who'd looked terrified when I'd mentioned

Arietta's name, to Derwin, who was such a broken man, he'd cracked and killed his own sister.

Arietta zoomed around the room, dropping the temperature a good five degrees. "Before you hand the evidence to the Magic Council, I want to confront Derwin. I need to hear his confession."

"That's not a good idea."

"If you want me to wake Sol and give you back that flea-bitten familiar, you'll do as I say."

"No. I'm taking this to the Magic Council."

Arietta rushed at me, but I dodged away. Her icy fingers skimmed the back of my neck, and I ducked. I scuttled out of the way, sparking magic on my fingers.

"Don't defy me." Arietta lunged again.

"You're pushing your luck. I found out who killed you, but that's it. I'm not helping with your revenge plans. I want nothing more to do with this. We had a deal. Your killer's been found, so now I get Sol and Tuffin."

"Bring me my brother!" Arietta screamed in my face.

I threw a spell at her, knocking her off track, but it lacked power. Tiredness made my bones ache. I'd barely slept, had had no opportunity to recharge my magic with powdered pumpkin, and my eyes were stinging with tiredness. And if I looked in the mirror, there'd definitely be new stress lines on my forehead.

Arietta circled me. "If you don't bring Derwin here, I'll kill him. Do you want that on your conscience?"

"I should ask you that question. You talk about killing a family member like it's something to tick off your to-do list."

"He killed me! I'm the victim. Don't support him."

"Are you surprised Derwin snapped? Until I met you, I'd always thought there was good in people, but you're awful, and you take advantage of everyone. You're doing it to me right now. Maybe if you'd changed your ways, none of this would have happened."

Arietta shrieked and shot around the room so fast she left behind an ice trail.

I sank back on the couch and rested my hand on Tuffin's side. After a few minutes, Arietta stopped swirling and hovered in front of me.

"Have you gotten over your temper tantrum?" I said.

She glowered at me. "I didn't want to die."

"I'm sure no one wants to die, but it's the one thing in life that's inevitable."

"Not like this. It wasn't fair. I had so many plans. I knew what I wanted for my future. People always say I'm cold and calculating because I don't give up on what I want. If I was a man, they wouldn't say that. They'd say I was bold and brave, and everyone would want to be my friend. It makes me sad." Arietta sniffed.

"You're not catching me out a second time. You did the 'woe is me' act earlier, and I fell for it."

She shrugged. "I want justice. Bring Derwin here so I can talk to him."

I sucked in a deep breath and let it out slowly. I always tried to see the good in people, but Arietta was making it hard. "That's all?"

"Yes."

"He'll have to confess once we show him the evidence."

"Derwin must realize his actions were caught on the trackers. He won't be able to explain this. I'll enjoy seeing him squirm. And he can try, but once he's done, I will kill him."

"No! No killing." I used my scarecrow command voice to get her attention and was surprised when her form shimmered and shock flickered across her face.

"Don't use your power on me, witch."

"I don't want to, but you're leaving me no choice. Besides, don't you want to know why Derwin killed you? Once he's dead, he could cross over and you'd lose your chance to find out."

A sullen look crossed Arietta's face before she nodded. "I suppose so. But that snake is living on borrowed time. Bring him here before he makes a run for it. It's just the cowardly sort of thing he would do."

"Derwin may be thinking about running, but would he leave behind Regan?"

"To save his skin? Most likely. After all, we're related. We always look out for ourselves first. Everyone else is an afterthought. Get him. There's a private line to the house in the office next door. The family knows that, when that phone rings, they'd better answer it."

"I'll make the call. But behave yourself. And when Derwin gets here, give him a chance to speak before you do anything." I headed to the next room and discovered an old-fashioned white telephone with a cord and a turn dial.

"Dial one," Arietta shouted. "That'll link you to the house."

I made the call, and when Eva answered, I asked to speak to Derwin.

He came on the line a moment later. "Odessa. You gave Eva a scare when the business line rang. Only Arietta used that."

"Sorry. But I need you to come to the distillery in Witch Haven. We've found something important relating to Arietta's murder."

"Oh! Do you want us all there?"

"Just you."

"Me? But... why? I had nothing to do with her death."

"You'd better get here as quickly as you can," I said. "Otherwise, Arietta will pay you a visit. And you don't want that."

"No, of course not. I'll be there immediately." The line went dead.

"Derwin's coming to us," I said to Arietta once I'd returned to the other office. "He sounded panicked."

"As he should. It'll take Derwin a while. He's such a ditherer."

A moment later, the air around me heated and Derwin appeared, looking pale and sweaty.

"Well, what do you know? I didn't think he could do transportation spells," Arietta said. "Is my brother hiding more than just my murder? Is he more powerful than I realized?"

Derwin staggered to the side and grabbed the edge of the desk. "Sorry. I'm not used to powerful magic. I took a potion from the distillery reserves in our basement. Arietta kept a store of magic down there."

"I hope you paid for that," Arietta said. "That was my personal supply."

"I appreciate you coming so quickly. So does Arietta," I said. "We found something on the magic trackers you'll find interesting. Come take a look."

Derwin hurried along behind me as I led him to the staffroom. "Did you see the killer?"

"Yes. Take a seat." I ran the magic tracker recording back a few minutes and set it to play.

Arietta hovered close to Derwin as he looked at the screen. "Why isn't he looking nervous? He must know what's about to happen."

I waved her away, but she stayed where she was.

Derwin shuddered. "Arietta's here, isn't she?"

"She's right beside you," I said. "And she's not happy."

"I'm used to that. She always had a temper, even when she was a child."

"Stop talking and look at the screen," Arietta growled.

Derwin sank back on the couch and shuddered again. A strange noise came out of his mouth as the image of him appeared on the screen. He jerked forward as if he'd received an electric shock. "Wait! That looks like me. That's my shirt."

"That's because it is you, idiot," Arietta said. "You shot me."

Derwin jumped up and raced to the screen. "That's impossible."

"You don't have an alibi," I said. "You were in your bedroom on your own."

His gaze was fixed on the screen. "I wasn't feeling well."

"Are you sure no one saw you going into your bedroom?" I said.

"They wouldn't have seen him, because he was busy killing me," Arietta said.

Derwin raked a hand through his hair several times. "I... Things are complicated. I don't want to get anyone in trouble."

"You weren't alone?" I said.

His shoulders slumped, but he remained glued to the screen. "I don't know how this is possible."

I walked over to Derwin. "Who were you with that night?"

His lips pressed together. "I can't say."

"He doesn't have a girlfriend," Arietta said. "No one would put up with someone so weak."

I glared at her, but kept my focus on Derwin. "You need to say what really happened that night. You've been recorded with a gun in your hand just before your sister was shot. If anyone can give you an alibi, you have to tell me their name. If you don't, I'll take this evidence to the Magic Council. They'll arrest you for murder, and your life will be over."

He remained silent for over a minute. "It's not fair. She's done nothing wrong. I can't drag her into this."

"Unless he paid someone to spend the night with him, he was alone," Arietta said.

"When we met at the house, I noticed Eva was concerned about you," I said. "Is that because she's good at her job, or is something going on between you two?"

Arietta snorted a laugh. "We don't associate with the hired help. That's beneath us. Derwin knows the rules."

"Derwin, are you and Eva in a relationship?" I said.

He turned to me, and his eyes were wet with tears. "She's a kind woman. We've been friends for years. It developed into something more about five years ago."

Arietta groaned. "Are you kidding me? He's messing with my staff."

"Were you with Eva the night Arietta was killed?" I said.

Derwin bowed his head. "Yes. I often stay at her chalet. But we had to keep our relationship quiet. Arietta would have thrown Eva out if she'd learned about it. She was strict about who was an appropriate person to date."

"How dare they break the rules and go behind my back." Arietta snarled in Derwin's face and jabbed him in the belly with a finger.

Derwin winced, his hands covering his stomach.

"So you were together when Arietta was killed?" I said. "Eva will confirm that?"

"Yes! And that's why I'm so shocked by this image of me. It can't be me. Even though... it looks just like me."

"You wear distinctive shirts. And the Frost red hair makes you easy to identify."

Derwin shook his head. "I can't explain this. It looks terrible."

"It does. But if Eva can confirm your alibi, you're in the clear," I said.

"And if she gives him an alibi, I'll fire her," Arietta said.

I turned on her. "No, you won't. Leave Eva alone. And don't touch Derwin. He hid the relationship because of your prejudice. If they're happy and not hurting anyone, then it's none of your business."

Derwin tapped me on the shoulder. "Err... you shouldn't speak to Arietta like that. She doesn't like it."

"I hate bullies, and Arietta could get a distinction in being mean to other people."

"Don't forget, witch, I have your little friends. And I will hurt them if you keep testing me," Arietta hissed in my ear.

"We give Derwin a chance," I said to her. "Let's speak to Eva."

"But how can this be explained?" Derwin gulped loudly as he pointed at the screen.

"He could be lying," Arietta said. "I didn't think he had it in him, but I'm learning new things about my brother."

I studied the image. It really looked like Derwin, although it could do with enhancing, just to be sure it was him. If it wasn't him, then he must have a doppelganger walking around out there. That idea was almost as scary as Arietta.

"I promise, that's not me on the tracker," Derwin said.

Arietta shoved him, and he recoiled. "If you're lying to me—"

"Arietta's frustrated," I said as I batted her away.

"I'll take his head from his shoulders if it was him." Arietta grabbed for Derwin, but I blocked her and whacked her with my hip, giving her a hefty shove to encourage her to back off.

"Go home," I said to Derwin. "But don't go anywhere else. We need to check your alibi with Eva."

"Do you have to? We worked so hard to keep our relationship a secret so she doesn't get in trouble."

"She won't get in trouble, but if you want to clear your name, we must involve Eva."

His jowls wobbled. "Can I take time to consider this some more? The family won't approve."

"You kept your relationship a secret because of Arietta's disapproval. Now she's dead—"

"I'm still here. They have to break up." Arietta swirled around us in an icy spiral of indignation.

I ignored her. "You can have a relationship with Eva without having to worry."

"What about Arietta? I can tell she's unhappy. What if she won't cross over until I split up with Eva?"

"I'll do that. Just to spite him. I'll ruin her."

I glared at Arietta. "No, you won't. You stayed to figure out who killed you. Once we've done that, you move on. You're done threatening your family and controlling them. Look where it led you." I slid my finger across my throat.

Arietta slowed down. "I don't like it when my employees talk back."

"It's a good thing I'm not an employee," I said.

"How angry is she?" Derwin was trembling.

"Arietta understands. Come on. Let's go visit Eva and clear your name." I herded him to the exit, using my body to block Arietta from getting too close.

"You're still siding with my family," she snarled in my ear. "You'll pay for this."

"You keep threatening me, and I keep getting bored. Let's get out of here and find your real killer."

Chapter 8

Eva sat hunched in her seat in the small chalet she lived in behind the main house. Derwin had wanted to come with us when we visited her, but I insisted he go home.

"Take your time, but I do need an answer to my question." I was trying to keep calm, but the swirling malevolence that radiated from Arietta was testing my cool.

"If I answer, will I lose my job?" Eva's voice shook.

"Yes," Arietta snapped.

"No. But it's important I learn who you were with the night Arietta was shot. I have information to suggest your alibi wasn't correct. Is there anything you want to tell me?" A quick glance around the small living room showed Eva had made the most of the space. There were fresh flowers in a vase, a clean cloth on the small table in the corner, and the furniture smelled like it had recently been polished.

"Is this just between us?" Eva said.

"And Arietta, for now. Although I can't promise I won't share this information if it becomes relevant to her murder."

Eva shook her head, her lips pressed together. "I told him we shouldn't have kept quiet about it. And I knew keeping silent would get him in trouble, especially after the threat he made over dinner."

"Who are you talking about?" I said softly.

Eva let out a sigh. "Derwin. He was here when Arietta was shot. We were together when we heard it."

"He was in your chalet?"

She nodded, her hands clasped in her lap.

"And why was Derwin here that night?"

"We already know the disturbing answer to that," Arietta said.

"I don't want to get in any trouble." Eva's voice was barely a whisper.

"You won't. But you could be helping yourself and Derwin out of a mess. You're still suspects in Arietta's murder. You must want to clear your names."

She closed her eyes for a second. "Derwin is a kind, sweet man. We just want a quiet life. I had a crush on him for a long time but never thought he noticed me. Then one day, he brought me some wild flowers and suggested we take a walk. He said he noticed I liked to go walking around the grounds in the evenings. I was so surprised. I thought, like the rest of the family, I was invisible to him. That's my job, you see. I make sure they have everything they need, and I don't get in the way. That's how it's supposed to be."

"That's the way I trained her," Arietta said. "And until this unfortunate incident, Eva was always adequate at her job. It seems she's been deceiving me, along with everyone else. You can't trust anyone."

"You and Derwin are dating?" I said to Eva.

"Yes, for about five years. I hated keeping our relationship a secret, but I understood the cruelty of his family. Arietta would have ruined me and forced Derwin to give me up if she found out we were dating." Her gaze flashed around the chalet. "I'm assuming she's here, listening to this?"

"She is. And I'll be honest with you, she's not happy. But Arietta will understand. Love finds you in strange places. You can't always decide who you fall in love with. It just happens."

Arietta snorted a derisive laugh. "This has nothing to do with love. This is an attempt at scrambling up the social ladder. Eva won't get her hands on my money, though. If Derwin and Eva marry, I'll make sure they're penniless."

I waved a hand at her. "Arietta is adjusting to the news. Tell me what you did the night of her murder."

Eva settled in her seat, seeming less stressed now her secret was out. "I served the family, tidied the kitchen, and then came back here. We had a routine, and Derwin would come here most evenings. Sometimes, he spent the night, but sometimes we'd sit and chat, and then he'd go to the main house. That night, he came over stressed and unhappy. He told me Arietta had announced the sale of the business."

"He wasn't happy about it being sold?" I said.

"Derwin has no love for the distillery. He always said... I don't like to say anything bad about Arietta in case she hurts me."

"If she does, I'll hurt her right back," I said.

Arietta growled. "I'll behave. I want to hear this horror story."

Eva pulled back her shoulders and sat up straight. "Derwin thought Arietta exploited people and didn't pay them enough when they handed over their power."

"Everyone got a fair rate," Arietta said. "Sometimes, the powers they offered weren't as good as they made out, so I cut the fee. You see, everyone lies."

"Derwin wasn't interested in taking on the business?" I said.

"Never. He wanted out, but he felt trapped. Arietta had control of everything." Eva glanced around again. "I'll make her angry by saying this, but I think it gave her pleasure to control people. Derwin even tried to get a job away from the magic distillery, but Arietta made a phone call, and it vanished. It happened several times before Derwin admitted defeat."

"He didn't try hard enough," Arietta said. "He should have found a workaround. I was testing him, and he failed. Derwin always fails."

I shook my head at Arietta. "So, Derwin was here that evening. What did you do?"

"After Derwin ranted about Arietta and the business being sold, I suggested he take a bath. I thought it would help him relax. I ran it for him, then left him to it. I brewed some chamomile tea to help relax him and was bringing it to him when we heard the shot."

"What did you do?"

"We hurried out of the chalet. I didn't stop to think that it might look odd to the others that we arrived at the same time, but everyone was so shocked, they didn't notice."

"And the rest of the family were there when you arrived?"

"Yes. They were just ahead of us. Chay and Fontayne arrived first, but Regan was right behind them."

"Which gave none of them time to shoot Arietta, hide the gun, and get back without being spotted," I said, more to myself than Eva.

"It wouldn't have been possible," Eva said. "It couldn't have been any of them."

"I'm deeply unimpressed by this betrayal," Arietta said. "Tell Eva she's fired."

I resisted the urge to roll my eyes. I'd do no such thing. "Arietta is glad her brother's name has been cleared."

A small smile crossed Eva's face. "Did she really say that? I imagine she's telling me I don't have a job anymore."

Arietta snorted and crossed her arms over her chest. "She's got that right."

"Understandably, Arietta is surprised by this information. But it's good news for you. It means you and Derwin are in the clear."

"Explain the magic tracker evidence," Arietta said. "Derwin is on there. He can't be in two places at once."

I was thinking that over. I didn't have a proper explanation yet, but I'd work it out.

"Shall I pack my things?" Eva said.

"No," I said.

"Yes," Arietta said.

"Arietta's not in charge of this estate anymore." I caught hold of Eva's hand and squeezed. "She has no control over you."

"I'm right here. I could whip that pathetic excuse for a housekeeper into shape even though I'm a ghost."

I kept my attention on Eva, who was vibrating with tension again. "And I know a thing or two about ghosts. Arietta's energy can only be sustained for so long before she needs to recharge. She's no longer all-powerful. You're free of her. And you won't need to hide your relationship with Derwin."

Tears sprang into Eva's eyes. "It would be nice to meet Derwin and not worry about people watching us. We used to sneak out and take midnight walks to make sure no one would see. Now, it feels like I have my freedom back."

"Don't be so sure about that," Arietta muttered. "Odessa, I need a word with you. I'm not happy."

"Thanks for being honest with me. That's all I wanted. I'll leave you to it," I said to Eva.

She stood from her seat and led me to the door. "What will happen now?"

"I'll keep investigating."

"I haven't lost my job?"

"You should," Arietta said.

"No. Stay right where you are. And make sure you and Derwin spend lots of time together. You never know how long you've got."

Eva's mouth opened, and she stared at me. "Why not? Do you know something bad is going to happen? Is Arietta plotting against us?" Her trembling hand covered her mouth.

"Oh! No, sorry. You have nothing to worry about. I was speaking from personal experience. I... I lost someone a while ago. Don't take your time together for granted. That's all I meant."

She let out a sigh. "Sure. Got it. Thanks."

I left the chalet with Arietta ranting beside me, repeatedly attempting to shove me, and making me dodge out of her way to avoid landing in the dirt.

"I know you're not happy," I said, "but their alibis tally. Derwin and Eva were together. They're not your killers."

"Unless they're covering for each other," Arietta said. "And why were you so nice to the hired help?"

"Because I'm a good person, and so is she. You could learn from us."

"When I want to figure out how to be a doormat, I will."

I shook my head. "And I don't think Derwin and Eva were in on it together. It would have been impossible for either of them to have shot you and return to the scene of the crime at the same time as the rest of your family."

Arietta swirled around me. "I don't like it when you're right. Where does that leave us?"

I shrugged. "Back at square one."

***

Something cold slapped the side of my cheek. My head jerked up, and I came face-to-face with an angry-looking Arietta. "Urgh. What time is it?" It felt like I'd only been asleep for half an hour.

"It's time you woke up. Stop being lazy."

I yawned loudly. "It's still dark outside."

"You've had a few hours of sleep. That's enough. Get up and solve my murder. You've gotten exactly nowhere since I employed you."

I rested my head against the wall. I hadn't planned on sleeping and had settled next to Sol so I could keep an eye on him. But I was tired and hungry and hadn't eaten any of my energy giving powdered pumpkin for ages, so I must have dozed off. My protesting back and butt told me I'd been on the floor for too long.

Arietta jabbed me several times with her icy fingers.

I sparked a spell and flicked it her way, knocking her back. "When my scarecrows finally catch up with you, they'll whip your behind."

Arietta cackled a laugh. "I'm not scared of them. What can they do to me?"

"Some have the ability to catch ghosts."

"Lies."

"Truth. It's something I invented after a customer reached out to me with a problem haunting. I can call back that scarecrow and set him on you. You wouldn't like him. He's big, mean, and eats ghosts for breakfast. Yum, yum."

"See me shaking in my designer boots." The smirk on Arietta's face didn't look as potent, though. "I could take down a scarecrow if I had to. After all, I've already gotten rid of two."

"Which you're still not forgiven for." I looked at Sol. He was curled on his side, his chest slowly rising and falling. "Will you wake him?"

"Will you stop being so useless?"

I sparked another spell, but it flickered and died on my fingers. "You've been draining me in my sleep, haven't you?"

"I took a small amount. As you rightly pointed out when you were talking to that simpering idiot of a housekeeper, I need to keep my energy up, and you have plenty of power to spare."

"I won't have if you keep taking it without my permission."

"It has a sparkly pumpkin tang to it. I don't object."

"I do. I'll soon be too weak to continue this investigation. Then you'll be lost and stuck forever until you turn into a ghost ghoul and the Magic Council issues an order for your destruction."

"No, you won't. And you have an excellent incentive to keep going." She pointed at Sol. "And I haven't forgotten the furball in the staffroom. You won't let them down."

I shuffled closer to Sol until I reached the edge of the magic barrier trapping him in place. "I need to make sure my incentive is okay. Wake him up."

"I'm not sure you deserve it."

"I've ruled out two suspects in your murder. That deserves something."

"You're so demanding. You remind me of myself when I was younger. Although I was much more forceful."

I glared at her until she laughed. She zoomed through the magic barrier and placed her hands on either side of Sol's head. She backed away as his eyes flickered open.

"Sol! It's Odessa. Can you hear me?" I tried to reach him, but the magic barrier was still up.

"You can't get too close," Arietta said. "He can stay awake for now, providing he doesn't cause trouble."

Sol rolled over and stared at me. For a few seconds, there was no comprehension in his eyes, but everything suddenly clicked into place. He rushed over and slammed into the magic barrier.

Arietta whooped out a laugh. "He's good-looking enough, but not all that smart."

"Take it easy," I said to Sol. "You've been out for a while."

He pressed his hand against the magic barrier. "What happened? The last thing I remember was running from the Magic Council."

"Long story short, we met the ghost of Arietta Frost. Apparently, she was murdered and has decided I must solve the crime. She's holding you until I do. Tuffin, too."

"Another murder?" His gaze flickered over me. "Are you okay?"

"Yes, I'm fine. And I'm only helping Arietta because she's holding someone I care about."

"You mean Tuffin?"

I laughed, partly in relief but also because I was so glad to have Sol back by my side. "I do. And maybe you. I don't want to see you hurt."

Sol smiled. "You really care about me?"

Arietta made a gagging sound in the back of her throat.

"Haven't you got somewhere else you can go or people to annoy and be horrible to?" I said to her.

"No, I'm staying right here."

"The ghost is here?" Sol said.

"Yes. And she's demanding and rude."

"Let's get rid of her. I know how powerful you are."

I shook my head. "Arietta is strong and ruthless. And she's not giving me a chance to recharge my magic. She keeps draining it. I want to kick her into next week, but I can't."

Sol settled on the floor. "We'll figure a way out. You can solve any problem."

"I'm sorry this happened to you," I said. "You must hate me for dragging you into this."

"It's impossible to hate you. You know how I feel about you."

"You shouldn't. I keep getting you in trouble. First, the Magic Council arrested you, then I forced you to do a jailbreak, and now you're a prisoner to an angry ghost."

"Life with you will never be dull," Sol said. "But I can handle that. Every relationship has its ups and downs."

"I thought you two weren't in a relationship," Arietta said.

"Stop listening to a private conversation," I said.

"No. And he's cute enough to date. I like the big hairy bear type of guy. Although the ones I marry are more refined. I need to be able to take them into all social events without eyebrows being raised."

"I can't hear what that ghost is saying, but I can tell you're not happy about it," Sol said.

"She's being rude. Arietta has a habit of using people to get what she wants and then abandoning them. That includes her husbands."

"She's had more than one?" Sol said.

"Yes. How many men have you been married to?" I asked Arietta.

"Five."

"Whoa! She's on her fifth marriage."

"Arietta's been busy," Sol said.

"It's not my fault most men are dull."

"She's being rude again," I said. "But right now, I'm stuck with her, and so are you."

"We'll get through this. And I can get involved now I'm awake. I could set up a suspect board like we did the first time."

"First time?" Arietta said. "What's this?"

I waved her away. "That's a great idea."

She prodded me. "What's he talking about? What suspect board? What other murder?"

I eased to my feet and rolled my shoulders. "I got involved with helping someone else who was murdered. He was haunting the family home, and they asked for my assistance."

"And did you help him?"

"Yes. It turned out, his entire family tried to kill him."

"Wait! Is this Eldridge Talbert? I read about all the arrests."

I rubbed the back of my neck. "It seems like that happened ages ago, but you're right. We'd just solved Eldridge's murder when the Magic Council arrested us."

"And you used a suspect board to help you?"

"Yes. It was Sol's idea. It was useful having the suspects laid out beside each other and seeing their motives, alibis, and opportunities. Although that last issue has me stumped when it comes to your death."

"Why didn't you ask for a suspect board?" Arietta whacked me over the head.

"Stop!" I shot a spell at her. "It slipped my mind. Being blackmailed is stressful."

"If you keep me awake, I'll help," Sol said.

"We don't need a man involved," Arietta said. "He'll start mansplaining and showing off."

"Sol isn't like that."

"All men are like that. It's why I mainly employ women in my business. You get plenty of bitchy comments, but no one gets all chest-puffed-out and pompous on you."

"Sol helped me figure out how Eldridge died. We need him." And this was an opportunity to get Sol free and away from Arietta. "It would mean we solve this problem faster."

Arietta tilted her head, her gaze sliding over him. "I'll let Sol work for me, providing he takes his shirt off."

"That's disrespectful, possibly sexist, and definitely inappropriate."

"Don't tell me you haven't drooled over this gorgeous hunk of man when he's been toiling in your fields."

My cheeks flushed. "Arietta, stop it. Sol could be useful. But only if he can freely work."

Her eyes narrowed, then she nodded. "Make him promise not to run away."

I looked at Sol. He wasn't going anywhere while I was stuck in this mess. "I don't have control over Sol, but I think he'd like to help."

"I'm in this with you," he said. "We can work on the case together."

Arietta zoomed around the room. "I'm not convinced. Neither of us needs a man to solve this. We can manage on our own."

"Why don't we forget he's male and simply an extra pair of hands working this problem?" I lifted a shoulder at Sol. Arietta had serious hang ups when it came to trusting guys.

"A word of advice." She swirled down to me. "Don't invest too much affection into any guy. They easily break your heart."

I thought of Brodie and how shattered my heart had been when he'd died. I'd been working so hard to get him back that I'd closed myself off from anything else. I hadn't seen a way forward with another man. I looked at Sol, and his warm smile made my closed off heart flicker to life.

Arietta whacked the top of my head. "Don't get dopey over a guy. I get what I want from my men and then ditch them."

I rubbed the back of my head and smoothed down my hair. "Were you planning on ditching Chay?"

"Eventually. But Chay knew the score. Any man who entered a marriage contract with me knew what they were getting. Make sure you do the same with this one."

"We're not... I'll consider it." I gave Sol a what-are-you-gonna-do hand gesture.

"Chay knew he was onto a good thing with me," Arietta said. "All the evidence is against my idiot brother. Even though he has Eva as an alibi, he must be involved."

"Derwin has a great alibi. Everyone does. But we still need to look into Chay, Regan, and Fontayne," I said.

"This definitely calls for a suspect board," Sol said.

"I agree. Arietta, we're recruiting Sol to our team."

"If we must, but you're responsible for him. One wrong move, and he'll go straight back to sleep."

"Understood," I said.

Arietta lowered the magic barrier around Sol. He jumped up and wrapped me in his arms, holding me tight and lifting me off my feet.

I returned the embrace. His inviting applewood smoke and pumpkin scent surrounded me, and I breathed it in and closed my eyes. He smelt like home.

"I'd suggest you two get a room, but we don't have time for your hanky-panky," Arietta said. "Solve my murder."

I reluctantly let go of Sol and stepped back, even though he kept his hands on my waist. "Are you doing okay?"

"I'll be fine now I'm with you." His stomach grumbled.

"I'll find you something to eat. Arietta is terrible at providing for us."

"You get fed when you do some work," she said. "Move it."

"Let's begin with pictures of the suspects," I said.

"We have a staff board with pictures, and I have photographs of Fontayne and Chay on my desk. And there's a family photo album somewhere in my office." Arietta gestured toward the offices. "Go take a look."

An hour later, we stood in front of our new suspect board. There was even a picture of Eva from a staff Christmas party, wearing a sparkly red sweater, her cheeks flushed with happiness as she stood next to Derwin. I'd also pinned the picture of the empty glass and plushie on it.

"How is this helping?" Arietta muttered.

"Let me think for a minute," I said. "The biggest motive for your murder is the money from the sale of this business. How much were you selling it for?"

"Twenty-five million."

I wrote the number on the board, and Sol whistled. "That's a lot of reasons to kill."

"And if this is the motive, it has to be someone from your immediate family," I said. "It rules out everyone else because they wouldn't get their hands on the money."

"Unless they killed me out of spite," Arietta said.

"That's very possible." I wrote the word spite on the board and circled it.

Sol held up a printed image from the magic tracker, showing Derwin with the gun. "It would be helpful if we could enhance this. We could be missing something. It's a little fuzzy."

I nodded. I'd gotten Sol up to speed on the clues and suspects as we'd searched for pictures for the suspect board. "I don't have the best computer skills."

"I could take a look. See if I can make it any clearer."

"Thanks. The hair and clothing suggest it was Derwin, but with his alibi confirmed, it must have been someone in disguise," I said.

"Could it have been a magic disguise?" Sol said. "There are spells that change a person's appearance."

I glanced at Arietta. "Could any family member have used magic to hide their identity, so they looked more like Derwin?"

"No. And even if they borrowed a spell from the distillery, it wouldn't have worked for more than a few seconds. None of us can change physical form."

"Which means someone put on a shirt that looked like Derwin's and maybe a wig. Although that red hair is distinctive. It would be hard to fake."

"Was anything like that found at the scene of the crime?" Sol said.

"Not that I know of."

"It wasn't. The Magic Council only found my voodoo plushie and an empty glass," Arietta said. "I watched them while they looked around."

I wrote wig and shirt on the board. "The Magic Council wasn't looking for a disguise, though. They could have missed something."

"More than likely," Arietta muttered.

"But whoever wore that disguise would have only had seconds to hide it," I said. "Where could they have put it so it wouldn't be found?"

"They could have thrown something over the disguise," Sol said. "They kept it on."

"Maybe. And then hid it or burned it when things got quiet," I said. "We need to see if we can find any clothing and wigs in the house that match these."

"You're wasting your time looking for the disguise. It's long gone by now. I've been dead six weeks. Only an idiot would keep such damning evidence around," Arietta said. "Although none of them are that bright. They could have messed up. We need better evidence."

"We do. And I've got an idea about how we get that, but it involves bringing someone else in on this," I said.

"Not anyone from the Magic Council," Arietta said.

"No, but it's time we call in the big guns. And she can be trusted. I need to contact my friend, Hettie."

Chapter 9

I got hold of Hettie on the phone while Sol searched for snacks and drinks, and explained I had another ghost situation. She'd been helpful when I'd dealt with Eldridge, so I hoped she'd come through again.

Sure enough, after a brief conversation, we arranged to meet that evening at the distillery.

"I found these." Sol returned with bags of salted caramel popcorn, dried fruit, and glasses of water.

"Great. Let's eat. I can't concentrate on solving a murder when I'm so hungry," I said.

We were stuffing our faces when there were three loud raps on the main door. I hurried over to open it.

"Be careful." Arietta lunged in front of me, blocking my path. "You don't know who it is."

"Then take a look outside," I said. "You're invisible to most people."

"Don't give me orders."

I squeezed my eyes shut for a second and clenched my hands. "Arietta, this is for your benefit. It's most likely Hettie, bringing us your autopsy file. That file could give us clues about what happened to you. However, if you don't want your murder solved..." I turned back to my popcorn. When I glanced over my shoulder, Arietta was gone.

She zoomed back through the door a few seconds later. "It's Hettie. She's gotten old!"

I inched open the door under Arietta's fierce glare and peeked out. "Hey! Thanks for coming so quickly."

"Of course. You know me, always interested in anything dead. And I was intrigued when you said you were dealing with another potential murder." Hettie's eyes gleamed in the gloom.

"Were you able to get the file without any trouble?" I ushered her inside.

"Of course. No one questions me when I ask for information. They wouldn't dare unless they want to find themselves transporting cadavers for the next year. I might even suggest they dig the holes to put them in." Hettie stepped inside and looked around. She was a retired coroner and a full-time horse handler, who occasionally free-lanced with the dead when things got busy. "I've never been in here before."

"It's our sort of temporary hideout." I motioned at Sol.

Sol nodded a greeting at Hettie. "You're welcome to join us for food. Although it's nothing special."

Hettie peered at the sad contents of our meal and shook her head. "No thanks. I have a sensitive stomach. I don't eat anything that comes out of plastic."

"How do you know Hettie?" Arietta hovered close by, making slow circles around our visitor.

Hettie batted her hands in front of her face. "I don't see ghosts, but I sense them. Back off, Arietta. I don't play well with the dead if they mess with me."

"Arietta, be nice. And I got to know Hettie when she helped me investigate what happened to Eldridge."

"I'm getting a buzzing in my ears," Hettie said. "If she doesn't calm down, I'm taking this file and leaving her to fend for herself."

"Arietta! Stop." I zapped her with a weak knockback spell. "Sorry. She gets a bit intense. She's feeling impatient about finding her killer."

"Don't apologize for her. I've encountered the Frost family and their employees more times than I care to remember. Magic distilling is dangerous. I've handled five fatalities from this business over the years."

"Maybe Arietta cut corners with the safety measures," Sol said.

"I'll send him to sleep if he keeps saying stupid things," Arietta said.

"Sol, how about you get the suspect board? We can add any new information to that while we talk."

He nodded and left the table.

"Your ghost isn't a fan of Sol?" Hettie said.

"She's using him as collateral. If I don't help her, she'll hurt him."

"She's a charmer." Hettie's gaze ran over me. "Are you feeling well? You look tired."

"Being blackmailed by a ghost will do that to a witch. I'll be fine once this is over. And I'm hopeful the information you have could be useful. Shall we look at the autopsy file?" I said.

"That's what I'm here for. You can't keep it, though. And I want all the details on how you got entangled with another ghost."

I led Hettie to the table, with Arietta hovering close by. Sol returned with the suspect board and made a space for Hettie.

"I don't want you getting in trouble for helping us," I said. "If I tell you too much, the Magic Council might look into you, too."

"I'm too old and jaded to care about Magic Council rules. Besides, they need me. The guy who's supposed to be dealing with the dead bodies is still off sick. If they cause me trouble, I stop working and leave the mysteries to pile up in a rotting heap of limbs."

I shuddered at the gruesome image, then gave Hettie a summary of everything I'd discovered about Arietta.

She leaned back in her seat once I'd finished, her gaze cutting around the room. "It makes sense now why you're in the distillery."

"Did you meet her when she was alive?" I said.

"We never had any direct dealings, but I knew her by reputation."

"I always had an excellent reputation," Arietta said.

"She had a huge ego, an attitude problem, and from what I heard, took delight in putting people down," Hettie said.

"I don't like her," Arietta said. "It's time Hettie went."

"Not yet," I said.

Hettie chuckled. "Our ghost isn't happy?"

"I don't think I've seen her smile yet. But Arietta's murder has me stumped. There are plenty of motives for wanting her dead, but the suspects have alibis. They all arrived at the scene of the shooting at the same time, and none of them had a gun."

"But you still think it was one of them?"

"If the motive is to get access to the money that would come from the sale of the business, it has to be a family member. No one else would benefit."

"Maybe that's not the motive. You said Arietta was selling off that snobby Crown Copse village. Maybe a resident took offence about losing their home."

"I carefully vet the people I allow into Crown Copse," Arietta said. "None of them may bring weapons into the village, and the magic trackers inform my security if anyone breaks the rules. It's not any of them."

"Arietta doesn't like that motive," I said. "It sounds like she had everyone who lived there so terrified they wouldn't burp without her permission."

Hettie shook her head. "I like a woman who knows her own mind, but Arietta took it to the extreme."

"Let's take a look at her file, and then you can get out of here," I said. "I don't want you getting on the wrong side of Arietta."

"Don't worry about me. And I want to be involved. It gives me something else to think about other than horses and dead bodies." Hettie opened the file and arranged the pages and photographs. "I dropped by your farm on the way here. The Magic Council is there. They were all focused on a locked barn."

My heart beat faster. "Which one?"

"The one right at the end. They were having trouble getting access to it. What have you got hiding in there?"

"They still haven't gotten in? That's good. I didn't have time to—" I bit my tongue.

"Well? You aren't hiding anything from the Magic Council, I hope." Hettie arched an eyebrow and grinned at me.

"Not hiding, exactly. But I like to come up with new designs for my scarecrows. Some of them are unusual, and I'm not sure everyone would approve."

"Tell me all about it. I like unusual."

"Focus on my murder," Arietta said. "I'm the most important person here."

"In a second. I'm thinking," I said.

Arietta knocked the file on the floor.

"Is Mrs. Queen of Exploitation getting her panties in a twist?" Hettie retrieved the paperwork.

"She's used to being the center of attention."

"Bad luck," Hettie said. "Odessa will get to you when she's got the time. Her scarecrows are important to her."

"I'll put Sol back to sleep and get rid of that annoying snoozing furball if you don't do as I say, when I say," Arietta said.

"We'd better get on with this before she does something awful to one of us." I flipped open the file.

"Just before we do, I heard a rumor Selma Black is involved in the investigation at your farm," Hettie said.

"She is. She was the one who issued the warrant. Do you know her?"

"Yes, and she's a nasty piece of work. Be careful."

"Olympus has already warned me about her. But it's too late to be careful. Selma has marked my card."

"I'm talking specifically about your scarecrows. The thing about Selma is she hates animation magic. And anyone who uses it gets in her little black book of wrongdoers."

"But it's so useful. And it's a key part of what I use to bring my scarecrows to life. Why would Selma have a problem with that kind of magic?"

"Because of what happened to her aunt. It was a long time ago, but I was working as the coroner and had to deal with the case."

"What happened?" I said.

Arietta floated closer, most likely drawn in by the ominous note in Hettie's voice.

"A dark magic user reanimated a doll that was a childhood toy of Selma's." Hettie pursed her lips. "The doll ate Selma's aunt."

I jerked back in my seat. "When you say ate, you mean, it took a chunk out of her arm or something like that?"

"Well, the doll only ate part of her, but it was the aunt's brain, so a pretty important part."

"Wow! I see now why Selma is so against animation magic."

"Maybe, but I don't approve of her prejudice against your scarecrows," Hettie said. "I've never had a problem with the one you've loaned me to work at the stables. Even the horses have gotten used to him and don't run anymore."

"My scarecrows would only eat someone if they posed a threat to me. I almost feel sorry for Selma, but she could be more understanding."

"Selma thinks the worst of everyone, and she uses underhanded tactics to find faults in businesses. And she'll keep digging until she finds dirt on you." Hettie tapped the file. "So I hope whatever you're hiding in that barn doesn't mean you get closed down for good."

I bit my bottom lip. It would. Selma would take one look at the humanlike scarecrows and think I was up to no good. I had to get back to my farm and empty that barn without anyone seeing.

"I also saw Indigo. She caught me up on a few things. Including your arrest and subsequent escape," Hettie said.

I grimaced. I still had that to deal with. "What did she say?"

"I figured you might be interested in that, so I asked a few questions, and there's good news. The Magic Council has no plans to charge you at the moment. And Olympus convinced them you had nothing to do with the explosion at the headquarters. The evidence shows it came from the outside. And there's even a recording of you being carried away by a scarecrow. Sol, too."

"Err... that's only because they run faster than I do," I said. "I ordered them to carry us."

"You keep that to yourself, because there's also bad news. Olympus and Indigo figured that the only way to clear your name was to implicate the scarecrows. They said some had gone rogue and abducted you and Sol. Apparently, Selma loves that idea."

"They can't blame the scarecrows. If the Magic Council catches them, they'll be destroyed." I stood from my seat. "I sent Shamrock and Marmaduke to the farm. They could be at risk."

"I didn't see any scarecrows when I was there," Hettie said. "But I can keep an eye on the place if you like."

"Thanks. Please. I can't let them be taken. Selma wants to run creepy experiments on them. She already has several she's examining."

"No problem. I'll do it in exchange for all the free pumpkins I can load into a horse cart, of course."

"Take what you need. I have to know what's happening to my scarecrows." I sank back into my seat, feeling slightly better Hettie was looking out for me, even if it meant I was down a crop of premium pumpkins.

"If any useful information comes my way, I'll let you know. Will you be staying here?"

"Yes, as long as the Magic Council doesn't notice I'm using this place. And don't tell anyone about me being here."

"I'm not one to gossip." Hettie leaned forward in her seat. "One more piece of advice. Stay out of the way until Selma has been dealt with. And don't go near the farm. I wouldn't put it past her to lay a few traps in the hope you'd return."

I stifled a groan. I needed to get back and rescue my humanlike scarecrows, or Brodie would never come back to me.

"Odessa, I don't say that for fun. If Selma catches you, it's game over. You've got some breathing space thanks to your friends, but she won't give up."

"I get it. I'll be careful."

"And don't sacrifice yourself for the scarecrows," Hettie said. "I like getting all the free hay and pumpkins off you. You're the most reliable supplier I've ever had. If you get locked up, I'll be stuck."

Arietta cleared her throat and jabbed my shoulder with an icy finger. "Have you forgotten I was murdered?"

"That's impossible to forget," I said. "Let's look at this file before the ghost's head explodes."

"I'll show you the important bits," Hettie said. "The cause of death was obvious. It was a single gunshot through the heart. Arietta died instantly." She pulled out several grisly photos and laid them on the table.

I looked at them for a second before averting my gaze to the wall. "It was Arietta's gun. The family all heard the shot."

"I examined the bullet. It's an unusual way to kill a magic user."

"Arietta has a thing about guns. Maybe she liked to look her victims in the eye when she pulled the trigger." I arched a brow at Arietta.

"I never pulled the trigger when I was pointing the gun at anyone. But there's nothing like having a weapon like that in your hand. You can feel its primitive power," Arietta said. "It's intoxicating."

"And dangerous. As you found out," I said.

"Just keep looking at my file."

Hettie turned another page to show a sketch of the body with the injuries marked on it. "I found something interesting during the autopsy. Arietta was stabbed in the leg not long before being killed."

"Stabbed! Was it a bad injury?"

"Superficial. It went through fat rather than muscle, but she had to get treatment for the wound."

I looked at Arietta. She refused to meet my gaze and floated away. "Do you know who stabbed her?"

"After she'd received treatment, Arietta claimed it was an accident," Hettie said.

"Arietta, do you want to make any comment here?"

She didn't reply.

"Did it look like an accident to you?" I said to Hettie.

"The blade went in her right calf from the inside edge of her leg. It's not impossible, but it would have been difficult to do to herself."

"Arietta, get involved in this conversation. Who stabbed you?"

"It's not important."

"It could have been a first murder attempt," I said. "It's crucial."

She floated back, a scowl on her face. "It wasn't a fatal injury. My boy got angry. He may be an airhead, but I've taught him never to run from a fight."

"Hold on now, Fontayne stabbed you in the leg?"

"Not with a knife. It was a silver letter opener off my desk. We had a disagreement, and I made the mistake of turning my back on him. The next thing

I know, there was a pain in my calf, and the letter opener was sticking in me."

"That must have been some argument to make Fontayne stab you. What were you arguing about?"

"I don't remember. Now I'm a ghost, I'm forgetting things."

"Like how to tell the truth," I said. "If Fontayne tried to kill you once—"

"He didn't try to kill me. He's just a badly behaved young man, who let his anger get the better of him."

Hettie pulled out her phone. "Young people are obsessed with social media. Let's see if her boy said anything online about why he stabbed Arietta. Check the date for when Arietta was brought in to have the leg wound dealt with."

I looked through the file. "It was August thirtieth."

"You won't find anything useful online. Fontayne wouldn't put up anything damning for someone to see." Arietta hovered around Hettie, an anxious look on her face.

"A lot of people share everything online," I said.

"My boy isn't the brightest diamond, but he wouldn't tell everyone he stabbed me."

"His girlfriend is pretty." Hettie showed me her screen.

Arietta zoomed away. "I don't know her."

I leaned over to get a better look. There were dozens of pictures of Fontayne and a petite brunette with a big smile. "They look happy. What's her name?"

"I don't remember."

"This is interesting," Hettie said. "There are no new pictures of the happy couple after August twenty-ninth. Why would that be?"

"Arietta, did you make Fontayne breakup with his girlfriend?" I said.

She didn't reply.

"And look at this. Fontayne posted lots of sad faces and changed his relationship status to single," Hettie said.

"My boy's young. He doesn't want to settle for just anyone," Arietta said.

"Whoever she is, it looked like she made Fontayne happy. Maybe he was in love," I said.

"I can tell you why Madam Pompous was unhappy with this relationship," Hettie said. "Look at the girlfriend's family. Witches have married non-magic users."

I studied the pictures and names attached to them. "Which dilutes the magic. And Arietta wouldn't want anyone weak joining the family. Isn't that right?" My gaze flicked to Arietta.

She returned to the table and glared at the phone. "They were getting serious. I have a reputation to uphold, and magic in the Frost family isn't as strong as it should be. I had to make sure it didn't get diluted further. That girl's mother fell in love with someone with no ability. She even moved out of her magic community to be with him."

"Arietta, what did you do?"

"Protected my family. Fontayne came to me and said he was thinking about asking to marry Bambi Shaw. I mean, the name should have told you everything. I had to stop it. I told him he had a choice of the family or the wide-eyed girlfriend. He knew, if he walked away from me, he'd be left penniless. And I'd make sure he never worked."

"From the way your nose is wrinkling, Arietta is saying something deeply unpleasant," Hettie said.

"She forced Fontayne to break up with the love of his life because Bambi Shaw didn't come from the right family." I shook my head at Arietta. "And by doing that, you gave him the perfect motive for wanting you dead."

"It is a great motive," Hettie said. "Love makes people do insane things."

"It's also the wrong motive," Arietta said.

Hettie's phone buzzed with an incoming call. "I need to get this. I'll leave you to argue with your ghost." She collected the file before answering her phone. "Hettie Crane. Hold the line if you want to talk to me about horses or dead people."

"Thanks, Hettie. And help yourself to any pumpkins when the Magic Council has cleared out of the farm." I jumped up and walked with her to the door.

"Will do. And it'll give me an excuse to see what they've been up to. Stay safe." She stopped by a gurgling pipe and tapped it. "You should get that fixed. Sounds like an air lock."

We said our goodbyes, and she headed out, her phone against her ear.

Arietta slammed the door shut. "You're wrong about Fontayne."

"I don't think I am. Let's go talk to your son. He's now got an incredible motive for wanting you dead."

Chapter 10

It was getting more of a struggle to keep a hold on my magic as we snuck back to Crown Copse that afternoon. I had a sneaking suspicion Arietta was covertly draining me to keep me weak.

I needed to get my hands on some powdered pumpkin. That would fix me up. I may even feel strong enough to take on Arietta and get out of this mess.

"I'll go ahead and give Fontayne a warning you're coming," Arietta said.

"Don't do anything mean to him," I said, but she simply laughed and zoomed away.

It was easy to get past the troll guard again since my name was still on the approved visitor list, and after checking in, I headed to the family home.

There was a yelp from inside an upstairs room in the Frost house, and a moment later, Fontayne raced out the front door in some green fitted boxer shorts and nothing else. He almost collided with me in his haste to get away from whatever Arietta had done to him.

He saw me at the last second and skidded to a halt, his breath panting out of him. "I think my mom just threw me out of bed."

"Sorry for the rude awakening. You do know it's two o'clock in the afternoon, right?" I said.

Fontayne looked back over his shoulder, not bothered he had so little clothing on. Oh, to have the body of a twenty-year-old again. "Sure. But I had a late night. What's wrong with Mom?"

"Shall we go back inside? You can put on some clothes, and we can talk."

He looked down at himself and patted his flat abs. "Sure. So long as Mom's not going to keep being mean to me."

"I'll do my best to keep her under control. But we have a few questions for you."

Arietta hovered in the doorway, shaking her head. "He always was a lazy layabout."

We headed inside to be met by Eva in the hallway. "Is there a problem?"

"Hopefully not. I just have a few questions for Fontayne," I said.

"Fetch us some coffee, Eva," Fontayne said, "and something for my head."

She nodded and hurried away.

"You can wait in there if you like." Fontayne gestured to a room by the front door. "I'll get dressed." He bounded up the stairs.

I walked into the room to discover a messy space with several state-of-the-art computer consoles and a pool table at the back by the large windows.

Arietta zoomed around the room. "Eva isn't keeping on top of things now I'm not here. This place is appalling."

"She has other things to worry about," I said. "And I expect she's spending more time with Derwin now you're no longer a threat to their happiness."

Fontayne returned a moment later, wearing a pair of slouchy dark jeans and a hooded sweatshirt. "You wanted to ask me something?"

I gestured to the seat opposite me as I sat. "Yes. I have questions about the fight you had with your mom before she died. The one where you stabbed her in the leg with a letter opener."

He stared at me and blinked rapidly. "She said she wouldn't tell anyone about that."

"And she didn't. But the wound was recorded in her autopsy report. What happened between you two?"

Fontayne sank into the seat and raked his hand through his messy red curls several times. "She is here, isn't she?"

"Yes, but she won't hurt you," I said.

"That all depends on what he did to me." Arietta heaved out a sigh as I glared at her. "No, I most likely won't hurt him."

"You're safe," I said to Fontayne. "But what happened?"

He stared at the ceiling for several seconds before looking at me. "I had no relationship with my mom. She was always bossing people around and had to control everything. So long as I turned up at her social events with her highflying friends and posed in the family pictures to make it look like we were one big happy family, she left me alone. I got my allowance, and I could do what I liked."

"And you thought you could date who you liked?" I said.

Fontayne sat forward with his elbows on his knees. "Mom never paid attention to the girls I dated. But then I met Bambi, and everything changed. She was different from all the princesses I'd hung out with in the past. She wasn't interested in clothes, partying, or drinking all the time. She volunteered for an environmental charity, and she has a cute three-legged dog she adopted that goes everywhere with her."

"She sounds nice."

"Yeah, Bambi's great." Fontayne shook his head. "And when I saw her with her mom and dad, I realized what a real family should be like."

"We were a real family," Arietta muttered.

"Go on," I said to Fontayne. "What did you see?"

"Bambi's parents are amazing. They're so kind and always telling her how smart she is and how much they love her. And they support her dreams." A sad smile played across Fontayne's face. "Bambi wants to be a vet, but they didn't have much money, and the training is expensive. But they saved every penny to make sure her dream could come true. Her dad even took a second job just to help her."

"They do sound great."

"Yep. I even offered to help her, but Bambi said she didn't want me for my money. That was the first time any girl said that to me. When I've been out with other girls, they expected me to buy them stuff and take them to expensive dinners. Bambi gave me cute homemade gifts she made herself. And her favorite food is takeout pizza. I took her to a smart restaurant once, but she said she felt uncomfortable. She was a breath of fresh air. It made me see there was a different way to live. A better way."

"And you fell in love with that," I said.

"I reckon I did. And I still love her. But I asked Mom about getting engaged to Bambi, and she went ballistic. She yelled at me and threw things when I argued back. Mom said I had to marry up and find someone from a powerful magic family. She said I needed to strengthen the Frost family name. I didn't care about that. We're already powerful and wealthy. Why couldn't I marry for love?"

"He's a foolish boy who doesn't know what he's talking about." There was no anger in Arietta's words. In fact, when I took a peek at her expression, she looked sad. Maybe her son was getting through to her.

"You broke up with Bambi?" I said.

"Mom threatened to ruin Bambi's chance of becoming a vet. She said she'd report her to the university she studied at and make sure they took her place." Fontayne ran a hand down his face. "Mom also threatened to take away my inheritance and stop me from getting work. I knew she'd do it. I've seen her do it with other people."

"Arietta, would you really have done that?" I said.

"Fontayne has to learn how difficult the world is. And I know him best. He'd have been miserable with this weak magic user. The novelty would have worn off. I was saving him from years of heartache." Arietta was looking out the window as she spoke.

"Or preventing him from years of being blissfully happy with a young woman he clearly cares for," I said.

"I broke Bambi's heart when we split up," Fontayne said. "But I had to keep her safe. Letting her go was the best thing for her."

"You shouldn't have hidden this from me when I first came to speak to the family."

"Why? I don't see how it's important."

"It gives you a great motive for killing your mom. You'd previously fought, and Arietta got injured," I said. "Did you tell the Magic Council about the fight?"

He shook his head. "They'd only think the worst, just like you. I'm still angry with Mom, but I wouldn't shoot her. I've wanted to leave and get out of this family's shadow. I've felt trapped for ages and was sick of her scaring away people I like. She's done it with friends, but she shouldn't have done it to Bambi. It hurt."

"Arietta, is there anything you'd like me to pass on to your son? Maybe an apology?"

She bared her teeth at me, but then looked at Fontayne. "I didn't realize I'd hurt him so badly. I thought Bambi was a crush he'd get bored with. She wasn't good enough for him. He must see that."

"You can never be sure where your heart will take you," I said.

"Only if you're an idiot," Arietta said. "I taught him better. Don't get attached. Find a partner to have fun with and then move on. That way, no one gets hurt. You get your needs fulfilled, and everyone is happy."

"What she's saying?" Fontayne said.

"Your mom's realizing she made a mistake."

"I didn't say that," Arietta said.

"You were working up to it. Maybe you can rekindle things with Bambi," I said to Fontayne.

"Bambi hates me. She won't return my calls." Fontayne slumped back in his seat. "I should leave. I only stayed because of the money. And I expect Mom's got everything tangled up in some complicated will, and I'll get nothing. We're still waiting for the reading. Even if I get something, it wouldn't be enough to stay."

"Your mom's not around to mess with your life anymore."

"She's right here!" Fontayne said. "Although I can't see or hear her, I keep getting chills running up and down my spine. I always knew when Mom wasn't happy. I'd get this cold ball of tension in the pit of my stomach. If I date Bambi again, she'll come after me. I sometimes hated her."

Arietta gasped, but had turned away so I couldn't see her face.

"Fontayne, I have to ask this question. Did you shoot your mom?"

Eva hurried in with coffee mugs and a full cafetiere. "I don't like to interfere, but Fontayne wouldn't do that. He's a good boy."

"Put down the coffee and go," Fontayne said. "This is none of your business."

Eva opened her mouth as if to say something more, then shook her head and set down the tray.

"Thanks, Eva," I said.

She nodded at me just as her pocket buzzed with an incoming call on her mobile. She hurried out into the corridor to take the call.

"Are we done?" Fontayne stood. He grabbed a mug and poured himself a coffee. "I hated my mom and everything she did to me, but I didn't shoot her. I was with the others that night."

"That's all I need from you for now." I followed Fontayne into the hallway and watched as he ran up the stairs. He had a great motive, but a solid alibi.

"Are you sure you can't do anything more?"

I tilted my head at Eva's panicked tone. She was standing outside the front door. I pressed a finger to my lips and gestured Arietta to move closer.

"I've been here so long. I must have some rights," Eva said.

I furrowed my brow and looked at Arietta. What was Eva talking about?

Arietta simply shrugged and looked mildly bored.

"I understand. Thank you." Eva pulled open the front door, her eyes widening when she saw me standing there. Her face was pale, and she was shaking.

"Eva, what's the matter?" I went to take her arm, worried she might faint.

"Nothing. I've just had some bad news. If you'll excuse me." She dashed past me, heading to the stairs.

"Who was she speaking to?" I said.

Arietta floated past me. "Who cares?"

"Eva's still on our suspect board. All information could be useful."

"Do you want her phone?" Arietta grinned at me. "I could get it for you."

"Err... sure. But she's not going to hand it over and let me check her call history. That would be weird."

"Leave that to me. I'm good at scaring the truth out of people." Arietta zoomed off after Eva.

"Don't scare her to death," I called out.

Arietta raised a hand as she headed up the stairs.

I stepped out the front door to wait for Arietta, then walked around the side of the building to stretch my legs. I froze when I spotted Selma, Olympus, and Indigo. I ducked behind a row of bushes and crept closer. What were they doing here?

"The reports have come to nothing. Odessa isn't in Crown Copse." Olympus had his arms crossed over his chest.

"Why would someone lie about seeing her here?" Selma said.

"It doesn't matter if she is here. You can't keep harassing my friend." Indigo stood toe-to-toe with Selma. "She's done nothing wrong. You've had investigators at the farm for too long. If there was anything to find, you'd have discovered it by now."

"The investigation will go on for as long as I see fit." Selma flicked a glare at Olympus. "Control your girlfriend."

Eek! That was the wrong thing to say. I inched a little closer.

Olympus rested a hand on Indigo's shoulder. "Selma knows not to overstep any boundaries. And she's almost done at the farm, aren't you?"

"There's still a barn we can't access. There's magic preventing us from getting inside. We must have full access to everything. And there's still the jail break to deal with."

"There was no jail break. Odessa creates powerful scarecrows, and they look out for her. She didn't order them to break her out," Olympus said. "We've already discussed this. The matter is closed."

"But she hasn't come forward," Selma said. "That's suspicious. It's because of what's in that barn."

"That old barn is full of equipment or spare parts for scarecrows," Indigo said. "Go look for real criminals. Odessa has done nothing wrong."

"She's hiding something," Selma said. "The magic around that place feels weird."

"It's not weird. She's a powerful witch, who uses reanimation magic."

"Which can go wrong fast." Selma grimaced. "Something that has died should not be brought back. Ever."

"Odessa doesn't use her power to raise the dead. She uses it for good. And her scarecrows are amazing," Indigo said. "You're jealous of her ability."

"Watch your step. Odessa had outside help to escape. And since you're her best friend, perhaps you were involved, too."

"Selma, that's enough. We've established the scarecrows acted independently," Olympus said. "We have recordings of them setting the magic charges. Odessa couldn't have contacted them after she was arrested. You restrained her magic."

"There was something else involved," Selma said. "I caught a blur of movement on the security tracker. It was small and black. Don't you have a spider familiar, Indigo?"

Indigo kept glaring at Selma. "Maybe."

"If I find out you helped your friend escape, I'll arrest you."

I bit my bottom lip. Selma must have seen Hilda. Indigo couldn't get involved with my dramas. She had a checkered history with the Magic Council and had been close to having her magic taken from her for good. She wouldn't want to get on the wrong side of Selma, or she'd get in trouble again.

"Selma, this isn't getting you anywhere," Olympus said. "Finish your investigation at the farm and close the case. And stop chasing rumors about Odessa. She's not a criminal."

"I won't close it. I'm not happy with my findings."

"You've got nothing to charge Odessa with. And do I need to remind you how heavy-handed you were when you arrested Odessa and Sol?"

Go Olympus! I was so glad Indigo dated a guy from the Magic Council.

"She's dangerous! Odessa attacked me. I had every right to use any force necessary."

"Odessa defended her scarecrows as you ripped them away from her," Indigo said. "That was like stealing someone's children. It's no wonder she reacted so strongly."

Selma sniffed. "That's ridiculous. A scarecrow can't be compared to an infant."

"Odessa's magic keeps them alive. They're connected to her," Indigo said.

"Which makes it even worse. If Odessa loses control of her magic, the scarecrows will run riot." Selma was shaking her head and scowling.

"Odessa is within her rights to lodge a complaint against you for how you handled her arrest," Olympus said. "Under paragraph eighty-five of the Citizens Charter for Inclusion, you broke the law."

Selma's mouth dropped open. "I did no such thing."

"Let's put that to the test." Indigo smirked at Selma. "Shall I lodge a complaint on her behalf?"

I was glad my friends were on my side, but I needed to be careful not to get them too involved with my mess. The problem was, I wasn't sure how to keep them away. I couldn't reveal myself, or Selma would arrest me on the spot.

A scream from the house had my heart thundering, and I raced back to see what was going on. A few seconds later, a small black object was launched from an upstairs window.

I raced over and discovered a mobile phone on the ground. I grabbed it up.

"Don't let the screen lock!" Arietta flew out the window, cackling with laughter. "I grabbed it while Eva was texting."

A quick change of the phone's settings meant it wouldn't lock, and I tucked it into my pocket. "How did you get it?"

"I conjured a little scare or two. Eva might need to change her underwear after that, but I got you the phone."

"Let's move. The Magic Council is here. If I'm found, this investigation is over, and I'll be stuck with you." And I didn't want to spend a second more with this mean ghost than I had to.

Chapter 11

We'd made our way back to the distillery in Witch Haven, and I was sitting at the table with Sol. Arietta was hovering around as I accessed the phone's call history.

"Sol, look up this number for me." I held out the display, and he tapped it into his own phone.

"It's a local solicitor," he said.

"What does Eva need legal representation for?" Arietta said. "She's got nothing of value and no house or assets to protect."

"If it is a legal matter, there's no point in calling to find out. If Eva's a client, they won't tell me anything," I said.

I scrolled through the phone. There were several voicemail messages. The last one had been received this morning from the same number as the solicitor. I opened it and put it on speakerphone so everyone could hear.

Miss Whiteflower, this is Gideon Salamander from Bloodstone, Smith, and Salamander. I've been through your contract and can confirm there's nothing we can do for you. I understand the Frost family has employed you for many years, but your contract is clear. If the business passes to a new owner, they're under no obligation to keep you on. I'm sorry I don't have better news. As the contract states in paragraph six, page four, you'll receive no financial compensation if your job becomes redundant. If you'd like to speak to me about this, please contact me, but I'm unable to take this case any further. You'll shortly be receiving our bill. Goodbye.

I ended the voicemail message and focused on Arietta, who'd moved away from the table once the contents of the voicemail message became clear. "Eva was losing her job because you were selling?"

"What of it? I don't keep track of all the staff comings and goings."

"But she's been with your family for years. Why get rid of her because you're selling?"

"That's not a concern of mine."

"Make it your concern." I slapped my hand on the table. "Or I won't help you anymore. You'll be stuck as a ghost for the rest of your miserable afterlife. And I hope you turn into a ghost ghoul. You deserve it. Then the Magic Council will hunt you and destroy you. I might even help."

Arietta scowled as she drifted closer. "I didn't want complications when I sold the business. The new owner wanted a fresh start. That meant I had to shed the dead wood."

"You were planning on getting rid of everyone? Even Regan?"

"Regan was staying, but it was likely she'd have had a pay cut and her role would have merged with someone else's. She'd have understood. It's just business. Nothing personal."

"That's doubtful," I said. "What about Eva's contract? You got her to sign a deal that left her with nothing. And she lives in the chalet behind your house. Where is she supposed to go?"

"She'd have managed. Although she is slowing down. Maybe she could have taken early retirement."

"She's not even fifty! And I expect you don't pay Eva enough to save any cash, so she has nothing to live off when she looks for a new job."

"What my employees do with their money is no concern of mine. If they don't handle it responsibly, it's their fault."

"When was the last time you gave Eva a pay raise?"

"I... I don't remember. I don't deal with the payroll."

"When was the last time anyone, other than you, got a pay raise?"

"People get rewarded when I see results."

"Which means not often. You should be ashamed."

"I have nothing to be ashamed about."

"You were kicking Eva out and making her homeless!"

"Eva's disposable, just like my business. I wasn't going to ruin an excellent deal because of some sad-faced housekeeper who's been seeing my brother behind my back. I'm glad she's out of the way. She deserves this."

"What she deserved was respect for having served you loyally for years. You gave her a contract that left her with nothing. When people get made redundant, they get a payoff."

"Other employers are far too generous. It's why they go out of business. And why would I give someone money when I no longer need them?"

"Because it's the responsible thing to do," I said.

"This is Eva's fault for having no ambition. And she should have protected herself. She should have read through her contract and raised any queries before signing it."

"You... you really are a terrible person."

"I look after myself and make sure I don't get exploited. There's nothing wrong with that."

As much as I wanted to argue with Arietta, it would get me exactly nowhere, other than angry, frustrated, and regretting ever setting eyes on this mean ghost.

"And rather than complaining to me, this is good news for you. Eva has an excellent reason for wanting me dead," Arietta said.

"She does. And she should have shot you years ago. But Eva was with Derwin when they heard the shot. She didn't do it."

Sol looked up from his phone. "What about the husband, Chay? If I was married to this jerk, I'd want to kill her."

"That's enough from you." Arietta grabbed Sol's head and wrapped herself around him.

"Hey! Get off my... employee." I leaped to Sol's defense, attempting to pry Arietta loose, but she didn't let go.

He groaned and slumped on the table, his phone falling from his hand.

I mustered magic from the bottom of my almost empty power well and shoved Arietta away. "Stop! Sol was being helpful."

She snarled at me. "We're running out of time. And Sol is a distraction. You can't afford to have anything taking your attention. Find my killer, or I'll kill your boyfriend and turn you over to the Magic Council."

"You won't. You still need me." Although I was aware of just how disposable Arietta considered people. Once she was done with me, I'd be in trouble.

Arietta lifted Sol and moved him to the floor. She swirled around him, forming a barrier to stop me from getting to him. "That gets him out of your way. Now you focus on me."

"We were both focused on you. Sol suggested Chay could be your killer, and I haven't properly looked into him." I studied Sol through the hazy barrier of magic. He was unconscious but didn't look to be in any pain. Maybe he was better out of this. It only took the smallest thing to provoke Arietta's rage.

"Stop staring at him like some lovesick teenager and get to work."

"I will, so long as you stop threatening to kill people."

"Very well. Maybe I'll just maim him the next time you lose focus."

"I'm keeping a note of all these threats. They'll come back to bite you."

Arietta simply cackled a laugh, proving I was lousy at making threats. I just wasn't a threat making kind of witch.

I grabbed Sol's phone and looked at what he'd been researching. There were several tabs open, all containing information about Chay. "Where did you meet unlucky husband number five?"

"He was at a clinic I attended."

"What kind of clinic?"

"It was multipurpose. And exclusive. There was physical therapy, massage, and spa treatments."

"I was hoping you'd gone to get your head looked at," I said.

"There's nothing wrong with my head."

"That's debatable. Chay was there getting treatments, too?"

"No, he was a nurse."

"Huh! I figured he'd be a patient." I looked at a picture Sol had on his phone. It showed a much dowdier, sensible version of Chay. He had his hair slicked back and wore a pair of thick-framed glasses. It must have been the sensible nurse look he rocked when dealing with high-strung, elite patients like Arietta.

"How long did you know Chay before you became a couple?" I continued to scan through the documents on the phone.

"We dated for three months. Then I suggested we marry."

"It was your suggestion?" I stared intently at one of the documents Sol had discovered.

"Of course. Why do you ask?"

"Did you know Chay had been married before?"

"He mentioned it. It wasn't important."

I opened two more documents. They were scanned copies of marriage certificates. All three had Chay listed as the groom. "He's been married three times."

"What's your point? I've been married five times. It wasn't a competition."

"My point is, you shouldn't have knocked Sol out. He was researching Chay's background and coming up with useful information about your husband."

"I already know everything important about Chay."

"Did you know that, not only has Chay been married three times, but all his former wives died?"

"Let me look at that." Arietta attempted to snatch the phone, but I held onto it as I checked the information. "He didn't tell you about these deaths?"

"I wasn't interested in his previous wives. I knew one of them died."

"But not all three? He kept that from you?"

"I... I don't think it was mentioned."

I looked up at Arietta. "Chay has been lying to you. We could have a male black widow on our hands, and you were his latest victim."

Chapter 12

"I insist we visit him immediately. We've done enough research," Arietta said. "And if I married a serial killer, I need to know about it."

"If you did, I'm going nowhere near him," I said.

We'd spent hours going through the information Sol had discovered and found even more useful leads. Chay had used his job in the rich ladies' clinic to exploit vulnerable, wealthy women. Once he'd gotten what he wanted, he killed them.

"You have all the evidence. Chay deceived me. Maybe he's killed other women, too, but didn't bother marrying them. There could be bodies everywhere." Arietta swirled around, making the room uncomfortably cold.

"Not so long ago, you said you didn't care about his previous marriages."

"That was before I learned what a coldhearted monster he is."

"The two of you should have been a perfect match," I said.

"This is no time for your terrible humor. Chay is a dangerous man."

"He could be. Everything Sol discovered suggests Chay's been conning rich women for years."

"Chay could be at my house right now, stripping the contents. We must stop him." Arietta zoomed to the door of the distillery.

"We should get the Magic Council involved. I'm not equipped to handle a serial killer." I tilted my head. "Although I'm not certain what you need to deal with one. A knockout spell? Something to restrain him with? A defense against his charm?"

Arietta sighed. "Chay is charming. I had no idea about his true nature. I told you, never trust a man. Get what you want and move on."

"You certainly got more than you bargained for when you took on Chay," I said. "Did you really not know what kind of man he was?"

"The worst kind are always the most charming. But he's deliciously handsome, and he took great care of me at the clinic. He even gave me special massages."

"Yuck. I don't want to hear about your special massages."

She hovered by the table. "It was all an act. You must confront him. Chay will still be awake at this time of night. He's a night owl."

"I don't care if he's a night squirrel, I'm not getting into a risky situation with a serial killer."

"So you don't care what I do to Sol or Tuffin?"

"Arietta! You're asking me to put my life at risk by confronting a dangerous man. If Chay realizes we're on to him, he'll attack. He'll want me silenced."

"So use your magic on him."

"The magic you keep draining whenever I doze off, you mean?"

Her smug smile told me everything. "What are you talking about?"

"Don't play innocent with me. I feel like I've aged ten years since I met you. You're a strong ghost because you're taking my power without permission. Do you know how many laws that breaks?"

"It's probably fewer than you've broken. After all, you're the one wanted by the Magic Council."

I swatted her away but missed the target as Arietta zigged around me.

"Don't be such a wimp. We can catch Chay off guard. Take a weapon with you if your magic is weak," Arietta said.

"I want Sol with me. We can work together to deal with Chay."

"No, your hunky hero isn't an option."

"Then Tuffin." She might help me if she was in a good mood.

"Urgh! The furball. Must we involve her? Can't you find a hammer or something solid to whack Chay with if he misbehaves?"

"No whacking. And Tuffin has power. She can help us. It's Tuffin or no go."

"Very well. I'll unleash the furball." Arietta vanished, and a few seconds later, there was a hissing shriek. Tuffin raced out of the staffroom, her fur puffed out.

"Hi! It's good to have you awake." I gave her a wave.

She hissed, then spun around and glared behind her. "I was asleep when something cold bit me."

"That was Arietta Frost. The ghost. Welcome back."

"Welcome back? What's happening? Why am I so cold? I feel like I've been frozen. And what's happened to him?" Tuffin was staring at Sol.

"Long story. I'll tell you everything on our way to chat with a serial killer."

"A what now?" Tuffin's fur was still puffed out.

"You've missed a lot."

"Let's move. You have your weapon, and those claws do look lethal." Arietta shot past and out the door.

"That's the ghost who bit me?" Tuffin raced to the door and glared out at Arietta.

"Yes. And she'll keep biting, so watch your back." I eased open the door and peered outside. It was late, so there was less chance anyone from the Magic Council would spot me.

"Hurry up," Arietta yelled from the darkness. "We have to confront my lying, murdering husband."

After making sure I had all the information on Chay, I checked on Sol, who was still sleeping, and left the distillery.

I decided not to use a concealment spell. My magic felt so drained, and I hadn't had a sniff of powdered pumpkin for days. I was running on fumes, and didn't like it. I wanted to be back in my farmhouse, surrounded by scarecrows, with Sol by my side. Dealing with an angry ghost and serious withdrawal symptoms from a lack of sweet, powdered treats was awful.

As I filled Tuffin in on everything she'd missed, I kept to the shadows as we left Witch Haven and headed into Crown Copse. I was dragging my feet by the time we got to the Frost house. I needed sleep and food.

"I can't believe we're helping this monster," Tuffin grumbled.

"She has someone I care about trapped. She had you, too, but I negotiated for your freedom. Which I don't think you've thanked me for yet."

"What's there to be thankful for? You're dragging me to a serial killer's lair."

"Alleged serial killer. Although it's looking likely that he murdered his previous wives."

"And this one?" Tuffin's nose wrinkled. "We should make a run for it while we can."

"I'd make it about five steps." I looked down at Tuffin. We hadn't known each other long, and she had no reason to stick with me. "You can sneak off if you like. I'll handle this."

"And then leave me feeling mildly guilty when I hear the Legendary Serial Killer of Crown Copse gutted you. No thanks." Tuffin flicked her tail. "And if you were killed, who'd serve me overcooked, dry fish every day?"

I grinned. "No one. I serve the best overcooked, dry fish in the whole of Witch Haven."

"Stop dawdling." Arietta zoomed back and shoved me from behind. "I've already looked inside. Chay is in the kitchen. Go around the back of the house, and you'll find him."

I sucked in a deep breath, found a bit of energy, and stumbled my way around the house. Sure enough, as I looked in the kitchen window, Chay was sipping from a mug as he leaned against the black granite work top.

"Go in and confront him," Arietta said.

I tapped on the window, and Chay startled. He looked at me and tilted his head.

I gestured at the door, and he walked over and opened it. "Odessa? What are you doing lurking around outside at this time of night?"

"Arietta insisted I visit you." I looked around for any obvious weapons Chay could use to attack me. There was a large knife block I'd need to keep a watch on, but all other potential weapons were out of sight. "She said you'd still be up."

A wry smile crossed his face. "What my darling Arietta wants, she always gets, even though she's dead. Would you like to come in?"

"Thanks. I've got some information I wanted to talk to you about." I stepped inside the warm kitchen and happily accepted a mug of coffee from Chay. He might be a serial killer, but at least he had good manners.

"Oh, you wanted to speak just to me?" Chay glanced down at Tuffin as she strutted around, but made no comment. "I hope Arietta's not unearthed a dark secret from my past?" His chuckle died as he looked at me. "Or maybe she has."

My gaze landed on the large plate of delicious smelling pizza slices next to Chay. My stomach grumbled loudly, and I pressed my hand against it.

"Would you like some? I won't be able to eat this all myself." He pushed the plate my way.

"We haven't got time for eating," Arietta hissed in my ear. "Don't fall for his snake oil charm, or you'll be his next victim."

"Thanks. I am hungry," I said. "Arietta's not great at looking after me."

"That's odd. She was always good to me," Chay said. "She could get distracted by work, but made sure I had the things I wanted. And we'd often go for extravagant meals. She was a generous woman. I know many people didn't like her, but we got along."

I'd already eaten most of a slice of pizza while he was talking and nodded as I swallowed a cheesy, delicious lump of dough. "You were happy with Arietta?"

"Yes. I quickly learned that, so long as I agreed with her, life was much easier." Chay lifted a slice of pizza. "Does your cat want feeding?"

Tuffin was nosing around the trash can. "I do."

Chay tossed the slice of pizza on the floor. "Help yourself."

Tuffin sniffed it. "He's not your typical serial killer. I like him."

Chay stared at Tuffin. "What did the cat just say?"

"Um... we'll get to that."

Chay's gaze flickered around the kitchen. "It's getting cold in here. Did you bring Arietta?"

"Yes, I should have said. She's here, too."

Chay looked at Tuffin again and shook his head. "How are you, Arietta? How's the afterlife treating you?"

"Like he cares? After all, he black widowed me to death," Arietta said. "Tell him we know everything."

I greedily munched down another slice of pizza while Arietta floated around, raving about Chay's betrayal.

Chay shuddered and rubbed his arms with his hands. He reached down, and it was only then I noticed a large duffel bag by his feet. He pulled out a sweater and tugged it over his head. "I can't stand the cold. I was looking forward to a vacation with Arietta after the sale of the business was finalized. I was hoping we could go away for at least a month."

"Where were you going?" I edged closer to the knife block, just in case things got tricky when I circled back to the serial killer issue.

"We'd picked a beautiful tropical island. A place where you barely wear any clothes because it's so warm. It would have been great."

"If you think you're going on that vacation without me, you've got another thing coming," Arietta said. "I'll make sure the tickets are canceled. You won't be going anywhere other than jail."

"Arietta's hoping you'll get a long break from here soon." I finished my pizza and sipped on my coffee.

"That would be good. Not everyone here is my biggest fan." Chay bit into his own slice of pizza.

I'd delayed things enough. There really was no easy way to ask someone if they were a serial killer. I accessed the information about Chay's previous weddings on my phone. "So, the information I found. Were you honest with Arietta about your past relationships?"

He sucked in a breath, and his gaze went to the phone. "She knew I'd been with other people."

"And your previous wives?"

"Oh! Sure. You found out about them?"

"It wasn't hard to discover. Marriage licenses are public record. I'm surprised Arietta didn't do any research into you before you got married."

"I didn't hide them, but Arietta wasn't interested in who I used to be married to. She said I was her focus and to forget about the other women. I was happy to do that." His gaze stayed on the phone.

"I suppose it was easy to forget them because they're dead," I said. "Did Arietta know about that?"

Chay rubbed the back of his neck. "She never asked if they were still alive."

"And none of their ghosts came back to haunt you?"

"Err... no. Why would they do that?" He slowly set down his mug, and his easy expression hardened. "What are you suggesting?"

"That you targeted certain women, seducing them so you could get your hands on their assets. Then you killed them. Is that what happened with Arietta?" I blocked his path to the knife block.

Chay stared at me in silence for several seconds before bursting out in laughter. "I didn't murder my previous wives. Or Arietta."

"It's too much of a coincidence all of them are dead, especially when the only connection between them is you."

"No, that's not the only connection. You don't understand."

"Make him explain it," Arietta said. "How did his other wives die? Were they shot, too? All serial killers have a preferred method of murder."

"Arietta wants to know what happened to your other wives," I said.

Chay poured himself another coffee. "I can see, if you're looking at the facts, and you don't know the context, it would be easy to think I picked old, sick women, used them, and then, I don't know, gave them an overdose of whatever medication they were on."

"He just confessed." Arietta lunged at him.

"Wait!" I grabbed her and pulled her back. "Let's hear him out."

Chay had ducked as Arietta neared him, as if sensing the threat, and was looking around with wide eyes, one arm shielding his head. "Relax. I didn't overdose her with her meds."

"You worked in a health clinic, though," I said. "You must have medications on site. Were you able to access them?"

"Sure, but that wasn't my area of specialty. I sometimes helped the ladies with their pain relief if they were struggling, but my work was more physical therapy and massage."

Arietta struggled away from me. "He does have very strong hands."

I grimaced. "Did you meet your previous wives at the clinic?"

He nodded. "We specialized in helping wealthy women who needed a discrete place to stay and recover from their ailments."

"What kind of illnesses did you support?"

"Some were survivors of cancer or tumors. Some had recently had surgery and needed time to rebuild their muscles. Others were emotionally drained. They wanted a break from their lives, so they came to the clinic. We provided a discrete service. There was a large staff team, and we each had a small pool of clients. It was easy to get close to them, especially when they shared their fears or secrets with you."

"And once you knew their secrets, you exploited them?" I said.

"No, I grew to like these women. Sure, they were more mature than me, but they were sophisticated and confident. They'd seen the world and explored so many things. I found them fascinating. And I've always liked older women."

"How big of an age gap was there between you and Arietta?"

"Seventeen years. But that didn't matter to me. It was Arietta's fire and passion I admired."

"Not her money?"

Chay shrugged. "I mean, it helped. But I used to work seven days a week, so I was always at the clinic. That was my only opportunity to meet women. I didn't have time for the dating scene or time to get invested in anything serious."

"You admit you didn't marry Arietta for love?" I said.

"Neither of us ever talked about love," Arietta said. "That wasn't the deal. I understood that."

"I expect Arietta's yelling at you about the arrangement we had," Chay said.

"I'm actually surprised she isn't yelling." In fact, Arietta looked sad. "If you weren't in love, why did you get married?"

"To provide comfort and give each other security. I cared for all my wives."

"How did your other wives die?"

"Not by my hand. I'm a lover, not a fighter." Chay raked a hand through his hair. "My first two wives had serious heart conditions. They came to the clinic as part of their bucket list. They wanted to experience luxury. I developed genuine feelings for them. They weren't passionate love affairs, but we cared for each other. They both knew they didn't have long to live and wanted to enjoy every moment. I was happy to add pleasure to their lives."

"You were intimate with these women?"

"I was. And I had no problem with that. They were attractive and well preserved. They spent their money on looking after themselves, and they wanted a companion to share some amazing experiences with. My first marriage lasted a year before my wife died, and my second marriage lasted six months."

"What about the third wife?" I said.

"She was more complicated. My third wife shouldn't have died but had an undiagnosed mental health condition. She was also on strong painkillers for chronic back pain. One day, she decided she couldn't live with the pain and took too many of her pills."

"You didn't help her make that decision?"

"No! I was away on a week of training. Although I wondered for a while if leaving her pushed her over the edge. I still feel guilty about that. I was devastated when I heard the news. We were married for eighteen months. I wouldn't go as far as to say I loved her, but it was as close as I've ever gotten." Chay rocked back on his heels. "I decided to take a break from marriage after that. But the following month, I met Arietta."

"And I whisked him off his feet," she said. "I wish I'd known about his other wives, now. I missed out on an important part of his life. I always saw Chay as just an accessory, but there's more to him."

"You should be careful. You sound like you almost care," I said to her.

"What did Arietta say?" Chay said.

"That she'd have liked to know more about your past."

"She says that now, but she'd have just been angry. We both understood our arrangement. Arietta wanted someone to take care of her needs, make her laugh, make her happy in the bedroom, and not cause any drama. That was my job."

"What did you get in return?" I said.

"Like I said, a safe place and no money worries. Before I met Arietta, I was thinking about quitting my job and trying something new. I've always wanted to be an actor. Anyway, I could have done anything I wanted. Arietta gave me a generous allowance, and so long as I made her smile, it worked for both of us."

"Isn't true love amazing," Tuffin said. "Sign me up for a one-way pass to Single Town."

"Odessa, I assure you, I'm not a serial killer. I just met and married unhealthy women. I knew I wouldn't have long with any of them, but I enjoyed making them happy before they died. What's so wrong with that?"

"Arietta doesn't fit that mold, though," I said. "She was never ill."

"True. But I wanted a change. And Arietta assured me she didn't expect us to remain together forever. We had break clauses in our marriage."

"Break clauses?"

"The marriage was a business arrangement," Arietta said. "When you sign a lease on a building, you have a break clause so you can get out without incurring fees. I set up the same arrangement with our marriage."

"Is that legal?" I said.

"Perfectly. We had a contract in place before we married. At the three-year mark, we had the option to walk away from the marriage with no contest."

"Is Arietta explaining things to you?" Chay said.

"Yes, although I'm kind of shocked."

"Don't be. It worked for both of us. I got to live a life of luxury while I figured out what to do next. If the acting doesn't work out, I was thinking about going to university. I never studied much when I was younger, but I liked the idea of archeology or maybe Egyptology. I could be the next Indiana Jones."

"He'd make a dashing archeologist," Arietta said. "He'll also have the money for those plans if that's what he chooses to do."

"Arietta likes that idea. She also mentioned money. I'm assuming now she's dead, you'll get most of her assets."

Chay shook his head. "There's not a chance of that. I get something, but it's not an amount worth killing for. I signed a prenup agreement. It's rock solid. I knew exactly what I'd get if Arietta died."

Arietta jabbed me with a finger. "I knew you were wrong about the serial killer theory."

I rubbed my arm. "You didn't. You insisted we come here and confront Chay. Tell me more about the prenup."

"I've got it right here." Chay knelt and rifled through the duffel bag before pulling out a file. He opened it and extracted a sheet of paper. "Here it is. It was clearly set out. In the event of Arietta's death, I get a single payout of half a million. Nothing more. And you know what the business was being sold for if the sale had gone through. I won't see any of that."

"It's still a lot of money," I said.

"Not enough to live off for the rest of my life." He took back the paperwork after I'd looked through it.

"You just said if the sale of the business had gone through. Has there been a change of plans?"

Chay packed away the paperwork and zipped up the duffel bag. "You won't have heard, but the buyer is unhappy following Arietta's murder. They don't want to take on a business associated with something so dark. They're thinking about pulling out."

"What!" Arietta shrieked so loudly, Tuffin leaped in the air and hissed. I almost did the same.

"I think a lot of buyers will be put off after what happened to Arietta. Especially since her murder remains unsolved," Chay said. "There's even a rumor an unhappy customer attacked her. No one will want to touch the distillery business if it's considered a dangerous place."

Arietta snarled. "The business I slaved over is ruined. I'm surrounded by incompetent fools. How could they let this deal fall through?"

I looked at the duffel bag by Chay's feet. "Are you going somewhere?"

"Sure. I'm not welcome around here anymore. The family tolerated me because Arietta forced them to do so, but they've made it clear I don't have a place here for much longer." He shrugged. "I don't mind. I was only here for Arietta, and I don't want to be a stepdad to anyone. I definitely don't want to hang around with miserable Derwin. My time here is over. I'll take what I'm owed and move on. It's time to find wife number four."

"What's to say you weren't looking for wife number four while Arietta was still alive?" I said. "You might have had enough of her strong-armed tactics and been looking for an easier ride. When you found someone, you shot Arietta, collected the money, and planned your escape."

"It's not a terrible theory," Arietta said.

"There's one small problem with that. I have an airtight alibi. I was in the house messing around with Fontayne. Regan and Derwin will confirm that. Even if I'd wanted rid of Arietta, and I didn't, I couldn't have done it."

And we were back to that thorny problem. All my suspects had strong alibis.

"I guess that means you can rule me out," Chay said.

I glanced at Arietta, and she nodded, although she didn't look happy. "Stick around for as long as you can. After all, your wife was killed. Don't you want to find out who did it?"

"I mean, it would be good to get closure. Although I really am hunting for a new wife. I don't do well on my own." Chay grinned at me and winked. "You're cute. How rich are you?"

Chapter 13

My head was nestled against a warm, soft pillow. As I snuggled against it, I thought I was waking from a bad dream. One that involved an angry ghost, dozens of suspects, and a whole lot of reasons to kill.

It wasn't until I opened my eyes that I realized none of it was a dream. It was my hideous reality, and I'd fallen asleep in the distillery after coming back from confronting Chay and getting it spectacularly wrong.

And my pillow? That was Sol's chest. I froze as I realized I'd nestled against him during the night. *How had that happened?* When I'd fallen asleep, there'd been a magic barrier dividing us.

A cold draft of air flowed over me, and Arietta's face appeared a second later. "Having fun?"

I pressed a finger against my lips and reluctantly eased myself away from the warm comfort of Sol's body.

"He can't hear you. I've still got control of him."

"How did this happen?" I gestured to Sol.

"I thought you deserved a treat. After all, you discounted one suspect yesterday."

"Technically, I've discounted them all, since they all have alibis."

She shrugged. "I'm glad you discovered it wasn't Chay. He was good to me. We were good to each other."

"You still haven't explained this." I pointed at Sol again.

"After you went to sleep, I lowered the magic barrier and shuffled you in next to him. Someone needed to light a fire under you, or you'd never get together with this guy."

"Maybe I don't want to get together with him." Sol's face was relaxed as he continued his magic induced sleep. He really was a handsome man.

"Are you sure? He won't stay single forever. You should grab him while you can," Arietta said.

"I... I already have someone."

"Maybe Sol is a better option. Don't settle for something if it isn't working for you. What's so special about the guy you're with?"

I rolled to my feet and stretched out my back. "It's complicated. But he is special."

"Any time a relationship gets complicated, you need to leave."

"That worked for you?" I headed to the staffroom and made a mug of instant coffee.

"I never got my heart broken. Is that what you're worried about by getting close to Sol?"

"Maybe it's too late for that."

"Now, I'm intrigued. You're with a guy you're not happy with?"

"I was very happy with him. But... he's not around anymore. I'm waiting for him to come back."

"Never wait for a man. That's the way to ruin. What if he's found someone else? He could be living the high life, married with three kids and two mortgages, while you pine for him."

"Brodie's definitely not married with children," I said.

"That's his name? What's so magical about this Brodie?"

I sipped my coffee and gave her a pointed look.

"I knew a Brodie who lived around here, but he's dead."

I still didn't speak.

"It couldn't be him, though. He was a serial dater."

"It's definitely not my Brodie." He'd never be unfaithful.

She raised her hands. "I don't care. You look dreadful, by the way. And it's more than just tiredness. I've noticed a change in your magic."

"What kind of change?"

"When I first started draining you, you tasted sparkly, and the magic was infused with pumpkin. Now, there's only the faintest hint of that flavor. It's as if you were using something to enhance your powers."

I simply shrugged. I desperately needed some powdered pumpkin, but that didn't influence my power.

"What's changed?" Arietta said.

"I'm under a huge amount of stress, caused by a malicious ghost with a terrible attitude."

"You're hiding something."

"Nope."

"If you need a boost, there's still plenty of magic in the distillery. What's your flavor? We have all kinds here, from powerful translocation spells to invisibility."

For a second, I was tempted to take some of the magic Arietta had stored, but it felt wrong. The distillery was a place people came to when they were desperate, and I didn't want to get involved in that.

"Last chance. I'll even offer you a ten percent discount, since you're a new customer."

"You'd charge me for the magic?"

"Of course. No freebies."

"No, thanks. I want nothing to do with your shady business."

She pursed her lips and crossed her arms. "Are your scarecrows not a touch on the shady side?"

"There's nothing shady about them."

"They aren't pure. Although I couldn't get them to remove a business rival or two when I ordered the kill. But they were strong, mean, and ruthless. You use something strong to make them that powerful. I'd love to know what it is. I'd sell bucket loads of the stuff from the distillery. It would make me even richer. Well, it would if I wasn't dead."

"You've already got enough. And the magic in the scarecrows is legit. I simply have an affinity for bringing things to life."

"That's what I don't understand. Why scarecrows? You'd have a never ending supply of business if you used that ability to raise dead loved ones. People would give everything they owned to bring back those they cared about," Arietta said.

"And if you're looking for a business partner for such an opportunity, I'd supply the financing. For a majority stake, of course."

"That's not what my magic does. My family has created enchanted scarecrows for as long as I can remember. It's what we're known for. We're not necromancers. That's a whole darker shade of magic and one I want nothing to do with." I finished my coffee and considered having another one. The caffeine hadn't woken me up.

"You could do it if you had to?"

"Sure, but I don't want to. Once you go down that path, it's hard to come back." Dark magic got under your skin like an infection that was hard to shake off.

"I'm not buying this little miss innocent magic act. You're still hiding something. It has to do with that tangy pumpkin flavor to your magic."

"The magic you took without my permission. Stop draining me when I'm asleep. Otherwise, I'll be useless to you," I said. "Let's focus on your tangled life, not mine. Since we ruled out Chay, we still need to investigate Regan and figure out why someone tried to frame Derwin for your murder."

"They probably framed him to get him out of the way. He annoys everyone he meets," Arietta said.

I headed back into the main room. "You need to wake Sol."

"Why? He insulted me."

"He only spoke the truth. Get him awake. Sol discovered all that information on Chay. He has a knack for research. What if he can find more dirt on a family member? Dirt that'll solve this mystery.

We could miss important clues if we don't have him working with us."

"If he gets on my nerves again, I'm putting him back to sleep." Arietta drifted over to Sol, placed her hands on either side of his head, and did her magic mojo. After a few seconds, his eyes flickered open.

I lifted a hand when his gaze met mine. "Hey."

He groaned and rolled onto his feet. "Let me guess, I said something Arietta didn't approve of, so she zapped me?"

"You got it. But the information you found about Chay was valuable, so she's letting you back in the gang."

"I don't know whether to feel terrified or annoyed."

"Be terrified," Arietta said.

"We went to see Chay last night. We ruled him out as a suspect," I said.

Sol yawned and nodded. "That's great. You're one step closer to finding the real killer. How's Arietta been behaving?"

"She's being her usual monstrous self. Let me get something to help you wake up." I dashed to the kitchen, made a coffee, and returned. I sat next to Sol at the table, and we studied the suspect board. My gaze landed on the words voodoo plushie.

"Thanks for this." Sol sipped the coffee. "Did I miss out on anything else?"

"Not much. Although I still can't figure out why Arietta had this toy beside her."

"My voodoo plushies are works of art, not toys. They hold power. They give me control."

"Fine. Your creepy, evil voodoo magic wielding terror toy is still puzzling me, though. I saw the ones you made, and they're incredible. Intensely creepy, and I didn't want to go near them, but I could see the effort that had gone into them. The stitching was perfect and the colors vibrant."

"Why is the toy important?" Sol said.

"The one found by Arietta's body was a cheap knockoff," I said.

"I've already told you, that wasn't one of mine," Arietta said.

"It must have been. Otherwise, how did it get there?"

"Did someone give it to her?" Sol said. "Maybe they wanted her to add something to it. Sew on a button or fix the stitching. Whatever it is you do with a voodoo plushie."

"No, I don't remember that happening," Arietta said. "I make them from scratch. I don't do simple alterations. Each of my voodoo plushies is unique. They contain magic to help me control people. I wouldn't create the same effect if I'd gotten an off-the-shelf plushie from the store. The magic would be unstable."

"She says no. So how did it get beside you?" I said.

A quiet knock on the distillery door had me tensing. Arietta raced to the door and zoomed through it. She was back a second later. "It's Derwin. What's he doing here?"

I jumped up and headed to the door. I inched it open to see a nervous Derwin standing outside. "Hi. Is everything okay?"

"I need to talk to someone." His hands were clasped together and his face sweaty. "I was up all night thinking."

"This is about to get painful," Arietta said. "I'll check outside and make sure he wasn't followed. It would be just the kind of idiot thing he'd let happen."

I nodded at her. Since the family was under investigation for murder, Derwin might have been noticed sneaking away from the house, and I didn't want Selma Black discovering my hideout. Not until I could fully clear my name.

Arietta blasted past Derwin, shoving him out of her way.

"I take it Arietta's not happy I'm here." Derwin's wide-eyed gaze flicked around as if expecting to glimpse his dead sister.

"You know Arietta. It takes a lot to make her happy. Come inside. What's the problem?" I ushered Derwin through the door, checking outside to see if anyone was watching the distillery, but I couldn't see anybody.

When I turned, I discovered Derwin looking at the suspect board. I walked over and joined him.

"You're serious about this investigation," he said. "You really think it was someone in the family who shot Arietta?"

"I do. The Magic Council doesn't seem to be figuring things out, and she won't move on until her murder is solved. Which means, she'll continue to be a problem for all of us. I'm just looking for a quiet life. Solve her murder, and the problem is resolved."

At least one of my problems would be dealt with if Arietta crossed over.

"I'd love a quiet life, but I don't think I'm going to get it." Derwin turned to me. "You know, it only just hit me, but someone I trust and care about is trying to frame me for murder. They dressed up to look like me and got caught on the magic tracker with Arietta's gun in their hand, all because they knew I'd be arrested when that evidence was discovered."

"It looks like it," I said. "They knew what they were doing. This took planning."

"It's so hard to believe someone would be that cruel and try to ruin my life." Derwin's jaw wobbled, and he wiped away a stray tear. "Arietta worked hard at doing that while she was alive, but it seems it's never-ending. In my humble opinion, I must have done something wrong in a former life to endure this."

"Take a seat," I said. "You look about ready to collapse."

"Sorry, I don't do well under stress." Derwin sank into a seat, nodding a greeting at Sol, who'd just come out of the kitchen with more mugs of coffee.

I sat next to Derwin and patted his arm. "Have you got any idea who'd want to do this to you?"

He was quiet for a long time, occasionally sniffing and shaking his head. "The only person I can think of is Chay. He's not an immediate family member."

"Why would getting you out of the way benefit him?" I accepted a coffee from Sol, and Derwin also took a mug, his hand shaking as he brought it to his lips.

"That's just it. I can't figure it out. And no offence to Chay, but he's not smart. He keeps talking about wanting to be an actor, and I'm sure his looks will take him so far, but he's clueless about most things. And he has terrible time keeping. He'll miss all his auditions."

"I met with Chay last night. Did you know he had a prenup agreement with Arietta?"

"No, but I'm not surprised to hear that. Arietta wouldn't go blindly into any marriage. She always made sure her assets were protected. Her previous husbands left with a settlement of some kind, but I never dared ask her about it. Will Chay get a lot of money?"

"It should see him right for years, if he's careful," I said. "Although it would be eaten up if he buys a house in a nice area. I wouldn't say it was enough to kill for."

"So it's not a great motive."

"It's a motive, but there could be better ones out there."

He drank more coffee. "You said the murder took planning."

I nodded. "The disguise would have been bought in advance. And whoever did it would have needed to figure out how to get the gun without Arietta noticing."

"Then that also makes it unlikely it was Chay. He's a spur-of-the-moment kind of guy. He acts on his emotions. When he's happy, you know about it, just like you know if he's having a bad day."

"You're ruling out the one person you think did this?" I said.

"I... yes, maybe I am." Derwin sighed. "Planning this would have taken time and patience. The killer would have needed to get it just right. Even though I wish it was Chay, and not a family member, I'm thinking he should be ruled out. That's just my opinion, humble as it may be."

That odd gurgling sound Hettie noticed when she visited rumbled through the pipes, sounding like a troll with a bad case of stomach flu.

Derwin tilted his head. "That doesn't sound healthy. We have a blockage in the pipes."

"Does that matter?" I said. "Maybe it's just air."

"You don't get air bubbles in these pipes." Derwin stood and cocked his head as the noise came again. "If a pipe gets blocked, the magic running through it can mutate."

"Mutating sounds bad."

"It is. We could have an explosion. And there's a lot of magic in here. If one spell becomes unstable, it could take the whole place out." Derwin gulped. "It would be safer to leave."

I caught hold of his arm. "I can't leave. I have nowhere else to go. We'd better find the source of that noise and fix it."

"Oh, if you're sure. Are you certain you don't want to leave?"

"Positive." I didn't want to find another hideout. And Witch Haven didn't need an enormous explosion of magic messing with the harmony of the village.

Sol joined us as Derwin led the way, and we hunted along the pipes, listening for more ominous gurgling.

After a few minutes of searching, a burbling sounded close by my head. I hurried to the pipe and pressed my ear against it. It burbled again. "Over here."

Sol and Derwin joined me, and we all listened.

"Something is stuck," Derwin said. "Arietta used to make me crawl into the big pipes and fish out blockages. My skin turned blue for a whole month because I once grabbed some mutated magic."

I tried not to laugh as the image of an indignant blue version of Derwin came to mind. "How do we access the pipes?"

"There's an outlet valve at the end. If I'm careful, I should be able to open it and see what's going on." He grabbed three sets of goggles hanging on the wall and passed them around. "Just in case."

I quickly put on the goggles and hung back with Sol as Derwin moved to the end of the pipe and slowly turned a dial.

The gurgling increased, and there was a hiss. Derwin removed the cover and peered inside.

"Do you see anything?" I said. "Should we run, or is it safe?"

"There is something in here, but it's not a blocked spell. I can't make out what it is." Derwin grabbed a broom propped beside the pipes and stuck the handle into the hole. He slowly pulled it back. Hanging off the end was a red wig and a blue flowered shirt.

Chapter 14

I dashed over and grabbed the soggy offerings off the end of the broom. "This is the disguise! Whoever used the wig and shirt to frame you, they hid them in here."

Derwin stared at them and shook his head. "This shows I'm innocent. Someone is definitely out to get me."

I nodded as I examined the clothing and wig. They'd been stained with blobs of magic, but there could still be useful evidence on them. "Who has access to this distillery?"

"Anyone who's on the approved visitor list. We're all on it. Chay included."

I frowned. That eliminated no one. "Why would the killer choose this pipe as a place to hide the disguise? They must have known it could cause problems when the magic became clogged."

"Maybe they didn't have much option but to hide it here," Sol said. "With the Magic Council hunting for evidence, they needed somewhere the investigators would never think of looking. The killer snuck here while they had a chance and stuffed these in the pipe."

"Which is where they'd have stayed, if the magic hadn't started gurgling and alerting us that something was wrong," I said. "Where do you get your shirts, Derwin?"

"I order them online, but they're a generic brand. You can get them anywhere. All the stores stock them."

That wasn't much help. "Is this one of your shirts? Did you notice it missing?"

He studied it carefully. "It's a match for one I've got, but this is a different size. I wear a larger collar. It's not mine."

I examined the wig. "This is a great match to your hair. It's good quality, too. Whoever got this, they needed to make sure it was a good enough match to look just like you. The Frost family has such a unique hair color that this would have been hard to match."

"I know nothing about wigs," Derwin said, "but if you say so."

"Tuffin, I need your help," I called out. I hadn't seen her since I'd woken.

There was a shuffling and a quiet growl. "I'm asleep."

"Get your furry behind out here. I need you for an important mission."

"Send the boyfriend."

"You know Sol can't wander around Witch Haven at the moment."

"So, wait until he can."

"No fish for a month if you don't help. This has to do with solving the murder and getting rid of our least favorite ghost bully."

There was another growl, then a soft thump. Tuffin strutted out from behind a row of pipes. She did a full body stretch, shook out her fur, and cleaned one ear with a paw. "I just got comfortable on a hot air vent. I shall expect several large rewards for this. They must all be fish. Stinky, oily fish. And I'll expect it to be warm."

I tried not to gag. Oily fish was the gross gift that kept on giving every time you burped. "You'll get it. I'm sure Arietta will be happy to reward you once her murder is solved."

"What's this?" Arietta zoomed back into the room. "What have you got there?"

"The disguise the killer wore," I said. "And I was just sending Tuffin to see if she could find where this wig came from. It could have been bought locally."

Arietta whizzed over and inspected the shirt and wig. "Someone really did try to frame my useless brother. He can be immensely irritating. They probably hoped he'd get put behind bars for the rest of his life and be out of their way."

I looked at Derwin and smiled. "Arietta is happy you found the disguise. It's an important clue."

"You're a good person, Odessa, but my sister would never say that. I expect she used the words idiot, irritating, and useless plenty of times. In my humble opinion, she's wrong."

"Your opinion isn't humble," I said. "It's as valued and important as everyone else's opinion. Don't let the way Arietta treated you ruin your life. Be confident in yourself."

"That's decent of you to say, but you get used to believing something if someone tells you it enough."

"Arietta's bullying behavior shouldn't mess with the rest of your life. This evidence clears you and gives me a new lead." I looked down at Tuffin. "Are you up to the challenge of wig hunting?"

"Remind me what my reward is again?" Tuffin said.

"Gross, oily warm fish."

Tuffin's tongue appeared. "Yum."

"How about I don't shoot you in the fuzzy backside with my ghost magic? That sounds like a suitable reward," Arietta said.

Tuffin hissed at her. She grabbed the wig out of my hand and trotted away.

"Try not to worry," I said to Derwin. "We've got some loose ends to tie up, but we're a big step closer to finding the killer. Then your life can get going, free from your sister."

"I'm glad to hear it," Derwin said. "I should go. Eva's waiting for me outside."

"She's here?"

"She is. We've been spending a lot more time together. It's nice not having to hide our relationship anymore." Derwin walked with me to the door.

"I'm feeling queasy," Arietta said. "I can't stand seeing my brother in love and cooing over that ninny."

"I'd like to speak to Eva." I turned my back on Arietta, not prepared to acknowledge her rudeness.

"About what?" Derwin said.

"I found out some news about her job. It could be relevant to the investigation."

"Err... okay. But I don't know what you mean about her job."

"I'll explain it in a second. Where's Eva?"

"She's right outside. I'm not sure how she can help, though."

"Arietta, look around again to make sure no one's in the area," I said.

She zoomed close until we were nose to nose. "I give the orders."

I lowered my voice and stepped away from Derwin. "You'll be giving them to thin air if the Magic Council catches me and whisks me off. I can't be seen by anyone."

Arietta whizzed away, muttering about not being my slave and accepting orders from me.

"Sol, I'm just heading outside for a few minutes."

"Sure. I'll see if I can find us something to eat. More coffee?"

"Please. I need something to keep me going."

After I got the all-clear from my grumpy ghost, Derwin led me to where Eva was waiting behind a tree. She looked surprised when she saw me.

"Is everything okay?" she whispered.

"It's fine. But I need to ask you about your job at the Frost house," I said.

She glanced at Derwin. "What about it?"

"Were you planning on staying once the business was sold?"

"That's unlikely to happen now," Derwin said. "The buyer is pulling out. He's making a final decision tomorrow, but I don't think it'll sell. He's already asking for money off the list price since my sister's death has tainted the business."

"Maybe not to him, but it's still up for sale," I said. "Eva, do you want to stay working here?"

"I can't imagine working anywhere else. I've been here most of my life. It's the only place I've known as home since I was young, and my parents worked here before me, so it's something of a family legacy to stay."

"You must have been angry when you learned you'd be made redundant once the business was sold," I said.

Eva shot another quick glance at Derwin. "I wasn't happy about it. I didn't know I'd have to leave."

"And when you learned you wouldn't get any redundancy payment, what did you do?"

"Why is that relevant?" Derwin said.

"Because it gives Eva an excellent motive for murdering Arietta. She's dedicated her life to the Frost family. But once Arietta sold, Eva would have been kicked out. She'd have lost her home, she'd have no money to live, and I suspect Arietta might have been spiteful enough not to give her a reference. Eva's life would have been ruined because Arietta wanted to make as much money as possible."

Eva bowed her head. "I... I was angry when I realized what would happen. I begged her to keep me on and said I could be valuable to the new owner, but she laughed. She said I was past my prime and incompetent."

Derwin caught hold of Eva's hand. "My sister only said those things to be cruel. You're perfect as you are."

Her smile was sweet as she looked at him. "Thanks. I know. I've been around Arietta long enough to let her harsh words slide away without hurting too much."

"But what about the money you wouldn't get?" I said.

"I challenged her on the redundancy payout, but Arietta told me to check my contract. When I did, I was stunned. That's when I got legal advice."

"I didn't know about any of this," Derwin said. "And you shouldn't worry about money. I'll always take care of you."

Eva squeezed his hand. "I appreciate that, but your sister ruled your life as much as she did mine. I was worried she'd still have influence over you, especially since her ghost hasn't passed on. You could have changed your mind about me. You might have left me if she hounded you enough."

"I'd never do that." He glanced at me and cleared his throat as his attention returned to Eva. "I love you. You must know that."

Her smile faded. "I needed to know where I stood. I used the small amount of savings I had to contact a lawyer and have my contract analyzed. He confirmed what Arietta told me. I didn't have a leg to stand on. Once the business was sold, I'd be put on notice and have three months to leave. I'd walk away with only a few possessions. After dedicating my life to this family, I was being tossed out like trash."

"That must have been awful to find out," I said. "Arietta should be ashamed of herself for treating you so badly."

"Arietta's not ashamed of anything. She has no conscience," Eva said. "All I wanted was what I was owed, and to be with Derwin. It's not fair everything was being taken from me. And I knew that solicitor I spoke to was scared to handle my case. When he found out I worked for Arietta, he started shaking. He couldn't get me out of his office fast enough. I knew then, everything was lost. Arietta had won again."

"You must have hated that you had no power," I said. "Someone else had control of your life. It must have made you want to kill."

Eva sighed. "I know this looks bad on me, but I didn't shoot Arietta. You already know I was with Derwin in the chalet when the shot was fired."

I nodded. We were back to that problem. And there was the added issue of why Eva would dress in disguise as Derwin, the man she loved, to frame him? It made no sense. Unless...

"I have to ask. You and Derwin are happy, aren't you?"

Eva nodded as she smiled up at Derwin. "Much happier now we don't have to creep around behind people's backs."

"We are blissfully happy," Derwin said. "So much so that I've asked Eva to marry me."

"You have? That's amazing news. What did you say, Eva?"

She grinned as she held out her hand to show a sparkling diamond set in a silver band. "Yes, of course. I want to be with Derwin more than anything. I don't even care where we live. Although I don't want to live in that big house. It's too grand for me, and there are too many unpleasant memories."

"We can live anywhere you like," Derwin said. "We're happy, and we plan to spend the rest of our lives together. I'm such a lucky guy."

I indulged them with a smile as they gazed into each other's eyes. Even though Eva had every reason for wanting Arietta dead, she couldn't have done it. And there was no logical explanation why she'd dress up as Derwin to frame him for Arietta's murder. I was stuck.

"You will let me know when you hear anything about the disguise you found?" Derwin said.

"What's this?" Eva said.

"We found the disguise the killer wore," Derwin said. "It was shoved into a distillery pipe."

"That's great news," Eva said. "It shows you're innocent, and we'll soon know who murdered Arietta."

"Hopefully, I've almost solved this mystery." I tried to sound positive, but I really didn't know which way to turn. "And of course, I'll let you know as soon as I hear anything," I said to Derwin.

After saying our goodbyes, Eva and Derwin walked away, and I returned to the distillery.

Arietta came back a moment later. "I'm glad they're gone. I want nothing to do with Eva."

"I hope you're feeling bad after almost ruining her life," I said.

"Can't say I am."

I couldn't resist taking a little dig. "You'll be glad to know, Derwin has asked Eva to marry him. She'll soon be your sister-in-law."

"Then I really am glad I'm dead," Arietta muttered. "I won't be attending the wedding. And if they think they're getting a gift..."

"I'll buy something expensive on your behalf and charge it to your expense account," I said. "Or maybe you can pay for their honeymoon."

"Don't push your luck, witch, or the next time you go to sleep, you won't wake up."

"Your threats are as see-through as you. You won't hurt me until I'm no use to you."

"I could hurt Tuffin, though, or Sol."

"Or you could try being a decent human being, or ghost being, for once. It might be fun."

Arietta zoomed ahead, throwing out more threats. I was so used to them now, they barely bothered me.

"I hope you're being productive and not looking at naughty videos on your phone." Arietta floated over to Sol.

"I've been researching your family tree." He flipped his phone to show the screen. "None of your ancestors liked men much."

"I wouldn't say that. They have their uses. What makes you think they were all man haters?"

"Because I've been checking the online archives. Over the last three hundred years, it's always been the women who've ruled in the Frost family."

"You consider that a problem?" Arietta said.

"It's not a problem, but it is unusual." I joined Sol at the table and took a look at his phone.

"Not in my family. We've always passed our assets to a female heir."

I lifted my gaze. "That means Fontayne doesn't inherit everything now you're dead?"

"That's right. Experience has shown women do a much better job of managing things than men. One of my female ancestors, Magenta Frost, was left the estate after her hard drinking slob of a husband dropped dead of a heart attack. She fought tooth and nail to keep those assets and demanded a judge rule on the case so she could keep what was hers."

"What happened to her?"

"Magenta was given a year to prove herself. All the men thought she'd fail and looked forward to humiliating her at the end of that year, force her to marry one of them, and take it all. Instead, she doubled the profits, landed several successful contracts, and fired all the men. Ever since then, women have always been in charge. It works."

"Did Magenta marry again?" I said.

Arietta pursed her lips. "She was put off marriage for life. I can't say I blame her. But she had dozens of lovers. She was ahead of her time. I model myself on her."

"Doesn't that legacy leave Fontayne and Derwin out in the cold because they won't inherit anything?"

"They'll be fine. My son will be looked after, and Derwin will find his own way. After all, he's chosen to marry a poor servant. He must have figured out how to provide for her. I'm telling you this, it won't be with any of my money. And having a housekeeper as a sister-in-law is a humiliation too far."

"You know Eva's name. Use it," I said. "And she's a sweet lady. Much sweeter than you deserve."

"Her name is irrelevant. Derwin has chosen his path. He would have gotten something from my will, but I'll make sure it's changed. See how much he loves Eva when they're living in a hostel and surviving on tinned beans and favors."

"You can't change your will after you're dead," I said.

"I can. And I will."

"Nope. If that was legal, it would make a mess for the people left behind. Ghosts can't come back and change their minds because they're having a bad day. The last will you wrote will stand."

"I'll find a way to make sure Derwin doesn't get his hands on any of my money," Arietta said.

I stood in front of the suspect board, my hands on my hips. "None of your living male relatives get control of the business. Does that mean Regan is in line to inherit everything?"

"That's right. My niece gets it all."

I looked at Sol with raised eyebrows. "We've just found a prime motive for murder. I need to speak to Regan. She's got a lot of reasons to have killed her aunt."

Chapter 15

I waited until dusk before venturing out to speak to Regan about this inheritance discovery. I tried to muster a concealment spell as I left the distillery, but my magic flickered on my fingers and died.

"I've got a solution for that, if you want it," Arietta said. "Discounted rate, since you haven't been completely useless in discovering the suspects in my murder."

"It's still a no to using any magic you dragged out of your customers," I said. "Talk to me about Regan. Have you ever had any concerns about her?"

"She's never bothered me. Although I only gave her a job because Derwin begged me on his hands and knees to hire her." She tittered to herself. "I was planning to do it anyway, but it was entertaining to see my brother grovel."

"Have I ever mentioned what a truly awful person you are?"

"You have. But because I uphold my values, it doesn't make me bad. It makes me honest. Most people want to do the same things as me, but they don't have the courage."

"Or they have the morals not to," I muttered. "So, Regan. You must know something about her. She lives in your house."

"Regan lives in a part of the house. The place is big enough that we didn't bump into each other more than a couple of times a week."

"But she handles all the business's public relations work, is that right? You oversaw that."

"I don't deal with the gloss. I just sign off when things look good. I know when to delegate tasks to professionals."

"Did you ever work closely with Regan?"

"No, marketing isn't an area of interest. I took a look at things now and again and made sure the numbers were going in the right direction, but the rest I left to Regan."

"She's still young. She might have appreciated support from her aunt."

"No, you sink or swim in this business. It was a legacy left behind by Magenta. You figure things out yourself, or you go somewhere to flip burgers and daydream about riches you'll never have."

"I figured Magenta's legacy meant you looked after the women."

"Regan does fine. And my ancestors helped redress a serious power imbalance by seizing control and never letting go. I was carrying on the legacy. It's something I was proud to do. Women can be alphas, too. They should be."

"But Regan has been left to fend for herself. What about reaching down and helping her up? After all, she'll be running your business from now on. Didn't you want to mentor her?"

"She's big enough to leap up herself. And if she doesn't..." Arietta shrugged.

"You could have been civil to Regan. What if she makes a mess of the business?"

"She wasn't supposed to inherit a lucrative business. Remember, I was selling up and taking the money for myself."

"And leaving her with no job."

"Call it a test. I like to test people."

"Is that why you're so mean to Derwin?"

"I'm trying to get him to stand up for himself. Regan isn't like her father. She rarely cowers when I yell and comes up with reasonable business ideas. I don't object to her."

"She has a passion for the distillery business?"

"Regan does her job and doesn't ask too many dumb questions. That's about all I know."

Arietta was useless when it came to getting information about her family. She had so little interest in them that it was shocking, even after I'd been stuck with her for several days.

We headed past the security trolls and into Crown Copse. I was careful to keep to the shadows, since someone had reported seeing me here to the Magic Council.

I was walking up the driveway to the house when Regan appeared, pushing a cherry red electric scooter with black handlebars. She had a large rucksack on her back.

"She's still riding that ridiculous thing," Arietta said. "I keep telling her to upgrade to a Lotus or a Maserati, but she said electric scooters are the next thing in portable transport and good for the environment."

"She's not wrong. Reduce, reuse, recycle is the way forward. And scooters are much more environmentally friendly."

"Regan won't be thinking that when she hits a hole and ends up in a ditch with her leg broken. Foolish girl. That has to go when she steps into my role, or the business will become a joke."

I ignored Arietta as she ranted about Regan's scooter. It looked like a nifty way to get around. I lifted a hand as Regan noticed me and hurried toward her. "Hi. Have you got a minute?"

She shook her head. "Sorry, I've got a late meeting to get to. And I need to spend the night working on a new public relations blitz for the distillery."

"Why? What's going on?" I walked alongside her as she hurried along the driveway, pushing the scooter.

"The buyer for the distillery isn't happy. They noticed the numbers slipping since Aunty Arietta's murder. If I don't scramble to fix things fast, we might not have a buyer."

"And that would be a problem for you?"

"It's not the best news in the world. Although at least Aunty Arietta isn't here yelling at me to fix stuff." Regan glanced around quickly, and her cheeks flushed. "Although is her ghost here?"

"She's here. But she's not yelling. Well, only about your cute little scooter."

Regan rolled her eyes. "Of course. She loathed this thing. But it's cheap to run, and it's fast. I don't need an expensive gas guzzling car. I was always saying to Aunty Arietta that we needed to be more environmentally responsible."

"I bet she loved that idea," I said.

"She said there were more important things to worry about. But if we don't have a planet, then nothing else matters. It didn't matter what I said. Aunty Arietta dismissed every suggestion. She wouldn't even have paper recycling bins in the offices because they got in the way, and she was worried someone might trip over one and sue her."

"That was mean spirited of her."

Arietta scowled at me. "It was sensible. And if someone had tripped and injured themselves, I'd have been down a worker."

"I have a small confession to make." Regan grinned at me. "We did it, anyway. At least, where I work. We recycle everything. It's an almost zero waste office."

"That's impressive," I said. "It sounds like you enjoy working in the business."

"Um... not so much. But whatever I do, I work as hard as I can," Regan said. "Now, if you'll excuse me..." She put a foot on the scooter.

"Just one more minute. What plans do you have for the business?"

She cocked her head. "What do you mean? Are you interested in the PR plan I need to work out to boost numbers?"

"No. But you're inheriting the business. You must have a few ideas about what you want to do with it."

Her mouth dropped open, and she blinked rapidly. "I... what? I'm inheriting it all?"

"Sure. Isn't that what always happens in your family? The next female in line inherits. Your aunt must have talked to you about it." My gaze cut to Arietta, who had drifted away and pretended she wasn't listening.

"Well, that's true. That's what happened in the past, anyway. But you never know what Aunty Arietta has planned. She left it all to me?"

"That's what she told me."

"I... I'm not ready to take on a huge distillery business. I only specialize in marketing and public relations. I don't have the skills to be chief executive of some enormous, and honestly, unscrupulous company. You're mistaken."

"No one told you about the inheritance coming your way?"

"No! And we're still waiting to have the will read, so no one knows what they'll get."

"Arietta said nothing?" I shouldn't have been surprised, but this ghost still wasn't failing to disappoint me with the lack of interest and regard she showed her family.

"Not a thing. And the family lawyer was on an extended vacation when she died. Aunty Arietta only deals with him when it comes to personal family matters. He was supposed to do the reading when he got back."

"That's a long vacation," I said.

"He was away for three weeks but had a fall and injured his back and hit his head, so he has been recovering in the hospital. We're meeting him in a week's time to hear the will." Regan clutched the handlebars of the scooter. "I don't know what to think. I get the business?"

"You do. Everything."

"Everything! The houses, money, the lot?"

"Regan suddenly doesn't think my business empire is so unscrupulous now she knows what's coming her way," Arietta said.

"Aunty Arietta must have set up a holding company or a board to oversee things. I can't do this alone." Regan licked her lips. "Aunty Arietta, you wouldn't drop this all on me, would you?"

Arietta sighed. "Are you sure there's no way I can change my will?"

I shook my head. "Your aunt didn't give you a hint of what was coming your way?"

"No. I assumed I'd get something, but I figured Fontayne, Chay, or even Dad would get more involved in the business. I haven't even graduated from college. Aunty Arietta let me out on day release once a week, so I could finish my course. The rest of the time, I worked for her."

"There was no succession plan?" I directed the question at Arietta, but Regan was shaking her head.

"I never got around to it," Arietta said. "It's a bit like making a will. When you put things on paper, it hints at your mortality. If I'd written a succession plan, I was setting the clock ticking down to my death. I didn't like to think about it."

"You should have." I felt sorry for Regan, who was looking bewildered as she swayed on her feet. "Regan, this will mean a lot of changes for you."

"No kidding. I don't know what to say. Or do."

"Will you consider taking it on?"

"I don't know. I need to speak to my dad about this."

"She's wasting her time talking to Derwin. He'll take a month to make a decision and then change his mind. And he'd better not try getting any money out of Regan, or I'll wring his neck."

I brushed away her sharp comments. "How long have you worked for your aunt?"

"I started working here part-time when I was sixteen. Just doing basic things like filing and delivering the post around the different offices. And, well, I didn't love it, but it was expected of me. I mean, I don't mind my work, but Aunty Arietta was mean to people, and it felt wrong."

"Not mean, just direct."

"It made me sad to see desperate customers drag themselves to a distillery to give away what little power they had left in exchange for money. It felt like we were taking advantage of them." Regan shook her head. "I wondered if there was a better way of doing things."

"Is that why you're keen on making sure this deal goes ahead?" I said. "You want to sell it and forget about it?"

"I... maybe. I mean, I've just found out about the inheritance, so I never had a serious plan for the future of the business. It would be good to get rid of it. Although the buyer's already lowered their offer. We had a family meeting about it, and we're tempted to take the money and run. Although I guess it's now my business, so I'll get all the money."

Arietta cackled a laugh. "The money will change her. She hasn't even gotten her grasping hands on it, and she's already planning her future without the deadbeat family by her side."

"There's so much to think about. My head is spinning," Regan said.

"If you sold, what would you do with all that money?" I said.

"It's not something I've ever thought about. If this business was mine, I'd change things."

"I should demand a DNA test to make sure we're related. No niece of mine should talk like this."

"I just figured Aunty Arietta would go on for years, though." Regan glanced around. "She seemed unstoppable. I hoped I'd find the courage to get out and start my own company. I never planned to stay here forever."

"This isn't the news I want to hear," Arietta said. "This business will become Regan's life. She can't think about leaving. Not ever."

"If you hate it so much, why not just get out? Don't worry about what anyone else thinks," I said.

Regan arched an eyebrow. "Did you know my aunt when she was alive?"

"Only by reputation."

"And what did that reputation tell you?"

"That she was terrifying and not to be messed with."

"Aunty Arietta was scary. If she barked an order, you got your head down and did the work. And I pride myself on doing a good job. While I'm employed here, I make sure I turn in solid work."

I studied her expression. All I saw was shock and surprise, not the look of someone who was hiding the fact they were a killer. "Regan, I have to ask you this. Can you confirm what you were doing when Arietta was shot?"

"You already know. I was with everyone else."

"You weren't drinking and dancing with Fontayne and Chay, though?"

She chewed on her bottom lip. "No, they get on my nerves. Chay is always fake charming everyone, and Fontayne is just stupid. And they're always playing pranks on me, and I end up yelling at them. Fontayne is the worst. He pretends it's just a game, but those pranks can be mean."

"Talk me through what you did that evening," I said.

Regan sighed. "Sure. But my alibi is no different from the last time you heard it. I said goodnight to my dad, he left, and then I sat at the back of the room reading a book. I was sort of keeping an eye on Fontayne and Chay to make sure they didn't do anything too dumb, but I was mainly processing what Aunty Arietta had told us over dinner about the business. I couldn't decide whether it was a good thing."

"Have you come to a decision since then?"

"I'm still thinking. I was excited, because I hoped I could leave and have a life of my own. I didn't know what plans Aunty Arietta had put in place for my future. It's been a huge shock."

Arietta pursed her lips but didn't say anything.

"What will you do now you know?" I said.

"Keep doing my job, wait for things to become official, and make some plans." She looked back at the house. "I really get everything?"

"She does," Arietta said. "My houses, the business, and the cash. It's all hers."

I nodded at Regan. "You do."

"I could turn this into a legitimate business and use the money to make reparations to the people Aunty Arietta exploited."

"Absolutely not!" Arietta said. "The business must stay as it is."

"I love that idea," I said to Regan. "And I agree with you. It's wrong to prey on the vulnerable and take the only thing they value."

"They sign an agreement," Arietta shrieked. "I didn't force them to give me their magic."

I rubbed my left ear, which was ringing thanks to Arietta's incensed ranting.

"I tried talking to Aunty Arietta about it a few times, about how uncomfortable I felt working in this industry. I kept saying there must be another way, and we could leave customers with a small amount of power so they weren't defenseless, but she'd never listen." Regan shrugged. "Honestly, it made me sick to my stomach. I promote a place I don't believe in. A place that exploits those who are already suffering."

"I didn't know I had such a bleeding heart on my hands," Arietta said. "My business will not be turned into some goody two shoes environmentally driven nonsense. If it does, it won't last a year."

"Now it's yours, you can do what you like with it," I said to Regan.

"Maybe. I still don't believe it. I really should get going. Until this is settled, I have my old job to focus on." Regan looked around again. "Aunty Arietta, thanks for this opportunity. I hope I can make the business better if I keep it."

Arietta wagged a finger in Regan's face. "If you waste my money on helping those who don't deserve it, I'll haunt you for the rest of your life."

Regan's face paled, and she inched back, taking the scooter with her. "Is she mad at me?"

"She'll be fine. Arietta's just processing a few things. I get the impression she's not keen on change," I said.

"Change! This idiot will ruin everything."

Regan pushed a hand through her hair, looking older than her years. "Well, thanks for letting me know, I guess. I have to go." She rushed off on the scooter.

As I watched Regan go, I couldn't decide if she was being genuine, or if she'd known about the inheritance and everything that came with it. She had looked shocked when I'd told her she was getting the lot.

"Are you just going to stand there, staring into space?" Arietta said.

"Maybe for a couple of minutes. Your niece seems like a decent young woman. But is it an act?"

"I can't worry about that. You need to find out how I can change my will. She's not turning my business into a joke."

"You're stuck with that decision," I said. "And it's a great decision. Regan is a responsible person who cares about others. Although... we could have a problem with that description if she's your killer."

"That bleeding heart doesn't have it in her. She's just shown how weak she is. Just like her father," Arietta said.

"I wouldn't be so sure about that. Being handed these assets gives her a perfect motive. Regan is now obscenely rich and hugely powerful if she's stepping into your shoes as the alpha at the top of this business."

"But you heard her. Regan wants to waste my money." Arietta's entire body shook. "I have to stop this."

"The only way you'll be able to stop Regan taking control is if she's found guilty of murdering you."

Chapter 16

"This isn't good enough. You have to find out who killed me." Arietta swirled around the distillery, making the place icy cold.

Ever since we'd met Regan and heard about her plans for the business, Arietta had been unsettled. She was sniping and growling at me and Sol, and nothing I could say would calm her. In the end, I'd chosen the mature response and was ignoring her.

"How long is she going to behave like this?" Sol muttered as Arietta swooped over his head.

"I don't think Arietta likes it when someone beats her," I whispered. "And I didn't let on when I was questioning Regan, but I was impressed by her. She said she was thinking about making reparations to customers exploited by Arietta." I waited until Arietta had zoomed past before continuing. "She might be young, but that girl has courage."

"And you think Regan was being truthful? She doesn't want to carry on running the distillery?" Sol said.

"I wondered about that, but she seemed so surprised when she heard the news about her inheritance. And no one could have known for certain what Arietta had planned because of the delay in reading the will."

"Since Regan didn't know the contents of the will, it doesn't give her much of a motive," Sol said. "You're ruling her out as a suspect?"

"Almost. But Regan must have had an idea the assets would pass to her in the event of Arietta's murder. Maybe it was too much of a temptation, and she took a risk, hoping her aunt hadn't put some nasty twist into her will." I tapped my fingers on the table. "Although she was upfront about not enjoying her work and said she hoped to get free from the family business. Now, the opposite has happened."

"But there's no more Arietta terrorizing her," Sol said. "It's a win-win."

"Maybe not for Regan. Perhaps she was pushed over the edge by Arietta. She shot her aunt because she couldn't take it anymore," I said. "And she must have witnessed how awful Arietta was to Derwin. She was protecting her dad by killing her aunt. Urgh! There are still too many possibilities in this mystery."

"None of that explains the disguise," Sol said. "And why someone framed Derwin. Regan wouldn't do that to her dad."

"Yes, and it doesn't explain how Regan pulled the trigger. She was inside with everyone else." That was a huge piece of the puzzle I hadn't been able to figure out.

"Stop gossiping and focus on what happened to me." Arietta whizzed to the table and glowered at me. "If you continue to be this useless, I'll set the Magic Council on you."

"I'm not so worried about the Magic Council, anymore. From what Hettie said, they're not after me. Although I expect Selma Black is lurking about somewhere. It might even be safe to go back to the farm."

"You're not going anywhere. You're staying here. And if you attempt to leave, I'll destroy your boyfriend. Then, I'll take that scruffy, mangy cat, and —"

I jumped from my seat, focused my remaining magic into my palms, and slammed them against Arietta's head. "No, you won't. I'm done listening to your threats. All you do is make nasty remarks, or insult people, or threaten them. You did that when you were alive and look what happened to you."

Arietta squeaked and struggled to get free, but I didn't let her as a blinding anger overtook my exhaustion, peppered with frustration at how badly this ghost had treated me and the people I cared about.

"You're a ghost. And I'm one of the few people who can see you. Show me respect. I am helping you, even though I shouldn't, but you've been nothing but terrible to me. You're a horrible, cruel ghost. You're a ghost ghoul in disguise. You don't deserve help."

She fought to pry herself free, but my rage fueled me, and my grip didn't slacken.

"I could ignore you forever. And if you continue to hassle me, I'll shove you into a ghost jar. Then I'll put that jar in a hospice for three-legged cats that only have one eye. You'll be forced to see all the good deeds, love, and kindness that exist in this world. It would probably kill you all over again to endure that. You cold-hearted... meanie!"

Arietta's sharp glare softened. She tipped back her head and roared out a laugh. "There is fire in my witch."

"You'd push even the sweetest person into doing something awful. I wouldn't be surprised if Regan shot you. She seems lovely but having to spend every day working for you must have driven her mad."

"Regan was fine. I paid her well. I may not be warm and cuddly, but I know how to run a successful business."

"Using threats and intimidation?" I lowered my hands from Arietta's head, surprised by her continued laughter.

"There's a place for that, but I generously rewarded loyalty. I wasn't a complete monster. Maybe a partial one, but it made me fabulously wealthy."

"You were a monster to Derwin." My anger was fading, and a bone aching tiredness seeped in.

"You still don't understand me. That was a test. I want people to show me courage and passion. You just did. You stood up to me. That's what I respect. That's what I want from Derwin. I don't want his sniveling apologies, humble opinions, or cowering. I want him to show me his fire. Assuming he has any."

I sank back into my seat and massaged my aching head with my fingers. "Derwin may have had courage if you'd encouraged him rather than yelled at him."

"It's too late for that now," Arietta said.

My body trembled with exhaustion as I leaned back in the seat and closed my eyes. I felt stuck and desperate to get back to my normal life. It had been days since I'd seen my scarecrows, and I missed them. I also missed the smell of warm straw in the morning as I looked out the front door at my fields. And I missed the scent of fresh pumpkin in the air as I processed a new batch. Most of all, I desperately missed the hours I'd lost not working at getting Brodie back.

Arietta tapped my cheek with a cold hand. "You're not dead, are you?"

"Almost." Guilt shivered through me, and I wrapped my arms around my middle. Brodie. There'd been times when I hadn't thought about him. Brodie was always on my mind. But dealing with Arietta, worrying about Sol, and trying to puzzle through this murder mystery had made me lose sight of him. There'd even been times when I'd been more worried about Sol than Brodie.

"Boy toy, make her move. I don't like it when she's not being productive." Arietta prodded me again.

"Are you okay, Odessa?" Sol's gentle voice was soft in my ear.

"I'm not sure. Maybe." What was happening to me? I'd always had one man as my focus, and I didn't like that things were changing. I needed Brodie back in my life, but I had to make sure Sol stayed safe, too. And I wanted to see Sol every day, with his easy smile, kind ways, and solid dependability. There had to be a way to get the balance right. But until I solved this murder and got Arietta off my back, I couldn't see a way out.

There was a scuffling noise, and the main door leading into the distillery inched open. Tuffin wriggled through the gap, carrying several things in her mouth.

I stood and hurried over to her. "What have you got?" I pulled out the first item and instantly dropped it.

"That's not for you." Tuffin spat out the rest of the items. "I found that rat's tail on my way back."

My nose wrinkled. "And you brought it back... why?"

"To show you I can catch things when I choose to."

"You caught a rat?"

"No, just the tail. But it shows I'm a skilled hunter."

I petted her head. "You must be admired throughout the lion kingdom for your gross tail hunting prowess. Did you get anything useful, though?"

Tuffin flicked her tail, looking extremely smug with herself. "I found a rib bone."

"Um... brilliant? From a body?"

"From the Chinese takeout. It still had sauce on it and a few stringy bits of meat. Not as good as fish but still delicious."

I swallowed my disgust. "I meant anything useful about the wig. You did go look for where it was sold?"

"Of course. That piece of paper is a sales slip."

"Let me guess, for a Chinese takeout?"

She hissed at me. "For a wig!"

I grabbed the slightly soggy piece of paper. "You found out where the wig came from?"

"Have a look. There are two stores that stock that wig. And one was sold just over six weeks ago to a tanned guy who smelled of coconuts."

"Coconuts! Chay wears a cologne that has coconut in it. I smelled it on him the first time we met."

Arietta whizzed over and stared at the slip in my hand. "Chay bought the wig? He shot me?"

I lifted the slip closer to my face. It was dated just before Arietta had been shot. And, unbelievably, Chay had signed the slip. This clue was too good to be true.

"Is it legit?" Sol said.

I nodded. "It's all here. Would Chay be so stupid to leave such an obvious clue? He must have realized this would be discovered."

"Maybe not," Sol said. "After all, the disguise was hidden in here. Maybe Chay hoped we would never find the wig and shirt. Or the Magic Council wouldn't figure out he'd worn a disguise and simply arrested Derwin."

I took a moment to consider all the clues. "Chay wanted Derwin sent away for Arietta's murder. He made sure he was seen dressed as Derwin with the gun on the magic tracker, so there'd be a quick arrest. Derwin would have protested his innocence for as long as he liked, but with the evidence laid out, nothing he did or said would have stopped him from being charged with murder."

"Or it could simply be that Chay's not all that clever," Arietta said. "I didn't marry him for his brains, after all."

I looked over at her. The fire in her expression had faded. Arietta looked genuinely miserable. "Do you think he did this?"

"That's Chay's signature. There can only be one reason he bought that wig."

"We need to speak to Chay again," I said. "Ask him what he knows about the wig."

"We go now," Arietta said. "Let's finish this."

"I agree."

"I'll come with you," Sol said.

Arietta shoved him back into his seat. "Stay where you are, boy toy. We don't need a man getting involved."

"Sorry, Arietta wants you to stay here," I said.

Sol rubbed his chest. "I figured that out for myself."

"It won't be for much longer. With this evidence, we just need to figure out how Chay pulled the trigger with no one seeing him."

"If you're sure you don't need me."

"I... I do need you." I blurted out the words before my courage faded.

He grinned. "That's good to know. I need you, too."

"Men always get in the way," Arietta said. "I should never have trusted Chay. He deceived me. No men allowed. This is girl power in action."

"I don't want to be a part of your girl gang," I muttered. "At least Tuffin can come with us. She's female."

"Fine, the fuzz ball can come, but let's move. Chay may not have stuck to his word and stayed around. He could already have left Crown Copse." Arietta shot off like a bullet before I could caution her not to rip Chay's head off the second she saw him.

"Let's go, Tuffin."

She yawned and turned in a circle several times. "I need sleep. Then snacks. You can handle the easy bit."

"You're my familiar, now. You have to support me." I scooped her up and lowered my voice. "And I'm exhausted. If Arietta goes rogue, you'll have to handle her for me."

Tuffin wriggled onto my shoulders and huffed in my ear. "Very well. But you owe me."

"Yeah, I know. Send me the fishmonger's bill." I raced out of the distillery and back to Crown Copse with Tuffin, not able to keep up with Arietta, who was a ghostly blur in the distance.

When I got to the house, I heard voices and followed them around to the back and into an extensive yard. Chay was lounging by the swimming pool in an obscenely small pair of red trunks. Fontayne was there, too, wearing a pair of baggy shorts. Derwin was also there, sitting upright in a chair and not looking happy.

He noticed me first and raised a hand in greeting. "Odessa. How can we help you?"

At that moment, Regan came out of the house with a tray of drinks.

Arietta hovered by the pool, malevolence oozing out of her as she waited to strike.

I set Tuffin down, and she hopped onto a padded lounger and settled in for the show. "Chay, you need to explain this." I strode over and handed him the sales slip.

He stared at it, turned it over a couple of times, and shook his head. "I don't know what this is."

"That's your signature?" I said.

"Sure. How did you get it?"

"You left it behind when you bought a red wig six weeks ago from a local store."

His head jerked back, and a frown crossed his face. "A red wig? Why would I buy that?"

Derwin stood from his seat and approached us. "Let me see." He studied the sales slip. "Is this the wig you found in the distillery?"

"I believe it is," I said. "And this sales slip is evidence to show Chay bought it just before Arietta was killed."

"I know about the disguise from Derwin, but I didn't buy any wig. I don't like where this is going." Chay stood and adjusted his trunks.

"I'm sure you don't," I said, "because it shows you tried to frame Derwin for Arietta's murder."

"No, no, no! I didn't frame anyone for anything," Chay said.

Fontayne rolled off his lounger and walked over, Regan right beside him. "What's this about a wig?"

"Odessa's getting things wrong." Chay stumbled over his words. "She thinks I had something to do with what happened to your mom."

Regan's gaze ran over Chay. "I thought you liked each other."

"We did. This has nothing to do with me."

"If you didn't kill her, explain why you bought a wig," I said. "A wig that's the same color as Derwin and Arietta's hair. That hair color is a unique family trait."

"It wasn't me," Chay said. "And I had no problem with Derwin. I mean, sure, he can be a wet blanket, but we rubbed along okay. Derwin, I wouldn't do this to you."

Derwin stared at him with narrowed eyes. "Was it you? You dressed like me and got seen on the magic tracker. You knew when it was looked at I'd get arrested for Arietta's murder. You set me up."

"But... but I was inside with the others. Fontayne, you'll back me up on this." Chay's tan didn't hide how pale he'd gone. "We were doing shots and daring each other on."

Fontayne looked at Derwin and then at me. His gaze landed on the sales slip. "We were inside, but you were the one who insisted on the loud dance music."

"So what? We both like dance music."

"And you mixed those strong cocktails before we got started on the shots. I watched you pour half a bottle of vodka into one of the mixes. I don't mind a strong drink, but you were practically forcing them on everyone. It was like you wanted to get us drunk as quickly as possible." Fontayne crossed his arms over his bare chest.

"You've never complained about my cocktails before," Chay said.

"Did you drug us with them? My memory of that night is hazy."

"No! Why would I do that?"

"Fontayne, did you have problems remembering what happened the night your mom was killed?" I said.

His hands clenched several times. "I hadn't said anything before, but that night, I was so drunk, I blacked out a couple of times. Maybe that was Chay's plan. He wanted everyone so wasted to give him a chance to sneak out and shoot Mom."

"It couldn't have been me in that disguise," Chay said. "We don't even look alike. I'm taller for a start."

Derwin and Chay were standing next to each other, so I could see he was taller than Derwin by at least six inches. He was also broader in the shoulder.

"There are differences between you, but the recording from the magic tracker was from up high when I viewed it. It's hard to judge height from that angle."

"It wasn't me!"

"You took a risk that night. You got everyone drunk, cranked up the music, and snuck off to kill your wife," I said.

Chay held his hands up and backed away several steps. "That's not what happened. I never bought a wig and didn't sign that sales slip. You've got the wrong person."

"Don't let him get away." Arietta swirled around Chay.

"Don't do anything foolish, Chay," I said. "You need to go to the Magic Council and confess what you did."

"I'm not going down for this. I made Arietta happy. Ask her. I know she's here because I'm freezing." He kept inching away.

"Happy! I'm not happy that I'm dead." Arietta clamped her hands around Chay's head.

He groaned and staggered to the side as she drained his magic.

"Arietta, don't hurt him," I said. "We have to get a confession."

"Why? I know enough." Her form grew solid as she took Chay's magic.

"You can't kill him." My attempts to pry her away failed as my magic puttered out of me, and I was left grabbing air.

I looked at Derwin for help, but he shook his head. "I'm sorry, but Chay deserves this."

Chay sprang forward, knocking into me. I almost pitched into the pool but caught myself at the last second, my feet sliding on the slippery tiles on the edge.

"Get her off me. I liked you, Arietta. Don't do this." Chay tried to run into the house, but Fontayne blocked his path.

"You liked my money and privilege. I should have seen past the model looks." Arietta lost her grip on Chay for a second, but she was soon back, like a hungry monkey with a nut and a rock, bashing against him, determined to get the rest of his energy.

He dodged away, weaving and bobbing as he tried to avoid being caught by a ghost he couldn't see.

"Stop fighting," I said. "Don't make this any harder than it needs to be. Tell Arietta you'll confess to her murder, and she'll stop her attack." She might, but I wasn't feeling hopeful.

Chay's wild gaze hit me. "I'm innocent!"

Arietta grabbed him again. Chay swayed on his feet and shuffled back, just as Tuffin dashed over and caught his ankles.

With a yelp, Chay fell back into the pool. He went under with a huge splash, soaking me. His head bobbed up a second later as he spluttered curses. His hand shot out, and he grabbed Tuffin's tail. "Help me! I can't swim."

Tuffin yowled in dismay as she slid across the wet tiles, her claws not getting any purchase. Her huge amber eyes met mine for a second before she plunged into the pool with Chay.

"Tuffin!" I raced over, my feet skidding out as I landed on my knees by the edge of the pool and grabbed under the water.

Chay and Tuffin breached the surface at the same time. Tuffin slashed at Chay's arms, leaving a trail of blood as she hissed and spat her fury at him for her dunking.

He cursed again and let go of her tail.

I'd never seen Tuffin move so fast as she cat-paddled to the edge, her eyes huge and her teeth bared. "He dunked me! That's the last time I try to stop a killer."

I scooped her out of the water and held her against my chest. She looked like a soaked rat with her black fur stuck to her body. "Did you get hurt?"

"Yes! I'm soaked and cold."

I kissed her head, making her jump. "You'll be fine. And you did great. You stopped Chay."

Her nose wrinkled. "I... yes, I did. Although I was actually hunting a butterfly. Chay just got in my way. Do I still get a reward?"

"Always. I'll put it on the long list of treats you're owed." Typical Tuffin reaction, but this furball was growing on me.

Fontayne and Derwin hauled Chay out of the water, Regan standing close by, a spell flickering on her hand.

"Stay where you are," I said to Chay.

"He's not going anywhere." Fontayne loomed over Chay. "This guy murdered my mom."

Derwin nodded. "I should have known it was you. You only married Arietta for her money. Did you realize you weren't going to get everything so decided to cut your losses and run?"

"I don't know how many times I have to say this, but it wasn't me," Chay said. "I've been set up."

"I'll contact the Magic Council." I looked at Arietta, and she nodded. We'd finally cracked this case.

Chapter 17

It was just past midnight, and I was back in the distillery with Arietta, Sol, and Tuffin. Fortunately for me, it had been Olympus Duke who'd shown up at the Frost house after I'd made the call. He'd barely batted an eyelid when I told him I'd been helping another ghost get justice.

The evidence was gathered, and a soggy, sorrowful Chay was taken in for questioning. The case was solved. So why didn't it feel like it was over?

"Now you've found Arietta's murderer, we get to go home, right?" Sol said.

"I don't like this." Arietta had been saying the same thing since we left the house. "I still can't believe it was Chay. He could be a fool, but he was a sweet fool, and he rarely gave me any trouble. Not like the rest of them."

"Try really hard to believe it was him." Tuffin was super grumpy after her impromptu swim in the pool. "Chay tried to drown me, and he murdered you."

I sat back in my seat, with a second mug of coffee in my hand, and studied the suspect board. "I hate to say this, but I agree with Arietta. It feels like I've missed something."

"The evidence points at Chay," Sol said.

"I know, but I can't believe he messed up with that sales slip. He must have figured out someone would put the pieces together."

"Maybe not if it was only the Magic Council running this investigation," Arietta said. "They've been blundering about for weeks and gotten nowhere."

"They're not so bad. Well, some of them are decent. Olympus has been helpful."

"What about the department that's messing with your farm? You must hate them. You can't trust the Magic Council," Arietta said.

I huffed out a breath. "Selma won't be getting any special pumpkin deliveries anytime soon."

"Chay must be the killer," Sol said. "Let's finish up here and get back to having a normal life."

"If you call messing around with those scarecrows normal," Arietta said. "I can't believe you enjoy that work. I've seen the scars on your body."

"Scars? What scars? And when were you looking at Sol's body?" I set down my mug slowly and pierced her with a glare.

Arietta slid me a lecherous smile. "While he was sleeping. I had to keep myself entertained. Don't worry, I kept it above the waistband."

"Arietta! Sol was unconscious. That's wrong. Apologize."

She shrugged. "I'm so sorry for wanting a look at your abs. I'm simply a hot-blooded female."

"You're a dead, creepy, peeping letch. I should force you to cross over. You'll face your punishment when you get to the other side," I said.

"Punishment for what?"

I thumped against the table, forcing my anger down. Arietta did what she liked to people and cared nothing for the consequences. I turned to Sol. "What scars is she talking about?"

He looked away and shrugged. "Recently, your scarecrows have been harder to handle. Some get physical."

"They injured you? You should have told me. They're not supposed to attack people. When did this happen?"

"It's been happening on and off ever since I started working with you," Sol said. "I figured we needed to iron out the pecking order. But as you've been spending more time in the barn with your... you know whats, the scarecrows have been running wild."

"I don't know what. What are you talking about?" Arietta said. "Does Odessa have secrets?"

"It's nothing for you to worry about." I caught hold of Sol's hand. "I'm so sorry. It's not your job to be attacked by my scarecrows. I'll speak to them. Make sure they understand they need to follow your orders."

"They follow my orders fine. But sometimes, the magic in them goes wonky. It's like they're not in control. They get a vacant look in their eyes and then malfunction."

"That's impossible. They're connected to me. I'd know if anything was wrong with them. I'll look into

225

it." I squeezed his arm. "I never meant for you to get hurt."

"I heal. And there are only a few scars."

I wanted to believe him, but I had a horrible feeling Sol was downplaying how bad the situation was. My gaze turned frosty as I focused on my annoying ghost companion. "Arietta, it's time to go."

"No. I don't feel ready to move on. Where's the brilliant white light, soothing angels, and my old friends and family waiting to greet me?"

"Where you're going, I doubt the light will be that bright," I said.

"And you're assuming you have family or friends who'll want to see you on the other side." Tuffin was drip drying on a towel I'd found in the staff room.

"One more squeak out of you, and you know what'll happen," Arietta said. "I'll find another pool to dunk you in. I can smell the chlorine on you from here."

Tuffin hissed and turned her back on Arietta, which only made her laugh.

"Focus on looking for the light," I said. "And no more threats. You got what you wanted. Your murder has been investigated, and the Magic Council has Chay in custody. It'll only be a matter of time before they charge him."

Arietta hovered in front of my face, still not looking happy. "I gave him everything he asked for. And we had an understanding."

"He understood that he needed you dead," Tuffin muttered.

Arietta ignored her. "I know I can be occasionally difficult, but Chay got me. He knew when to back off and give me space. It worked between us. And I wasn't even mildly bored with him. The marriage would have lasted another three to five years before I traded him in."

"Chay isn't a second-hand car," I said. "Maybe he didn't like the idea of a ticking clock against his marriage."

Sol nodded. "I only caught your side of the conversation, but some people only want to marry once and that's it." His gaze was on me as he said that.

I stood from my seat and walked to the suspect board, pretending not to notice how flushed my cheeks were. That was exactly how I'd felt with Brodie. He was my one and only love.

My hand settled over my heart, which always felt like a piece was missing. Right now, it felt like Brodie was slipping away from me. I had to get to the farm and continue my work to bring him back. I'd lost focus on what really mattered.

Arietta drifted beside me, also studying the suspect board. "I know it looks bad for Chay, and I'm aware you want this finished, but take a final look at the remaining suspects. I... I don't want it to be my husband. They're supposed to support you, look after you, and be there when times get rough. Chay always was."

"You're showing your softer side again." I tried hard not to feel sorry for Arietta. She was such a tough cookie, but even they could have soft centers. "You loved Chay, didn't you?"

"Love is a complicated word. I didn't, but he was the best husband I'd had. I need to be absolutely certain it was him. What if he gets charged with my murder, and the real killer is still out there? They could get a taste for this and keep going."

"This murder was personal. You were the only target." My gaze flicked over everything we'd stuck or written on the board. "There's one thing still puzzling me. Actually, it's two things."

"Will those things prove Chay is innocent?"

I tilted my head from side to side as I got my thoughts in order. "It is possible Chay got everyone so drunk he was able to sneak out and shoot you, but he wouldn't have had long. Maybe a minute. And that recording of him on the magic tracker showed he was in no hurry. He strolled past."

"And that's important?"

"Even if Fontayne was passed out drunk, and Regan got so involved in her book she missed Chay leaving, his absence would have been noticed. How did he get in and out of the house so fast and hide the disguise and weapon? The timeline doesn't add up."

"Regan is such a bookworm. She gets lost in the pages of the dullest looking things. And my son, well, he's young. He can't handle his drink. They could both have become distracted. What's the second thing you're puzzled about?"

I pointed at the board. "Your cheap voodoo plushie. It's an anomaly. You said it wasn't yours."

"I stand by that. I don't even have to see it to know it wasn't mine."

"Maybe you should see it," I said. "A picture only tells half the story."

"I can't explain the plushie," Arietta said. "I don't care about it. Go through the evidence on Chay again. Find a fault."

"It's all here on this board."

"What was his motive?" Arietta said. "I took excellent care of him. He was fed and entertained, and he got to spend all his time with me."

"There's your motive," Tuffin said. "You drove him over the edge."

"It could have been the payout from the prenup that motivated Chay." Sol yanked Tuffin out of Arietta's way as she swooped at her.

"It was hardly an enormous amount, though. He'd have had a few good years of living off that money, but then would have needed to go back to work and deal with difficult women making demands on him," I said.

"Like Arietta, you mean?" Tuffin said from the relative safety of Sol's arms.

Arietta pointed a finger at her. "You're on your final warning, furball."

"You must have been difficult to live with," I said to Arietta. "Chay may have decided the luxury lifestyle wasn't worth the hassle."

"Not true. He cared for me. And you never saw us together when I was alive," Arietta said. "I was never cruel to my husbands. I picked them because I liked them and knew they'd take excellent care of me. Chay was no different. I could see there was a compassionate man beneath the tan and cologne. And with that face and body, he was destined for bigger things than toiling every day in a place like that. I made sure we were compatible, and it worked."

"Maybe the excitement you offered wasn't enough. People change," I said. "They grow apart."

"And they find other people they care about." Sol was looking at me again.

"I don't know about that," I said. "But when I think about what I was like as a teenager and how I am now, I'm a different person."

"Chay wouldn't change that quickly. And we were only married for a year. He gave up everything to move here. He only had me."

"He did it because it meant he could get away from a monster. It seems like an excellent motive to me," Tuffin muttered.

Arietta lunged at Tuffin and attempted to grab her off Sol's lap, but she dodged out of the way and leaped onto some overhead pipes.

"Arietta! Stop taking your frustrations out on Tuffin. You need to move on. Focus on your future. Stop looking for problems. Otherwise, you'll be stuck here."

"You don't believe he's guilty, either," Arietta said. "Otherwise, you wouldn't be standing in front of that suspect board picking holes in the evidence against Chay."

I tipped back my head and groaned. "I'm feeling physical pain from thinking you're right, but the timeline and the plushie are nudging me."

"Would seeing the plushie help?" Sol said.

"Possibly, but that could be tricky. It'll be in the evidence store," I said. "I only got this picture because I asked Indigo to twist Olympus's arm."

"We need a friendly face at the Magic Council, who'll let us look at the evidence," Sol said. "How about getting Olympus to help again?"

"He'll be tied up interviewing Chay. I won't be able to reach him until tomorrow morning."

"We have to deal with this now," Arietta said. "Before Chay is charged, and it's too late."

I looked up at Tuffin who'd plastered herself against the pipes and was swishing her tail from side to side. "How would you like to go on a covert operation?"

"What's in it for me?"

"I don't chase you for the rest of your miserable life," Arietta said.

"How about fresh salmon?" I said. "I could order in a special batch. I'm sure Arietta won't mind paying."

"I violently object," Arietta said. "That cat's been nothing but a problem. I don't know why you have her as a familiar."

"She's new to the role, but Tuffin is useful. She found the source of the wig, and that led us to Chay being your killer. And she stopped him from running. Kind of."

"A year's supply," Tuffin said.

I couldn't handle my kitchen smelling of salmon every morning for the next year. "How about two months?"

"Eighteen months. Final offer."

Arietta chuckled. "She negotiates like me. Very well. I know an excellent fresh fish supplier. He handles the orders at the house. Give him my name, and you'll get a discount."

Tuffin hopped down from the pipe and shook out her wet fur. "What do I have to do?"

"A tiny bit of breaking and entering," I said. "Are you up for retrieving something from a secure evidence room?"

"You want me to fetch something?"

"Yes. But discreetly."

Her eyes narrowed. "I'm not a dog."

"Nooooo! You're much better than a dog. And don't forget, you're getting twelve months of fresh salmon delivered to the farm door."

"We agreed on eighteen months."

"Ah, so we did. You'll do it?"

"I will. You'd better order enough salmon, or you'll find a hacked up hairball in your shoe."

"You'll get your salmon. But if we're going to do this, we should go now. Magic Council employees keep regular hours, so there won't be trouble getting into the evidence room at this time." I glanced at Arietta. "You and Sol be the lookout, while Tuffin sneaks in and grabs the plushie."

"We can keep a lookout on our own. We don't need him."

"This isn't up for negotiation. We can't get caught breaking into a Magic Council office. I need every pair of eyes we have. That means Sol comes, too."

Arietta stabbed a finger at Sol. "One false move, and you know what'll happen."

He glanced my way. "Is Arietta yelling at me?"

"Kind of. But you're in."

We were soon out the door and heading into increasingly risky territory as we walked toward the Magic Council office in Witch Haven.

I tried a concealment spell, but my magic flickered and died on my fingertips. I couldn't wait to get away from Arietta. Hopefully, the bone weary tiredness that ran through me would vanish once I was done with this toxic ghost.

Thanks to the late hour, we encountered no one on the streets and were soon hurrying around the back of the office.

Arietta slid through the back door to check anyone was inside. She was ejected a few seconds later, yelping and covering her head, her ghostly form streaked through with black. "There's magic protecting this place. You should have warned me."

"I didn't know about the magic. Although it makes sense there'd be something to stop intruders." I studied the door, trying to detect a spell. "Is anyone inside?"

"No." Arietta swiped her hands down herself, shaking off the spell.

"Did you get the evidence room unlocked?"

"Almost. The cat will have to deal with the rest on her own. Urgh! I need a shower. I feel unclean."

Tuffin strutted to the door and sniffed the gap at the bottom. "I'll get the plushie."

Sol returned from checking the windows and doors. "Everything is secure. I couldn't get anything to open, so I'm not sure how Tuffin will get in."

I glanced at his hand. The silver ring that channeled his magic was missing. "Where's your ring?"

He raised his bare finger. "Otherwise engaged, so I can't spring anything open with magic. How about you?"

"Thanks to Arietta, I'm almost out." With very little magic on our side, I had no choice but to do things the old-fashioned way and break a window as quietly as possible. The second I did, a green glow appeared around the windowsill.

I grabbed Tuffin and hoisted her inside. "You've probably got two minutes before someone arrives, so hurry."

Tuffin dashed inside, and there was nothing I could do but wait with the others, surveying the alleyway and counting down the time.

There was a scrabbling from the other side of the window, and Tuffin's face appeared. In her mouth, she clutched a large, dark purple plushie in the shape of a hippo.

I caught hold of her and slid her out the window, careful to avoid any glass shards. "Everybody, run." I kept hold of Tuffin as we dashed away.

We'd just rounded the corner when lights flared on in the front of the Magic Council office.

I gestured everyone back into the alleyway, but a sigh of relief slid out when I saw it was only Olympus. I couldn't risk him seeing us, though. I'd just broken into his office and stolen evidence in a murder investigation. That would get me in trouble, no matter how friendly we were.

"Let's go behind the empty bookstore," Sol whispered. "The place has been vacant for months, so we won't be disturbed while we check the plushie."

I waited until Olympus was no longer visible before hurrying across the street with everyone. We dashed behind the bookstore, and I held up the plushie for Arietta to examine.

She looked it over a few times, then shook her head. "Poor stitching and a cheap design."

"Are you sure you didn't make it?"

"No. And I'd be embarrassed if I had. It looks even worse now I see it up close."

"If it isn't yours, why was it by your body?" I said. "Did the killer leave it as a calling card?"

"The Loathsome Plushie Bandit," Tuffin said. "They're making a name for themselves by leaving soft toys at crime scenes."

"It's not a toy." Arietta passed her hands over it several times. "It doesn't even have magic attached to it. Check for yourself. All my plushies have voodoo magic."

I inspected the plushie and couldn't find a hint of magic. "This is no help to us. I thought if we saw it... I don't know, it might jog a memory."

"It hasn't helped," Arietta said.

"We need to get this back to the evidence room before Olympus notices it's missing."

"There's no way I'm going back in that office. I'll get arrested," Tuffin said.

"Let's hold on to it for now," Sol said. "You're friends with Olympus. You can convince him to sneak it back in for you. He'll understand what we're doing."

I wasn't so sure about that. "Olympus can be straitlaced with his work." I risked a peek at the Magic Council office to see the lights still blazing and another person arriving. There was no way we were going back over there.

I kept hold of the plushie and turned it over in my hands. "We need to go to your voodoo plushie room. I want to compare this with the others." I held the plushie to my chest and then pressed it to my ear. I squeezed it, and the stuffing bulged out. I squashed it against my face.

"Have you lost your mind?" Arietta said.

"Most likely, since I've been working with you. But looking at this toy has given me an idea. As soon as it's dawn, we're going back to your house. This puzzle has something to do with your toys. Or rather, this one, in particular."

"How many times do I have to tell you they aren't toys?" Arietta said.

"Whatever they are, this little guy could be the key to solving the mystery." I pressed the plushie against my ear again.

"Does that mean you think Chay is innocent?" Arietta said.

"Possibly." But to find out for sure, we needed to face a room full of voodoo magicked toys, find the hidden piece of this puzzle, and come out the other side.

Chapter 18

The sun was peeking over the horizon as we snuck to the Frost house. I didn't want to confront any of the family until my theory could be proven, so we were going in early.

I'd kept hold of the plushie from the evidence store and was still playing with it. Well, testing a theory. This toy would make an excellent muffler. It was the perfect thing to disguise a gunshot.

But we had the wrong plushie. This little guy was a decoy. The real plushie, the one Arietta had been working on before she'd died, had been hidden by the killer. And what better place to hide it than in plain sight, surrounded by nine hundred and ninety-nine other voodoo plushies. No one would think to look in the seriously creepy plushie room.

The killer must have known that. And they'd also know Arietta worked on those disturbing plushies every evening. Without realizing it, she'd given them the perfect tool to assist in her murder.

But before I could prove any of that, we had to find the plushie.

"One of my plushies didn't murder me. They're vicious little beasts when I activate them, but they wouldn't turn on me." Arietta had been hovering around me ever since we'd snuck away from the Magic Council office, demanding to know what I was thinking.

"I'm certain one of your plushies was involved in your murder." I kept a close watch to see if anyone spotted us approaching the house, but there were no lights on in any windows.

"That doesn't make sense."

"It will. I'm working on a theory, but I need to see the plushies."

"Work faster. I don't like being kept in the dark."

"Getting a taste of your own medicine sucks, doesn't it?"

"Meaning?"

"You now know how your family feels about you hiding the business sale from them."

She hissed at me.

"Be useful and open a door so we can get inside."

Arietta led us around the side of the house. She whizzed through a set of double doors, and they opened a second later. "Derwin sleeps at the back of the house, so he won't hear you as long as you're careful. Regan's room is near my voodoo plushie room, and she's a light sleeper, so don't knock anything over."

"Where's Fontayne's room?" I said.

"On the top floor. He won't hear a thing."

I crept up the stairs with Sol and Tuffin and headed to the voodoo plushie room. I sucked in a deep breath, my hand on the door, preparing myself for the sight of all those magically enchanted voodoo plushies. The door opened, and there they were in their magnificent, scary glory.

We hurried inside, and I eased the door shut, risking turning on the light so we wouldn't miss any sudden movements from these spine shuddering creations.

"Whoa," Sol said. "Talk about creepsville."

"They're so beautiful," Arietta said. "I miss my plushies. This one's of the mayor." She lifted a pale green doll that looked like a troll with a bright tuft of purple hair. "And this is Cordelia Norwood. I've even got one of Silvaria Digby around here somewhere. Ah! Here she is. I turned her into a porcupine. She's a prickly character and morbidly obsessed with her cemetery, so I gave her a reaper's scythe, too. It has a real blade."

"A plushie for everyone you want to control," I muttered.

"You've got a plushie for everyone in the village?" Sol touched a plushie with the tip of his finger, and it growled at him.

"Tell the boyfriend to be careful. But yes, I have a plushie for almost everyone, although there are a few exceptions. I have one for each resident of Crown Copse and one for people I do business with," Arietta said.

"You're sure you don't have one for me?" I started hunting through the plushies.

"No, but that can be remedied." Arietta grabbed my hair and yanked on it, taking several strands with her when she moved away.

"Ouch! Don't you dare make a plushie of me." I rubbed the sore spot on my head. "I've done nothing but help you."

"I won't misuse your plushie. Call this a demonstration of how useful they can be." There was a wicked smile on Arietta's face as she grabbed a half-finished plushie shaped like a duck.

Sol moved over to me and leaned down so his mouth was by my ear. "This is one powerful ghost. I just got a glimpse of her, and I don't usually see spirits. She keeps growing more powerful."

I turned away, so Arietta couldn't see my face, just in case she could lip read. "She's been feeding off me. And probably you, too."

"That's why I've been feeling so tired?"

"Yes. And it doesn't help that you don't have your ring to keep topping up your magic. Where is it?"

"I needed to put it to good use. A friend was in trouble. I'll get it back."

"Stop whispering about me," Arietta said, "or I'll make this voodoo plushie experience less than pleasurable."

"I doubt anything to do with your plushies is ever pleasant," I said. "Come on, we're here to find the plushie you were working on when you died. Do you remember what it was?"

"No. Maybe a were bear or a unicorn." Arietta zoomed in front of me. "Why do you think it's here?"

"Hide something important in a place so obvious, no one will look for it."

She gestured at me. "Keep going."

"Your plushies are stuffed with excellent sound muffling foam."

"I don't use foam! I use pure virgin premium fibers. It's the best you can buy. Foam loses its shape."

"Foam, virgin... whatever, that's not important. But the inside of a plushie would muffle the sound of gunfire," I said. "What if the plushie you were working on was used to silence the shot that killed you?"

"Not possible. Everyone heard the shot."

I was rooting through the plushies again. "They heard a shot. If I'm right about this, we're looking for a plushie with a big hole through it and powder burns on its fur."

Arietta jabbed me with a finger. "If someone misused a plushie in such a horrific way, I'd know. I love them more than my child. Much more."

"You won't remember the moments leading up to your death," I said. "It's the way this works. If you did, you'd have pointed out your killer and wouldn't have blackmailed me. Your plushie was involved. I'm sure of it."

Arietta scowled at me before bending over the duck plushie and pulsing magic into it as she wound my hairs around its leg. "Maybe. I'm certain I'd have kept the memory of plushie mistreatment, so I could get my revenge."

I glanced at Sol. "Any sign of our wounded plushie?"

"No. I'm about to check the creepy ones with the fangs and horns."

"Careful they don't bite."

"They do. And hard." Arietta watched us hunt through the plushies. "This is cruel. Whoever did this knew how much I loved my plushies."

"It's payback for years of torment." Tuffin's voice was muffled by the pile of plushies she'd dived into, so I couldn't see her.

No one spoke as we continued our search, and I kept an ear on the door to make sure we wouldn't be interrupted.

"The cat can go, but I like you two as a couple," Arietta said. "You work well together."

I didn't respond, frantically lifting plushies and looking them over for signs of damage. If I couldn't find this clue, I'd have to admit defeat, and Chay would go to jail.

"I'd have married Sol and had fun with him if I was still alive," Arietta said.

"Apparently, Arietta likes you," I said.

"I'm flattered," Sol muttered. "But I'll pass."

"You're not the marrying kind?"

I glanced up, also interested in that question.

"What did she say?" he asked.

"Arietta wants to know if you're interested in getting married."

"I am. With the right woman."

"I could be the right woman. Or I could have been. A successful business, plenty of money, and I'm not the jealous type. You'd have had your freedom with me. And I'd never tie you down and expect you to toil on my farm every day." Arietta's laugh was hard. "You must really like Odessa to put up with those scarecrows."

I flashed her a glare, but she was right. I couldn't offer Sol an exciting life of luxury. My days were long and the work hard. And, as I'd discovered, Sol had been suffering at the hands of my scarecrows and hadn't said a thing. I was a terrible boss, and by Arietta's standards, not a great catch.

My scarecrow obsession ruled me, and I needed a better work-life balance. But it was more than that. My determination to get back Brodie colored every part of my life. Even when I took time off and hung out with friends, I was counting down the minutes when I could get back to the farm and run more experiments.

Had I pushed things too far? Was my life so out of kilter I was missing important things?

"You're not even the tiniest bit interested in this boy toy?" Arietta said. "He's a hard worker. And he's obedient. The best husbands always are."

"Stop talking about Sol like he isn't in the room," I said. "And my relationship status is complicated."

"It doesn't have to be. Be clear and open with the men you choose. Lay out what you offer, and if they don't like it, move on to the next one."

"How many men turned you down before Chay accepted you?" I said.

"None. I was the one turning down a proposal most weeks. I had a lot to offer a man."

I glanced up from my plushie search. "It never bothered you they were only with you for the money and what you could give them? Didn't you ever want true love?"

"As I've said, my previous husbands knew the relationships were only for fun and not life. When

I got bored or they ignored me for too long, I moved on. So did they. And they got a payout. I had prenups for all my marriages." Arietta settled the duck plushie on the floor. "Make sure you do the same if this one convinces you to put a ring on your finger. You must have money tied up in that farm. You don't want to lose it when the love goes sour."

"Sol would never do that to me." My cheeks heated to my hairline.

"I've thought about marrying you," he said.

"Oh! I didn't mean that. Arietta was talking about something else. Well, prenups and paying off husbands. I meant you'd never take the farm from me if things went wrong between us. Not that there is an us." I pressed my lips together to stop putting my foot in it anymore.

He grinned. "Fair enough. But I'm serious."

I turned to him, a pink unicorn plushie in my hand. "After everything that's gone down between us, you still like me?"

"I sure do. My life became much more interesting since getting involved with you. I mean, the farm and you. Things are always changing. Although I never knew I'd end up helping solve murders, I like it. I want to keep doing it. Forever, if you'll let me."

"Never say forever," Arietta said. "It can be an awfully long time."

I dragged my gaze away from Sol. "I believe in one true love that lasts forever."

Arietta honked a laugh for several seconds. "True love is for movies and losers. My five husbands enjoyed themselves, we all got what we wanted, and no hearts got broken."

I pressed a hand against my chest. It would be nice to have a healed heart, one that didn't quiver away from the prospect of being in love. But I didn't agree with how Arietta operated, even though there was a cold logic to it.

"It's got you thinking, hasn't it?" Arietta said. "My way is the right way."

"I... I always wanted to marry Brodie," I said. "I still do. And even though we never made it official, I felt married to him."

"Why didn't you marry?" Arietta said. "If that was what you wanted, why didn't he make it happen if you were so right together? If this Brodie was such an amazing guy, he must have known what you wanted."

"Um... He did. But Brodie was saving up for a special ring."

Arietta laughed again. "That's an excuse."

I bit my bottom lip. I'd wondered that occasionally. "I'd have accepted a ring off a drink's can. The special ring didn't come, though, so I decided we were as good as married. A ring on my finger made no difference."

"And there's your problem. You compromised too much," Arietta said. "Ask Sol if he'd make you always compromise in a relationship."

I shook my head. "Every relationship needs its give-and-take."

Sol nodded. "True, but you always want to make the other person as happy as possible."

"I imagine he'd treat you like my husbands did me." Arietta winked at me. "You'd be his queen, he'd make you ridiculously happy in bed, and you'd have delicious arm candy to show off to all your drooling friends."

"That's not how real relationships work," I said. "Let's keep looking for this plushie."

"It worked for me," Arietta said.

I threw down the plushie I'd been examining. "What did your boy toys get out of these cold, detached arrangements?"

"Privilege, a generous allowance, and me."

Tuffin snorted a derisive laugh from behind a pile of plushies.

I sorted through another dozen plushies. We weren't getting anywhere, other than me being lectured on the state of my relationship. Or lack of one.

I glanced at Sol. He was always sincere with me. He'd always been honest, and I'd kept shoving him away. Should I change? Could I? Relationships were about compromise, though. Sometimes, when I'd been with Brodie, it had felt like I'd been the one doing all the compromising.

"Make an offer to Sol," Arietta said. "I can see he loves you."

"We're not talking about that anymore," I said.

"I'll ask him how he feels." Arietta shot over and grabbed Sol.

He staggered back, his eyes widening. "Err.. hey, Arietta."

"You can see her?" My breathing stalled as I watched him trapped by the ghost.

Sol nodded. "What's on your mind?"

Arietta's smile was smug as she glanced my way. "Do you love Odessa?"

His gaze flicked to me. "I do." The certainty in his voice made my head fuzzy. "She knows exactly how I feel about her."

"I bet you'd do anything for her," Arietta said.

"Stop!" I waved a gray plushie that looked like a cross between a giraffe and a vulture in the air, desperate to stop her meddling in my affairs.

Arietta kept hold of Sol. "I'm helping you. Thinking about your missing lover is unhealthy."

"He's not missing. Brodie is dead," Sol said.

Arietta sucked in a breath. "Interesting. So it was the Brodie I knew."

"You never knew him," I said.

"I did. Maybe it was before you got together. He was a ladies' man."

"No, that's a different guy."

"He did something in mining."

I glared at her. "Stop talking about Brodie."

"Well, that confirms my thoughts on your odd relationship. Having experienced being a ghost, I know I've changed."

"Why is that important?" I lowered the plushie. I'd wondered numerous times if Brodie would be different when I got him back.

"You don't want to deal with the dead when it comes to love. We shift and evolve. You don't want something that broken in your life. And you don't want a cheating ghost messing with your head."

"Brodie isn't broken. And he wouldn't cheat on me." I threw the plushie at her.

Sol sucked in a breath. But when I glared at him, he turned his head and focused on a row of demon-like plushies with glowing eyes.

"Ghosts aren't people. You can't always save us or fix us," Arietta said.

There was something like kindness in her voice. Or was that pity? I didn't care. I wasn't listening to her poison. "We aren't just people, though. Not with our magic."

"Ghosts are... other. When we sit between realms, we can't avoid being damaged. I'm already thinking dark thoughts the longer I stay."

"Then go. You're only here for revenge, anyway. What's darker than that?"

"No, I'm seeing this through. But, Odessa, some advice woman-to-woman. Let go of your past. It'll trap you, and you'll miss what's right in front of you."

"Spoken like a true serial marriage maker. When I bring back—" I bit my tongue.

"Yes? When you bring back what?" Arietta hovered around me, an intense look in her eyes. "Are you thinking about using your reanimation magic for no good?"

"Forget it. Let's focus on the toys." I yelped as a stabbing pain lanced through my calf. I dropped to the floor and grabbed my leg, expecting to see blood running down it, but there was nothing there. "What the heck was that?"

Arietta held up the duck voodoo plushie. "How many times do I have to tell you, these aren't toys? That was a demonstration of how powerful they are."

I rubbed my calf as the stinging pain faded. "Okay. They're not toys. But if you put me out of action, no one will solve your murder. And Sol definitely won't help you."

He nodded. "Although I appreciate the relationship advice."

Tuffin head-butted my leg. I turned and looked down at her. She had a plushie in her mouth, and there was a hole in it with a burn mark around the edges. She spat it out. "Is this what you're looking for?"

Chapter 19

I scooped up Tuffin and kissed her head. "You're a genius."

She grumpily accepted the kiss before squirming out of my arms. "I know I am."

Arietta swooped over and glared at the damaged plushie. "How dare they! Who used my plushie against me?"

"I'm working that out. But we need one more piece of evidence to support my theory."

"I'm bored with gathering evidence. Give me a name." Arietta grabbed me, but I ducked her icy embrace before she could get a tight hold.

"Not here. You don't want to wake everyone."

"Is my killer in this house?"

"Maybe. Most likely."

"Then wake them all and get the killer to confess. If you won't, I will."

"Arietta, stop!" I blocked the door, even though she'd be able to whizz through me if she wanted to. "If we don't get everything we need to prove who did this, our hard work will have been for nothing."

"I demand justice!" She hovered an inch from my face.

"But you must also want answers and closure. And do you really want a murder on your hands?"

She growled at me. "Maybe."

"You'll never see the bright light if you kill someone," Sol said.

I glanced at him. "You can still hear her?"

"Yep. It seems we have a connection." He shuddered. "What a gruesome concept."

"I can bribe my way into paradise," Arietta snarled at him.

I eased her back. "It doesn't work like that. And you'll get brownie points for not going rogue and killing anyone. I promise, by the end of the day, this will be over. You can finally leave."

"And leave us in peace," Tuffin said.

"I'm not happy about this, but I'll allow you to continue. But if it's not resolved by tonight, nothing will stop me from terrorizing everyone here."

"Agreed. You do you, while I put the final pieces together." I looked at Sol, who nodded. We were so close to solving this. And with the disguise and plushie discovered, there was only one more thing I needed to prove my theory.

I returned to the Frost house at dusk with Sol, Tuffin, Arietta, and Shamrock. We reached the edge of the extensive backyard and headed past the pagoda and around the back of the house to the chalets.

"You know what you need to do," I said to Tuffin and Shamrock. "If we don't find this clue, there won't be enough evidence, and the killer will get away."

"Why won't you tell me who it is?" Arietta said.

"You know why. The second I say their name, you'll zoom off and do something awful. Justice needs to be served. Your killer will go to jail."

"A swift death would be a better option. A quick snap of the neck, and it'll be over."

"Would you do that, though? Or would you hound this poor person in death just as you did in life?"

"There may be a small amount of ghostly terrorizing." Arietta cackled a laugh. "Jail is too good for whoever killed me. They'll get a free bed and meals. I hear they have internet and televisions inside. How is that punishment?"

"No one is getting killed," I said. "And if you try to hurt them, I'll capture you in a ghost jar and stop you from ever learning the truth. Now, help Tuffin and Shamrock with the search."

"I can do this without the ghost's help," Tuffin said. "I'm already picking up a scent trail. There's something out here."

"Keep at it. But be quick. Olympus is on his way, so we won't have long. Sol, will you keep an eye on them?"

"Of course. We'll come join you as soon as we can."

I left them searching the grounds and headed to the house. I had to knock loudly for several minutes before a sleepy-looking Derwin opened the door.

He blinked at me several times, as if he didn't know who I was. "Odessa! Is something wrong?"

"I know who killed Arietta. Can you get everyone together?" I didn't wait for an answer as I pushed my way into the hallway.

"Err... you do? I thought it was Chay." Derwin rubbed his eyes. "What's going on?"

"It's not Chay. He's being brought back here by the Magic Council. He should arrive at any minute."

"Oh! Well, you'd better come through." Derwin led me to the kitchen. "I'll be back in a moment with everyone else."

I paced the kitchen, my stomach a riot of nerves. If the others couldn't find the missing puzzle piece, I'd have to bluff my way through and hope the killer cracked and confessed.

It took ten minutes and lots of complaining before Derwin, Regan, and Fontayne were in the kitchen with me.

Fontayne looked bemused, while Regan had a worried look on her face.

"Derwin said you had a development in Aunty Arietta's murder," Regan said. "Has Chay confessed?"

"No, and he won't," I said. The sound of the front door opening and closing had everyone looking down the hallway. "That'll be Chay. The Magic Council has released him."

"But it was him," Fontayne said. "He was caught wearing that disguise of Uncle Derwin. And that sales slip had his name on it. It had to be him."

"I'll explain everything in a minute. I don't want Chay to miss this. Or the Magic Council," I said.

Chay walked through the doorway into the kitchen, looking rumpled around the edges but otherwise unbothered by his time being questioned by the Magic Council. Olympus was right behind him. He nodded at me.

"Thanks for bringing Chay here," I said. "I figured he'd want to hear this after everything he's been through."

"I wasn't unhappy when I was told I was free to go." Chay raked a hand through his hair. "What's happening, though? Did someone else confess to killing Arietta?"

I stood in front of the group and looked at Olympus again. He gave me an encouraging nod. Before I began, there was someone missing. "Where's Eva?"

"Oh, she left." Derwin looked out the window.

"Why? I thought everything was going great between you two."

"I think Eva got scared about all the changes. She needs time to think." Derwin tugged at his bottom lip. "I'm worried she won't come back, though. What with everything Arietta did to her... it was all too much. And I don't blame her, but I will miss her. I just want her to be happy. If leaving here makes Eva happy, then that's what needs to happen."

"What about your engagement?"

"It's on hold for now. Things might change. I don't know. I'm thinking about our future. Lots to consider."

I narrowed my eyes at Derwin, then whistled. A few seconds later, Shamrock shot through the door.

"Shamrock, go get Eva. She's in the chalet behind the houses," I said.

"No! I already said she no longer works here. She's gone." Derwin went to block the door, but Shamrock shoved him out of the way so hard he bounced into the fridge with a bone-jarring thud.

The news about Eva leaving surprised me, but I had a niggling suspicion her departure wasn't voluntary. And if that was true, it would only help me solve this murder.

"Let's get started while we wait for Eva," I said. "When I first saw the magic tracker footage of what I thought was Derwin with a gun in his hand, this investigation seemed simple."

"But I was set up." Derwin rubbed his shoulder where he'd hit the fridge. "By Chay."

"It seemed that way," I said.

There was a crash against the back door, and a second later, Arietta whizzed through.

"That'll be my backup." I opened the door, and Tuffin bounded through, closely followed by Sol.

"Did you find it?" I whispered to him.

He nodded, and so did Tuffin. But she couldn't talk because she had something in her mouth. Something that would resolve everything.

"Arietta's here. She's been helping me gather the final piece of evidence to figure out who killed her," I said.

The group shifted around, none of them looking happy Arietta was back.

She scowled at them and swirled about the kitchen. "Which one of you did it? And where's Eva? Don't leave her out."

"I'm not. Shamrock went to get her."

"What's she hiding from?"

"Most likely, Derwin."

"What's this?" Derwin said. "Arietta's not happy with me?"

"When was I ever happy with you?" Arietta zoomed around him. "What's going on with Eva? Has this idiot messed up his relationship with the housekeeper? Honestly, the man couldn't keep a dead fly interested for more than five minutes."

I pressed my lips together. "Let's focus. Arietta is keen on solving this mystery."

"So are we. What evidence were you looking for?" Regan said. "We already know what happened."

"That's the problem. We don't. This investigation has been full of misdirection from the start," I said. "From the evidence on the magic tracker showing Derwin as the killer, then the discovery of the disguise to prove it wasn't him, and the fact all of you had alibis for that night."

Arietta swirled around me. "Give me a name. I don't care about the motive. One name."

I shot her a sharp look, but continued. "When it became clear Derwin was being set up, my attention turned to everyone else. And when I learned about Chay's previous wives, all of whom died, I became convinced he'd killed Arietta to get his hands on her money."

"I've always had my doubts about you," Derwin said to Chay.

"But as I explained, we had a solid prenup agreement in place. I get some money, but it's a fraction of what the business and this house are worth," Chay said. "I always understood that. I didn't marry Arietta for her money. Well, I liked the lifestyle, but I knew a divorce or her death wouldn't make me wealthy. If money's the motive, you need to look to the family."

"I don't disagree, but all the clues led to you. Fontayne even suggested you deliberately made everyone drunk, so you could sneak out with Arietta's gun," I said. "And then we found the sales slip with your name on it. It wasn't looking good for you."

Olympus made a noise of surprise but gestured for me to go on.

"We all heard the gunshot," Regan said. "And we were all together. I mean, maybe Chay snuck out for a few seconds, but if it had been any longer, I'd have noticed."

"Most likely, you would have. And that's because Chay didn't leave the house that night on his own. He didn't murder Arietta," I said.

"If it wasn't Uncle Derwin, and it wasn't Chay, are you suggesting it was me or Regan?" Fontayne said.

"You admitted you attacked your mom and injured her leg during an argument," I said. "You must still be hurting because she made you give up your girlfriend. It gives you a motive."

"Yeah, but I have the same alibi as everyone else." Fontayne's tone was that of a sullen teenage boy.

"And I was in the room with Fontayne and Chay the whole time. It definitely wasn't me," Regan said.

"But you're now a wealthy and powerful woman. You inherit everything from Arietta," I said.

Chay whistled through his teeth. "That's some motive."

"And I've already said I plan to change things. No more exploitation." Regan's expression was fierce, and I caught a hint of a young Arietta behind those blazing eyes.

"I'll be speaking to her about that stupid plan," Arietta muttered.

"No, you won't," I whispered.

"Go on, Odessa. How did you figure this out?" Olympus said.

"Something has always puzzled me about this murder," I said. "One of Arietta's voodoo plushies was found next to her body."

Derwin nodded. "That's no surprise. She worked on those things every night. That was her routine."

"The problem with this plushie was it was a cheap, commercially made one. Arietta made one-of-a-kind plushies. And she told me she'd never buy one off the shelf, but that's exactly what was found by her body," I said.

"Why is that important?" Regan said.

"It's important because this plushie helped misdirect the investigation," I said. "Arietta *was* working on one of her own plushies that night, and her killer knew that. They used that knowledge to their advantage."

"What advantage?" Fontayne threw up his hands. "What's this got to do with my mom's creepy toys?"

Everyone's rapt attention was on me. "The killer used the plushie she was making as a silencer when they shot Arietta."

No one spoke for several seconds, and even Olympus look stunned by this information. But my killer was playing it cool and not revealing themselves.

"Olympus, we found the plushie that was used as a silencer," I said. "It's upstairs in a room with a heap of other plushies. I'm sure, when you test it, you'll find gunshot residue and DNA evidence to show who held that plushie as they pulled the trigger."

Olympus nodded. "I'll secure the room and make sure no one goes in until the evidence has been collected."

I looked around the group. "Has anyone got anything to confess at this stage?"

They all looked at each other, but no one spoke.

"Then I'll carry on. The killer knew Arietta would be outside alone that night, and no one would disturb her. They'd most likely experienced first-hand what happened if Arietta's private time was interrupted."

"We all did," Derwin said. "We all kept away from her."

Everyone turned as a high-pitched squeaking grew near. The door opened to reveal Shamrock with Eva tossed over his shoulder in a fireman's lift. Eva was pounding his back and begging to be put down.

"Eva, it's okay. Shamrock won't hurt you." I hurried over and helped the trembling woman down.

"He... he grabbed me. I thought I was dead." Eva shied away from Shamrock. "Why did he do that?"

"We needed you here." I glanced at her hand. As expected, the engagement ring she'd shown off was gone. "I know who killed Arietta."

Her face paled. "I... I just want to leave. I don't want trouble."

I led her into the kitchen. "You won't get in any trouble. Shamrock will look after you."

Shamrock leaned over and petted her on the head.

I focused back on the group, keeping a reassuring arm around Eva's shoulders. "The killer got to Arietta and killed her without anyone seeing."

"So it wasn't any of us," Fontayne said. "We all stayed inside after dinner."

"You did. But Arietta was killed earlier in the evening," I said.

"No! We all heard the shot fired," Chay said.

"And I saw the plushie when we arrived to find Arietta's body." Derwin was staring hard at Eva, but she wouldn't look at him. "It wasn't damaged. It wasn't used to muffle the sound of a gunshot."

"The one you saw wasn't damaged, but that was because it was placed at the scene to throw the investigation off course," I said. "What you all heard, and were meant to hear, was the second gunshot. The killer fired that shot to get your attention. It would have been easy to assume the shot you heard was the one that killed Arietta. It wasn't. She'd probably been dead for at least half an hour before you arrived."

"I'm not buying this. Where's the proof of a second shot?" Chay said.

"In my familiar's mouth. Tuffin, would you like to spit it out?"

Tuffin spat out a bullet. It hovered in the air, surrounded by a small protective spell to preserve the evidence.

"Did you mark the location where the bullet was discovered?" I said.

"As you told us to," Tuffin said. "I put a magic cordon around it, so it wouldn't be disturbed."

"Olympus, can you check this bullet to see if it matches the bullet that killed Arietta?"

"Of course." He stepped forward and collected the bullet before storing it in an evidence bag.

"This is all very good," Arietta grumbled, "but I need to know who fired the deadly shot."

I nodded at her. "This bullet was found outside Eva's chalet."

"Eva killed me?" Arietta lunged at her, but I stepped in front of Eva to protect her and shoved Arietta away.

Eva scuttled back and licked her lips. "It wasn't me. I... I was with Derwin that night."

"I know. You didn't fire the shot that killed Arietta," I said. "But the person you were with did. Derwin killed Arietta."

Derwin snorted a noise of surprise. "Impossible! That makes no sense. You found the wig and shirt. I was framed."

"You knew your sister's nightly routine, since you've lived here all your life. After you shot Arietta, using her plushie as a silencer, you went to Eva's chalet to give yourself an alibi. She told us you took a bath while she made you a herbal tea."

"That's all true. I was there. Eva, tell her."

I looked at Eva. She was still shaking and pale and simply shook her head.

"While you were in the bathroom, you leaned out the window and fired the shot that everyone assumed killed Arietta," I said.

"But... the disguise!" Derwin's gestures were wild. "Why would I disguise myself as myself and get caught on the tracker?"

"To frame Chay," I said. "You didn't want to risk him challenging the will, just in case he could get more money. And you definitely didn't want him around once Arietta was dead. On top of that, you needed everyone to doubt your involvement in the murder. You set this up to make it look like you were framed."

"This is ridiculous." Derwin turned to Olympus. "Are you going to stop this? Why are you letting this pumpkin growing witch do your job?"

"Everything Odessa is saying makes perfect sense." Olympus nodded at me again. "Keep going."

"The disguise problem and the plushie had me stuck. I expect you planned to get rid of the damaged plushie once the heat died down, but then Arietta got me involved, so you couldn't risk it. You figured no one would go in that room because its creepy factor is off the charts, so you took a chance and left it in there."

"And the sales slip with Chay's name on? Explain that," Derwin said.

"Chay likes a drink. You stole his card after he'd had a heavy night to make the purchase and faked his signature. You must have spritzed on his coconut cologne as well. And since you're good with disguises, you could have dressed up like him, too, when you made the purchase."

"That can be checked. I'll re-interview the sales assistant and get a handwriting analysis done on the slip," Olympus said.

Arietta was staring at her brother. "He really did it. All these years, he actually had the guts to get rid of me and attempt to frame my husband. Derwin almost has my respect for being so calculating."

I arched an eyebrow at her. "Getting yourself caught on the magic tracker was smart. It added another layer of doubt when I was looking at you as the killer. But I haven't forgotten you helped find the shirt and wig you'd hidden in the distillery. I didn't think it was odd at the time, but you led us straight to them. That added more doubt and made me believe Chay was the killer."

"I thought we were friends," Chay said. "You wanted to ruin my life. Why? I made Arietta happy."

"This wasn't about you, but it's no less than you deserve," Derwin said. "I know about your past and the other wives. You're a soulless predator."

Chay shook his head. "You know nothing about me. I cared for them all in my own way."

Derwin stared at me. "This is a fantasy. And Eva is my alibi. I was with her."

"Were you in the same room when you both heard the gunshot?" I addressed the question to Eva.

Derwin glared at her, and she stared back for a good thirty seconds before a soul shattering sigh slid from her lips. "He was in the bathroom, but I heard the water running and him splashing around in the bath. I didn't doubt him. But then—"

"Stop talking," Derwin said. "You're making things worse. I was with you that night."

"Eva, you've called off the engagement, haven't you?" I said. "I noticed the ring was missing."

She gulped. "I have."

"Did Derwin tell you something you didn't like about him?"

A tear trickled down Eva's cheek, and she nodded. "He confessed. Derwin told me what he'd done to Arietta, and I was horrified. He said he did it for us so we could be together and so Regan would get everything. He wanted Arietta ruined."

"Idiot!" Derwin said. "We could have had everything. This could have been yours."

"I want nothing connected to a murder," Eva said. "I loved you and wanted to spend the rest of my life with you, but you were wrong to do this. Arietta wasn't a nice person, but she didn't deserve to be killed."

I looked at Olympus. "Have you got enough information to make an arrest?"

"Yes. Thanks, Odessa. I'll take it from here."

"I don't care what you do to me now," Derwin said. "I've won. Regan gets it all. Arietta, you won't recognize this place in a year. Regan will make sure all the deceitful things you did to people ends. Isn't that right, darling?"

Regan stared at him, her face drained of color. "You killed Aunty Arietta?"

"Yes! For you. And for Eva, although she doesn't deserve it now," Derwin said.

"No, you killed Arietta mainly for yourself," I said. "She hurt you and made you feel small, so you got revenge. This murder wasn't about protecting other people."

Arietta shrieked. "You hateful, sneaky loser!" She lunged at Derwin, slammed him into the wall, and pounded him with her fists.

Chapter 20

"I'm going to kill you." Arietta kept shrieking as she used her energy to slam Derwin against the wall again.

"Odessa, what's going on?" Olympus hovered around Derwin, unable to see the ghost as she attacked.

"Get her off me!" Derwin yelped and cowered against the wall, covering his head with his arms as her ghostly energy continued to pound into him.

"You did this. You killed me because you were jealous, spiteful, and pathetic." Arietta howled, and her form shifted, becoming barely human and a whole lot terrifying ghoul as her rage consumed her.

I fired up a containment spell, but my magic was too weak to hold it, and it dripped off my fingers like watery icing sugar.

"Here! Indigo thought you might need this." Olympus tossed me a bag of powdered pumpkin.

I could have kissed him as I stuffed the contents in my mouth and chewed, getting an explosion of sweet pumpkin goodness and a blast of magical energy.

My magic flared to life, and I flung out a powerful containment spell that wrapped around Arietta and dragged her away from Derwin. But she was strong and fought me every inch, raking her hands down Derwin's face, and leaving him a trembling, bloody, weeping mess.

"I deserve this. Let me have him." She twisted and turned in my spell, but I wasn't letting her go.

Everyone stood back as I battled this powerful ghost, our energies mingling and sending sparks of orange and red magic flickering across the room. As we tangled, I slammed into all kinds of strange magic attached to Arietta, including some of my own and a hint of Sol's power. All this time, she'd been feeding off people to keep her ghost form strong.

I grabbed her when she was within reach and pinched her arms in a tight grip. "Arietta, you have to stop. You got what you wanted. Your killer has been found."

"It's not enough. I want more. I shouldn't have had everything taken from me, especially not by someone so pathetic." She almost broke through my spell, and I had to channel all my new energy into containing her, making me pant like an overheating werewolf on a blistering summer day.

Olympus stood beside Derwin, checking on him, although his gaze kept flicking back to me. "Is she under control?"

"Almost. I'm taking this problem outside. Shamrock, help Olympus. Make sure Derwin stays put. And don't let him near Eva." It took several minutes of fighting, but I finally dragged Arietta out of the house.

Tuffin strolled out behind me and sat watching as I struggled with Arietta.

"You know, familiars are supposed to support their witches." I dodged a swinging punch and almost got slammed in the face with a clawed hand.

"I know nothing about that," Tuffin said. "I'm new to being a familiar. Wasn't finding the bullet and the wig enough? I get a break now, right?"

"You're supposed to enhance my magic." I gasped and staggered back as Arietta ripped her claw-like hands through my spell.

Tuffin tilted her head. "How do I do that?"

I went down on one knee as an icy chill flooded through me. Arietta was gaining control. A few more seconds, and I wouldn't be able to stop her. "I don't know. I've never had a real familiar before. Indigo touches her familiars to get a boost."

Tuffin leaped and landed nimbly on my shoulders, digging in sharp claws to get a grip. The second we made contact, I was filled with a hot, spicy smelling magic. It blended with my pumpkin powers, and a blast of pale orange light shot out of my palms and entangled Arietta. Within seconds, she was cowering before us, all traces of her ghoul form gone.

"I'll behave. Just don't force me to crossover until I'm ready." She held up a wispy hand. "Don't banish me."

I gave Tuffin a quick stroke. "That was amazing."

Tuffin booped her nose against my cheek. "Agreed. I enjoy being fired up with your pumpkin magic."

I focused on Arietta. "It's time to go."

"Wait! I'm not ready. There's so much I have to do."

"Not anymore," I said. "You must release your hold over everyone. People need a permanent break from you."

Her scowl sent a shiver down my spine, but with Tuffin nuzzled against me, I wasn't afraid. "I don't want to. What if I don't like where I'm going? Will I be able to get back? Try again?"

"You're worried you're going to the dark, fiery place, aren't you?" Tuffin said.

"I'm not as bad as everyone makes me out to be," Arietta said. "I just don't suffer fools. You shouldn't be punished for that."

"You should have suffered those fools better." I kneeled next to her. "Arietta, you know what happened to you. You have no reason to stay."

She shook her head. "I can't believe Derwin used one of my precious plushies against me. He did it out of spite because he knew how much I loved them."

"He isn't as meek and mild as you thought."

Her form grew a little more solid, and she edged away but didn't look like she was going to make a run for it. "I'll eventually be impressed with his actions, but right now, I want to destroy him. Can't you give me five minutes alone with my lying, murderous brother?"

"No, Derwin will suffer plenty for what he's done. He'll go to jail for your murder, and he's lost the woman he loved. And from the look on Regan's face when she learned what he'd done, she won't be supporting him, either."

Arietta let out a long sigh. "I suppose that's something."

I glanced back at the house, but no one had come out to see how the fight was going. "Do you see a light? It'll guide you to your next adventure."

Arietta looked around. "I see a gray corridor. It doesn't look appealing. There's mold on the walls."

"It's better than a fiery black corridor and a guy with horns and a pitchfork," Tuffin said.

"Oh, hush." Arietta grinned sharply at Tuffin. "Never give up being sassy. It suits you. And it's important you keep this witch on her toes. Odessa will get bored if she doesn't have a few challenges on her hands."

"I'm done with challenges," I said. "I just want to get back to my farm, get the Magic Council off my back, and tidy up a few loose ends."

Arietta turned and stared at something I couldn't see. "Would one of those loose ends be Sol?"

He was a loose end, but I didn't know what I was supposed to do with him. "It's—"

"Don't say it's complicated," Arietta said. "If you do, it shows you haven't listened to my advice about relationships. You need a new start and a new guy. And I've been asking around about your Brodie. You can't afford any more of his shady business with your scarecrows, or you really will be shut down for good." Her gaze flickered away from me.

"Shady business? You've lost me." Did she mean the experiments in my barn? She couldn't know about that, could she?

Arietta looked over her shoulder, and her image flickered. "That light doesn't look so bad. I'm going to investigate. There might even be a few challenges of my own to tackle on the other side."

"Wait! You haven't explained what you mean by shady business and Brodie."

She nodded and opened her mouth, but her form was fading. A few seconds later, she blinked out of sight.

I stared at the empty spot. Apart from my experiments, my scarecrows were perfection. Occasionally out-of-control perfection, but I couldn't figure out what Arietta meant. And why was Brodie involved?

I returned to the house with Tuffin to discover Olympus had two more colleagues from the Magic Council with him. The voodoo plushie room was secured, Derwin was in custody, and the rest of the family was in shock as they came to terms with what had happened.

"Olympus, I don't want to distract you, but how are things going with my farm and Selma?"

He looked up from the form he was filling in. "It's a work in progress, but you're okay to go to the farmhouse. Selma doesn't have grounds to arrest you."

"Thanks for sorting things with her. I wasn't sure what to do after the breakout from the cell."

He glanced around and stepped closer. "Your scarecrows abducted you. You weren't involved in that breakout."

"Yes, but I—"

He held up a hand and shook his head. "No. Don't tell me anything. If I don't have the information, I can't get you in trouble. All we saw were two out-of-control scarecrows smashing through the wall and abducting you and Sol. You've been absolved of all involvement. Let's keep it that way."

"What about my scarecrows?"

"They'll have questions to answer if they can be identified. But they were moving fast, and their faces were blurry. And one scarecrow looks like the rest to me. That's what I keep saying, anyway." He raised his eyebrows. "Although you might like to send the ones that were involved away, just until the heat dies down."

"Of course. And thanks again. I'd have been stuck in a cell being grilled by Selma if it weren't for you and Indigo coming to my rescue."

"Don't get too excited. This is just a reprieve, and Selma will be back. Watch out for her and make sure your affairs are in order so she has nothing on you. You don't have anything to hide, I hope."

"Nope. And of course, I will. I'd better get going, if you don't need me here."

Olympus nodded. "You did a great job solving this murder. We were stuck as to who killed Arietta. I'd love to know how you figured out the whole plushie thing. Speaking of which, we had a break-in at my office. You wouldn't know anything about that, would you?"

"Um... I mean, if I did, would I get off with a slapped wrist because I solved the case?"

"Odessa!" Olympus glanced around. "Just put back anything that shouldn't have been taken, and we'll say no more. And drop by to make a statement as soon as you can."

"Sure." We said our goodbyes, and I raced outside.

Sol was standing there, waiting for me. Without thinking, I threw myself into his arms. He easily caught me and held me tight.

"You did it." He pressed me close against his chest.

"We figured it out."

"You figured it out. I'd have never made all the connections."

"It wasn't until I held that plushie that it got me thinking."

Sol stepped back and held my face in his hands. "And you're okay?"

"Yes. How about you?" A shiver of joy ran through me as I looked into his open, honest face.

"I'm good. Just glad you're safe and this is over. We can get back to normal, now."

I bit my lip. "I know this has been a whirlwind, and the last time we spoke, you were thinking about leaving..." I pressed on before I lost courage. "Have you changed your mind? Or are you still going?"

"I'll stay if you want me to. But we have a few things to figure out." His thumb brushed across my bottom lip, and I shivered again.

I couldn't keep hiding from Sol. I cared for him more than I should. I still missed Brodie so badly it made me want to ugly cry, but I couldn't imagine my life without Sol in it.

He tapped my forehead with a finger. "There appears to be lots of serious thoughts going on inside that head."

"Just one or two tiny thoughts. But we're good for now?"

"You're safe and with me. That means we're way more than good." He leaned forward and rested his forehead against mine. "So, Odessa Grimsbane, what are we going to do now?"

It was the end of a long and stressful day. After dealing with Arietta, solving her murder, and making things right with Sol, I'd gone to my beloved farm and spent the next twenty-four hours working with Sol and setting things back to how they should be.

The Magic Council had ripped through everything, but one place they hadn't been able to get into was my experiment barn. And it was only when I looked at it that I knew the reason.

"Sol, get over here." I wiped a hand across my sweaty forehead.

He hurried over. "What's wrong?"

"You're incredible." I kissed his cheek. "You used your magic ring to protect my barn." Sol's silver ring was wrapped around a thick metal chain that pulsed with magic. Nothing I'd tried had broken it open.

He shrugged. "I knew what was in there would cause a problem with the Magic Council."

"But you're almost powerless without it. No wonder Arietta had such control over you. It was a risk."

"It was worth taking. I'll always take a risk for you."

I was getting a gooey, warm feeling in my stomach when footsteps had me turning.

"There you are." Indigo strode toward me with Storm and Luna.

"Hey. It's good to see you," I said as we all hugged. I was so glad to be back with my friends.

"We figured you might need a hand tidying up," Indigo said. "But it looks like you're almost done."

"Your timing is perfect. We were about to stop for dinner," I said. "Join us."

"Absolutely," Luna said. "I've been missing out on all the fun gossip."

"Because you've turned into a crazy bridezilla," Storm said.

"I'm not crazy. I just have a demanding family and a bunch of intimidating werewolf almost in-laws to deal with. Keeping everyone happy is a nightmare. I've suggested to Cole we elope. I'm not even kidding."

"You won't elope." Indigo slung an arm around Luna's shoulders. "This will be the biggest and best wedding Witch Haven has ever seen, and you'll love being in the middle of it."

"I'm not so sure about that," Luna said. "But if I have all of you helping, I'll make it through with only a few bruises."

"You definitely have us," I said.

The others went ahead, and Indigo hung back as we walked to the farmhouse. "You were getting cozy with Sol when we arrived."

My cheeks flushed, but rather than denying it, I nodded. "We're working through a few things."

"You finally admit you like him?"

I grinned at her. "I might. I mean, I feel guilty about Brodie. And I haven't given up on him. But..."

"Maybe you're ready to move on?" Indigo's arm tightened around me. "This'll probably be the hardest thing you've ever done. You loved Brodie so hard, but it's time you found happiness. Living in your memories isn't really living. Give things a chance with Sol. I like him. And even Storm approves, and she hates almost everybody."

"What if it doesn't work out?"

"At least you tried, and you'll learn from it. You don't want any regrets. Sol is good for you, and you're good for him. Make the move."

"I'm giving it lots of hard thoughts."

"Less thoughts, more action. Pounce on the guy and devour him." Indigo nudged me with an elbow. "And just a heads up. I was talking to Olympus. Selma Black isn't done with you."

I frowned. "I don't know what her problem is. Well, I sort of do. The whole aunt getting eaten thing must have given her nightmares."

"The whole what?"

"I'll tell you about it over dinner."

She stuck out her tongue. "No, thanks. After dessert, maybe. Just be careful. Selma wants you shut down. Olympus is doing everything he can to make sure that doesn't happen, but keep your nose squeaky clean. And no more new scarecrows until Selma's investigation is done."

"I have to keep making them. Orders have backed up because I've been busy helping Arietta figure out who killed her."

"And I want to hear all about that, too. But those orders will have to wait. Get your name cleared, get Selma out of your hair, then you can carry on. People will wait a couple more weeks for one of your incredible scarecrows."

I wasn't happy at the thought of remaining closed, but Indigo had a point. "You're right. Once I've gotten Selma's thorn out of my side, things will be back to normal."

After heading inside and setting everyone up with drinks and pumpkin herb crackers, I left my friends in the kitchen and went to the washroom to freshen up. I hadn't felt this positive in a long time. Despite the Magic Council still interested in my scarecrows, things were looking up.

And I had Sol in my life. A glow radiated from my heart at the thought of spending more time with him. Maybe we could go on a date. I mean, one date, what would be the harm in that?

I shivered as the washroom grew chilly. I closed the window and pulled down the blind. The nights were closing in, and it would soon be peak pumpkin time. I loved autumn, when I could take out my favorite sweaters and long boots and sit by the fire with a mug of hot chocolate and a plate full of pumpkin and dark chocolate cookies.

After making myself less sweaty and more presentable, I headed into my bedroom and grabbed a light sweater. Once everyone had been fed and we'd caught up with the gossip, I'd get Sol alone and suggest something romantic. Nothing intense, just some fun, so we could get to know each other outside of work.

I grinned as I pulled the sweater over my head. Life was about to get interesting.

As I turned to the door, the air vanished from the room, and the world stopped turning as I looked straight into Brodie's eyes...

About Author

K.E. O'Connor (Karen) is a mystery author living in the beautiful British countryside. She loves all things mystery, animals, and cake.

If you want to be part of the Witch Haven crew, practice spells, solve a few murders, spend time with amazing witches and their talking familiars, and get a free book, join her weekly newsletter.

Sign up today.

Newsletter:
https://BookHip.com/QKGDWJW
Website:
www.keoconnor.com/writing
Facebook:
www.facebook.com/keoconnorauthor

Also By

Spells and Spooks
Hexes and Haunts
Curses and Corpses
Muffins and Moonlight
Cupcakes and Cauldrons
Pancakes and Potions
Hauntings and High Jinx
Hauntings and Havoc
Hauntings and Hoaxes
The Case of the Screaming Skull
The Case of the Poisoned Pumpkin
The Case of the Cursed Candy
Fire Fang
Silvaria

If you enjoyed

Hauntings and Havoc

turn the page to read an extract from the next Witch
Haven mystery.

HAUNTINGS AND HOAXES

ISBN: 978-1-915378-36-1

Chapter 1

It wasn't every day you saw the ghost of the man you'd given your heart to appear in your bedroom. I blinked once, twice, three times, and he was still there. This wasn't my imagination playing tricks on me.

Brodie Barclay's smile widened as his warm gaze flicked over me. "Are you going to say anything?"

I opened my mouth, but I'd forgotten how to talk. I pointed a finger at him and shook my head.

"Yep. It's me. I'm here. I've been looking for you for such a long time." Brodie's voice had the same deep, warm cadence that always made my toes curl.

I took a step toward him, but my knees buckled, and I hit the floor. Not only had I forgotten how to talk, I'd stopped breathing. Dizziness hit me so hard that I curled into a ball and squeezed my eyes shut. I'd waited so long to see Brodie, and I could do nothing but try to remember how my lungs worked.

"Odessa, what's keeping you so long?" Storm Winter yelled up the stairs. "We're starving, and you promised us dinner. I've already eaten all your pumpkin crackers. And is there anything in this house that isn't pumpkin flavored?"

I raised my head, not sure what I'd see when I did. Brodie was still there. After so many years of longing for him to return, this was too much. My eyes rolled back, and the room went dark.

Someone was tapping my cheek. I opened my eyes to find Storm, Indigo Ash, Luna Brimstone, my favorite scarecrow, Shamrock, and Tuffin surrounding me.

"She's awake." Indigo had her hand on my forehead. "What happened up here?"

I tried to speak, but only a croaking sound came out. I cleared my throat and tried again. "Brodie."

"What about him?" Luna said.

"He was here. You must have seen him." I tried to sit, but Indigo pressed a hand on my shoulder.

"Take your time. Did you hit your head on something?"

"No, my head's fine. But we have to find Brodie." I sat up with my friends' help, although they handled me as if I might break at any second.

Storm pursed her lips. "Brodie's gone. You're moving on. You've got a life with Sol."

"No, I haven't." My gaze flicked to the door, and I saw Sol Vossen standing there. He didn't look happy. "I mean, of course, I do. But not like I had with Brodie. Help me up. I knew he'd come back to me. I never gave up hope."

I didn't miss the worried looks that passed between my friends as they got me on my feet, but I couldn't care about how weird they thought I was being. My gaze shot around my bedroom. Brodie wasn't there.

"So, where's he hiding?" Indigo said.

"Should I check the closet? Or maybe he's under the bed." Storm yanked open a closet door. "No dead lover hiding in here."

"This isn't a joke. He was right here." I jabbed the air. "Brodie spoke to me. I've dreamt about this day so many times, but I wasn't ready. I let him down."

"Are you sure it was Brodie?" Indigo said. "I mean, you've been looking for a long time. And I've lost count of the number of times you were certain you spotted him in a crowd and it turned out to be someone else."

"Or you discovered his ghost in a haunted house," Luna said, a note of sympathy in her voice.

"This is different. It was him. I'm sure of it." I stepped away from my friends and their overwhelming compassion. I didn't need it. Brodie was back, and everything would be fine.

"If he's back, why doesn't he show himself?" Sol said, a quiet anger in his tone. "Or does he have something to hide?"

"No. Nothing! But this must be overwhelming for him, too. He said he'd been looking for me for a long time. I knew he'd gotten lost getting back to me." I pivoted on my heel, desperately seeking Brodie. "Come back. You know where I am now. This is your home, and we can figure everything out."

No one spoke as we looked around the room for Brodie's ghost. Well, I was looking. My friends kept shooting each other worried glances and shrugging.

"Give him a minute," I said. "You know what ghosts are like. If Brodie doesn't have much energy, he won't manifest."

"When you saw him, what did he look like?" Luna said.

"Just like Brodie."

"For real? But he's been a ghost for over three years. I figured he wouldn't be doing so well."

"He looked better than good, actually. Not even a hint of ghost ghoul about him."

"Which is impossible," Storm said.

I didn't like her sharp tone. "It's possible. Ghosts can linger for decades and not transform into something unpleasant. And Brodie has our memories to cling to. They kept him whole." I walked around the bedroom. "Brodie, follow my voice and come back to me."

I kept pacing and calling, but he didn't show. And every time I glanced at my friends, I could see they didn't believe me. "We need to split up. The farm is a big place. Brodie could have ended up in a barn. Maybe he got scared when you all came into the bedroom."

"Brodie knows us. He has no reason to hide," Storm said.

"There'll be a reason. Everyone go look for him. You can all see and sense ghosts, so make yourselves useful."

"I'll search the rest of this floor," Indigo said.

"I'll do downstairs and the basement," Luna said.

"That leaves me to check the barns and not get attacked by the scarecrows," Storm said. "What fun."

I appreciated my friends didn't hang around as they began their search. I stopped in the doorway by Sol. My initial excitement at seeing Brodie faded when I saw the grim expression on Sol's face. "I'm sorry, but I can't abandon Brodie."

He gave a slight shake of his head. "I'd offer to help look for him, but you know I can't see ghosts."

"I wouldn't expect you to, even if you could. And... this must be difficult for you. I never wanted it to be this way, but I was always honest with you. You know I've been looking for Brodie." I walked along the corridor, keeping a lookout for Brodie as I talked.

Sol walked behind me. "He's really here?"

"Yes. I'm certain of it. Tuffin, Shamrock, help me look, too. We need all eyes on this ghost hunt."

"I'm asleep," Tuffin said from the bedroom.

Shamrock lumbered into the corridor. He was holding a squirming Tuffin in his large, straw-filled hands.

"Help Storm search the barns," I said. "Come back and tell me if you find anything."

"Make this scarecrow put me down, before I shred him to pieces." Tuffin hissed in Shamrock's face.

"You go with Shamrock. Make yourself useful, too."

I ignored Tuffin's protests as I kept looking. Sol remained doggedly by my side, and although I was glad of his presence, I felt guilty. I'd been leading him on. I'd imagined a future for us and even contemplated going on a date with Sol. What had I been thinking? I'd almost missed the chance to reunite with Brodie because I'd lost focus. It wouldn't happen again.

We spent the next hour searching the farm and the barns from top to bottom. Brodie still hadn't appeared.

With every minute that passed, my frustration grew. I had seen him. It hadn't been my imagination. I hadn't even been thinking about Brodie when he'd appeared. I looked over to see Sol standing with his hands on the fence, staring out across the fields he tended. I'd been thinking about another man.

I gathered everyone in the kitchen and encountered lots more pitying glances and nods of sympathy. It was too much to bear, and I needed to be on my own. Brodie must want to see me alone. That was the reason he wasn't showing himself.

"What do you want to do next?" Indigo said. "There's no whiff of a ghost around here."

I forced a smile. "You're right. Maybe I imagined him."

My friends exchanged another set of annoying glances.

"You seemed so certain," Luna said. "Why the change of heart?"

"I made a mistake. I'm allowed to do that, aren't I?"

"You said you saw him," Storm said. "You even had me convinced. Well, almost."

I bit my tongue to avoid biting back at her sharpness. "I've had a stressful few days. I need to catch up with my sleep and get into my old routine, then I'll stop hallucinating." I hoped Brodie wasn't listening to this conversation and getting the wrong end of the stick.

"You think Brodie was a hallucination?" Storm shook her head, clearly not believing me.

"He must have been. Because as you said, there's no reason for him to hide. He knows everyone here, and he trusts me. Even if he's confused because he's been a ghost for a long time, it makes no sense." I looked out the window, so I didn't have to make eye contact with my friends as I lied. "This was my mistake. Sorry for wasting your time. You should probably all go."

"What about Brodie?" Luna walked over and wrapped an arm around my shoulders. "We don't mind staying and looking some more. Or we could have that long overdue dinner and see if he shows up. Maybe we did scare him. And if he's not himself—"

"He is himself. Really, it's best you go. And I'm not in the mood for doing dinner tonight. It's late, and I want to be on my own."

"I hate that idea," Storm said. "Someone should stay, especially if you're seeing things that aren't real."

"I can stay a while longer," Sol said. "There's nowhere else I need to be."

I didn't want anyone sticking around, but my friends wouldn't move until I compromised. "Fine. You stay. Everyone else can go, though. I'm embarrassed about what happened."

"Don't be embarrassed," Luna said. "Brodie was your guy. We all know how much you want to see him again. But it's time to move on, don't you think?" Her gaze shifted to Sol.

I nodded. "Thanks for helping. Sorry for wasting everyone's time."

"Don't be an idiot." Indigo walked over and hugged me. "I'm always happy to help you with a little ghost hunting."

Luna also hugged me and Storm gave me a half-hearted fist bump before they left.

I looked around the kitchen, excitement and anxiety bubbling inside me in equal measure. "Sol, I need your help."

"With what?"

"Your ring is still locking the barn with my experiments in it. I need to get inside. If Brodie is back, I have work to do."

"You didn't tell your friends the truth, did you?" Sol made no move from the doorway he stood in. "You're still convinced you saw Brodie's ghost?"

"They never believed he was here. It was pointless for them to stay."

"And you do believe he's back? Brodie is the only person you want?"

I wanted to tell Sol no and reveal I'd planned to ask him on a date just before Brodie had shown up. I cared about Sol and wanted him in my life, but I couldn't have him and Brodie. That was greedy. And I'd given my heart to Brodie so many years ago, I wasn't sure where to find it if I ever wanted it back. Not that I would. Brodie had always looked after it.

"I get it." Sol's sigh was heavy with regret. "You need to complete the magic for Brodie's vessel.

And I know you can make it work. Your power is amazing. You dazzle me."

"I appreciate you not judging me," I said. "I know this can't be easy for you."

"Your happiness is what I care about the most. I wanted to make you happy, but I see that'll never work. You've only got space in your heart for one guy."

I reached for his hand but stopped myself and stepped away. "It's how it's always been. It's only ever been Brodie for me."

"I never stood a chance? Even after everything we've been through?"

There had been a moment, just a flicker of uncertainty, that had made me reach for Sol. But that was me being weak and not true to myself.

"It's okay. You don't have to answer those questions. Let's go to the barn. Get you the happy ending you need so badly." Sol's steps were heavy as he went outside.

I waved over Shamrock and Tuffin, and we headed to the barn. My mind was whirring too fast for me to keep up with all the thoughts buzzing through my brain. There was so much I needed to do. I'd yet to perfect a permanent vessel that Brodie could live in. I was also aware the beady eyes of the Magic Council were still on me. I had to be careful not to be arrested again, but if I didn't take this risk, I could lose Brodie for good.

Sol caught hold of the ring that had protected my barn from unwanted Magic Council attention. A silvery glow covered his palm, and the ring slid off the metal chain holding the doors shut. He slid it onto his finger.

I stared at the ring and then my own bare fingers. I was so close to getting everything I wanted. When Brodie was back, we'd be married, we could start a family, expand the farm like he always wanted, and finally, I'd have my happily ever after.

"I should go," Sol said. "You got what you wanted from me."

"Don't be like that. I've loved having you around. I love everything you've done for the farm and the scarecrows."

"But you don't love me. And I accept that. It doesn't make me happy, but this is your choice."

I blinked back tears. "It's the right choice. I always knew one day my true love would return. And it's here. I can't let Brodie go. This is too important."

"You have to follow that," Sol said.

"I... yes, I do. But what about you? What will you do?"

"Figure something else out." Sol caught hold of me by the shoulders and drew me close. "I won't be sticking around for much longer. I've loved you for almost as long as I've known you, so it would be too painful to see you with another guy. When you get Brodie back, I'll be glad, but I can't watch. I need my own life."

I swallowed around the sudden lump in my throat. "I hope we can be friends."

"Maybe. In time." Sol stroked a hand down my cheek then stepped away. "Have a wonderful life. You deserve it." He turned and walked away.

Shamrock shoved into me and growled.

"What? This is the right thing to do. You want to see me happy with Brodie, don't you?"

He caught hold of my arm and made a two-way connection with us, the buzzing filling my head as our thoughts linked so we could communicate.

"Like Sol," he growled.

"So do I. But Brodie is everything to me. He's almost here. He's almost back with us."

"Brodie jerk. Not nice."

"Don't tell lies. Brodie was always good to you."

"Set me on fire once."

"Shamrock! That's not true. Don't be jealous because he's coming back. I'll still have time for you and the other scarecrows. You won't miss out on anything."

"Miss out on Sol. Like him."

I stepped away to break the connection. Shamrock had always had a possessive, jealous streak. He was only worried because Brodie was back and my attention would be elsewhere.

"You stay out here and check the perimeter. Tuffin, stay with Shamrock. I don't want anything to get in the way of Brodie coming back."

"I have no interest in meeting another ghost." Tuffin leaped out of Shamrock's arms and strutted away.

I headed back to the house and walked around, calling for Brodie, but no amount of pleading got him to materialize. I briefly considered a séance or a summoning, but that was extreme. He'd made it back to me on his own, so he could do it again.

I sank into a chair in the kitchen and rubbed my aching forehead. I wanted to cry in frustration. Where was he?

Automatically, I grabbed a pouch of powdered pumpkin on the table and went to take a huge scoop. I hesitated. I'd managed without it when I was helping Arietta Frost solve her murder. She'd constantly drained my power, and though I'd felt awful, I hadn't had any powdered pumpkin, and I'd survived fine. Maybe I was too reliant on my supercharged magical pumpkin dust.

I took a small amount and chewed slowly, welcoming the rush of energy.

There was a shift in the air, and I tensed. I jumped from my seat and looked around, almost too afraid to breathe in case something went wrong. "Brodie?"

Tuffin raced into the kitchen, her fur bristled and her eyes wide. "Something is here."

"I told you to stay outside." I was looking around, frantic for any hint Brodie was back.

"I don't like this," Tuffin said. "It doesn't feel right."

"You never met Brodie, so you don't know what his energy feels like. This must be him."

"He'd better not feel like this, or I'm moving out," Tuffin said.

"You've only just moved in, so that won't be hard to organize." I kept looking around. "Brodie, follow my voice. It's Odessa. I'm right here. Come back to me."

Something shimmered in the corner of the kitchen, and a few seconds later, Brodie appeared.

A startled laugh shot out of me. "It really is you."

Tuffin hissed and backed to the door.

Brodie strode forward and wrapped me in a tight, icy hug. "Hey, babe. It's me. I'm back."

Hauntings and Hoaxes is available in paperback and e-book

ISBN: 978-1-915378-36-1

www.ingramcontent.com/pod-product-compliance
Lightning Source LLC
Chambersburg PA
CBHW050801190726
48285CB00005B/1748